The Sailing Master

Book Three: Letter of Marque

Lee Henschel Jr.

Rocket Science Press

SHIPWRECKT BOOKS PUBLISHING COMPANY

Minnesota

Cover photo by Mark Willis
Cover and interior design by
Shipwreckt Books

For Raincloud

The Sailing Master
Book Three: Letter of Marque

Part One: Half-pay

1. Some frauds are so bold

London, July 1802

FitzRoi stood at his bay window gazing down upon Lombard Street. He patted his wig and was about to take another pinch, but then tucked away his snuff box when Rainey arrived.

"It took you long enough, lieutenant. I have no time to spare so I'll go straight to the matter. Can you name these two gentlemen sitting across from me?"

Rainey stiffened. "Who are you? And by what authority do you ask me to name these two?"

FitzRoi puffed indignant, his jowls colouring pink. "I'm Increase FitzRoi. A director at Barclays. There's been a forgery inflicted upon this firm and to begin my investigation I must establish the bona fides of these two men. They claim you can identify them, and further state that your current duty station is nearby, at Admiralty House. That's why I've had you summoned here."

Rainey raised a brow, glanced at Mr. Lau and me, then replied forthwith.

"The older man is Mr. Lau. I knew him as sailing master aboard HMS *Eleanor* when I served as first lieutenant. The midshipman is Mr. Harriet, though I knew him as a ship's boy aboard the same vessel."

"Then it's as I suspected. The forgery of which I speak seems to involve a misrepresentation of these two men. I've already described to them that a man stood in this very office on fifteen July, of 1799, claiming to be Mr. Lau. The man requested a transfer of the entire sum of Mr. Harriet's inheritance from his late uncle, Captain James Cedric. Now these two claim that the man I described resembles a certain Émile Coutts. Do you recall Mr. Coutts, lieutenant?"

"I do, sir. Ship's purser aboard *Eleanor*."

"Then what I ask next is critical to my investigation. Please recount, as best you can, the physical appearance of Coutts."

"About forty years old, I'd say. A scrawny fellow. Medium height.

Greasy hair. Long and black. Grey eyes and a grey, hatchet face."

"Any other notable characteristics?"

"Aye, sir. Coutts stank to high heaven."

FitzRoi nodded. "Very well. I believe that will do. You may leave."

Rainey took his leave, glancing our way as he departed.

FitzRoi turned to Mr. Lau. "It's settled then. You are who you claim to be."

"Of course we are who we claim to be, FitzRoi, and this incident is by no means settled. At the very least, I hold you incompetent."

"Mind what you say, sailing master."

"I will not. I demand to know how Coutts could be allowed to conduct such a boldface fraud."

FitzRoi discounted the demand. "Some frauds are so bold none would dare consider them other than the truth. I fear such is the case here. Coutts produced fair copy of Captain Cedric's will, along with sufficient proof of who he, as well as the boy who he brought with him, claimed to be. I had no choice but to honour his request, and transfer the entire amount held at Barclays." FitzRoi patted his wig, then went on. "However, a cautionary note is in order here. In his will, Captain Cedric listed all of his assets, as well as his investment shares. The total was listed at approximately one-thousand one hundred fifty-one pounds. But it seems that amount fails to take into account a string of setbacks regarding the captain's shares held in commercial trade. One of his holdings is verified lost at sea. Another's gone missing."

"So Mr. Harriet's inheritance is less than the amount stipulated in the will?"

"Quite so, Mr. Lau." FitzRoi turned to me. "Young man, I hope you've not entertained any notions of living an idle life derived from your endowment."

I shook my head no.

"That's good. The amount's still substantial but, after all of Captain Cedric's debt is accounted for, the remainder's far less than mentioned in the will. And his share of prize money for taking *Santa Isadora* remains to be adjudicated."

Mr. Lau wrapped on the desk with his knuckles. "Get to the

point, FitzRoi. What is the butcher's bill?"

FitzRoi referred to a slip of paper on his desk. "Mr. Harriet's bequest now stands at three hundred ninety-one pounds, seventeen pence." The room fell silent. A cart rumbled past on Lombard Street, its drover barking for people to stand clear.

I spoke for the first time. "Does that include the one pound fifty-three pence interest earned at four point seven-nine percent compounded to eight bells of the forenoon watch of this day, sir?"

"Mr. Harriet, rest assured that Barclays will calculate all interest due. Though I must say your estimate sounds about right, given the short time it just took for you to calculate it."

"It's most accurate, sir."

FitzRoi raised a brow and changed the subject. "Yes. Well, to return to this Coutts fellow, the miscreant asked for the entire sum to be transferred to an existing account held at Taylor and Lloyds of Manchester."

Mr. Lau stomped his foot. "Then I suggest you have Taylor and Lloyds return it immediately."

"Unfortunately, we can't do that, for the money's no longer there. However, I believe we know where it is. Due to the unusual nature of his request, we thought it prudent to remain in communication with Taylor and Lloyds regarding the activities related to this account. It seems that shortly after the Treaty was signed at Amiens, Coutts closed the account in Manchester and had the entire amount transferred to Nathan Mayer, in Calais."

Mr. Lau stood abrupt. "Enough of this palaver. Captain Cedric entrusted you to safeguard Mr. Harriet's inheritance and you have failed in every regard. I find your ineptitude verging on malfeasance and now I intend to seek legal counsel."

FitzRoi would not bear the goad, and replied hot, "I have never been accused of such . . ."

"Hear me out, FitzRoi. I served with James Cedric aboard *Zealous*, as well as *Eleanor*. He was my captain and colleague, and as such he named me guardian of his nephew's bestowal until the lad turns eighteen. Now Mr. Harriet has come here to request a portion of that legacy for the care and well-being of his simple and destitute brother, Albert, and you say the inheritance can not be recovered because it was released to a man whose identity has been proven a blatant lie."

"I say no such thing. In fact, I think Mr. Harriet's account may very well be recovered. I have people in Calais, and since you can readily identify Coutts I think you would expedite the matter by going there as well."

"To remove ourselves from London, no doubt."

"It's no concern of mine whether you or Mr. Harriet remain in London. But, if Coutts is still in Calais, you can personally identify him. It would facilitate the proceedings."

"We cannot travel to Calais. Since the Treaty has taken effect both Mr. Harriet and I are on half-pay, as is much of the Royal Navy. Travel to the continent is beyond our means, let alone paying the exorbitant cost of room and board in France."

"I understand, sir, and am willing to arrange a small loan against any recovery of Mr. Harriet's inheritance. And as it happens, you're in luck. I know of a boat captain who's begun channel service between London and Calais. He's in need of a pilot and deck hand just now. I'll recommend you to him and you can work your way to Calais."

I watched him scribe a name and address on a slip of bank stationery and hand it to Mr. Lau.

"Jean Dame-Marie is the man's name. His boat is the *Solitude*."

"Do you expect two Englishmen to board a vessel owned by a Frenchman and then sail into a French port? The ink's barely dry at Amiens, and the peace is tenuous at best."

"That may be so. But I assure you, even though the man's name is French, he's surely not from France."

"Then where?"

"Saint-Domingue. I'll say no more. Tomorrow you'll find both Dame-Marie and *Solitude* across from the Isle of Dogs. Stop here first and ask for Mr. Posey. He'll release ten pounds sterling, along with several hundred francs. I'll also have a packet for you to present to Lionel David once you arrive in Calais. Mr. David is my associate at Nathan Mayer and he'll extend you further credit. Find him on Rue Leveux. Go you now. I must try to determine how best to approach my colleagues with this wretched business."

2. I'll tell you what I know of Coutts

We grabbed our ditty bags and stepped into Lombard Street. The reek of London stung in my nose. I'd been at sea for near three years continuous and was not yet accustomed to the stench. George Town, off Sumatra, had stunk just as bad, but more of rotting jungle, open slops, and a strange foetor no Englishman ever knew how to describe. London stank of rot and open slops, to be sure, but also of thick, acrid smoke belching from a forest of blackened chimneys. The smolder hung low in a grey sky.

Of a sudden Mr. Lau cocked an ear and came up short. Despite his age the Sailing Master still heard sharp as any fox, and certain he'd heard something now that caught his notice.

"What is it, sir?"

"Over there, beyond that tall stack. Do you hear it?"

I listened sharp and then heard it plain. "That hissing sound, sir? And the clanging metal?"

"Aye."

"What is it? Some new weapon?"

He grinned and patted my arm. "No. What you hear is a steam machine."

I stared at him unknowing.

"A Beam Engine, lad. And I believe this one is hard at work pumping bilge into the Thames."

Mr. Lau winced, touching the fresh scar of his wound received on *Eleanor* ... a musket ball discharged by a French marine aboard *Hommage,* perhaps the last round to be fired before the Treaty. The wound would inflame at this time every day, yet he never spoke of it.

The press of London closed in. FitzRoi's news had taken us aback, and until we spoke with Mr. Posey in the morning, we knew not where to go, or what to do. I watched Mr. Lau's rheumy gaze settle on a nearby inn. I feared he might weaken and head straight for it, so I made ready to speak of his vow to remain sober.

I was spared the effort, though, when Lieutenant Rainey hailed us from the throng.

"Mr. Lau. There you are."

"Ah. Lieutenant, I hoped you might catch us up. Thank you for coming to our aid at Barclays."

"You're welcome. I see you've recently been wounded. Shot, I would think."

"A slight wound, sir, and of no consequence."

Rainey squinted doubtful. But he said no more of it and went on to other matters. "None of my business, of course, but are either of you in trouble with that FitzRoi fellow?"

"No. But it seems Coutts took French leave with Harriet's inheritance as soon as the miscreant returned from Port Mahon."

"Bastard. I wish to hear the details if I may, but not here on the street. Come, I have rooms near Tobacco Dock. I'd hire a coach for us but it's not very far, and it would serve you both to walk off your sea legs. Since the peace there are a great many seamen adrift in the streets of London and their rolling gait marks them as easy prey."

"Tobacco Dock has always been an uncertain place for a sailor, Rainey."

"Agreed. But I can afford no better. I'm on half-pay, same as you."

"Yet you had just come from Admiralty House to confirm our identity."

"I did. I'm off at at the end of afternoon watch though, and my landlady, that's Mrs. Dolan, is roasting a joint of mutton this evening. So I invite you to join me. Besides, I have information concerning Coutts."

"We will be pleased to hear your news, Rainey. But neither Harriet nor I can spare the cost of another full meal this day."

"I'd be honoured to provide you both with a meal. And even though Mrs. Dolan's a sharp trader, she has a soft heart for sailors. Her husband was carpenter on *Babet*."

"*Babet*? The brig lost off Jamaica Station?"

"Aye. Two years ago, and not heard from since. But the woman still holds out hope. Reads the *Gazette* every month for any news."

We walked for a mile along Lower Thames Street, past Tower of London, and then Wapping High, until we entered the Isle of Dogs. Finally, we arrived at Thirty Byng Street.

Mrs. Dolan's Room & Board was a wood frame wattle and daub standing back from the street, tucked between a tinsmith and livery. The place rose but one story, with a low overhang and a row of windows fronting the street. It faced Sawyer's, a public house direct across the narrow lane, with its heavy oak door still shut tight and in sore need of fresh paint. But Dolan's door stood open, so Rainey led us through to a great room with a long table and six trenchers set in place for the evening meal. Sturdy benches lined each side.

Rainey went in search of Mrs. Dolan, but before he returned, a substantial woman with a club foot limped from the kitchen. The savour of roasting mutton followed on as she stood before us, wiping her chafed hands on a broad apron. She gauged us shrewd before she spoke, and when she spoke, her voice boomed overloud.

"If you're here for a meal it's one bob each. Pay before." She looked at our ditty bags. "And if you wish for a room I have only one to let. But you can share. A shilling for the two of you. Pay before. I saw you come in with Lieutenant Rainey. Do you know him?"

"Ah, there you are, Mrs. Dolan. And yes, Mr. Lau and Mr. Harriet know me. I served with them at the Battle of the Nile. I'd like you to set a place for them at dinner this evening. You may put it on my bill."

Mrs. Dolan nodded, then turned to us. "Do you gentlemen wish for a room, then?"

"We will take it for the night, but we must be off in the morning."

"Very well. Your room's at the head of the stairs. Dinner's served in the last dog watch."

⚡

Two bells rang from the kitchen, seven o'clock, and Mrs. Dolan served dinner. Three others joined us at the table. Old salts, no doubt, for each one hooked a leg around a bench support as if running before a big sea. Not one of us spoke, for the roast and mash was toothsome, and deserving of our full consideration. The meal went down quick, and in not ten minutes all was complete. The others departed, leaving the great room to Rainey, Mr. Lau, and me.

Even in high summer dusk fell early in Byng Street, for the lane was cramped and the buildings, though humble, stood tall enough to block the late sun. The last few carts rumbled past, and soon the lane filled with foot traffic. Across the lane, Sawyer's door swung wide, with lanterns burning at all windows.

Mr. Lau groaned low, once more lifting a hand to his wound. Rainey noticed the discomfort. I think he meant to say something about it but changed his mind and spoke of something else.

"Now then, I'll tell you what I know of Coutts. In my capacity at Admiral House it's my duty to review the documentation of all civilian passengers transported in a ship of war, and I couldn't help but notice Coutts's name on the manifest of *Lapwing*, a brig deploying from Port Mahon in November of '98, and arriving in Portsmouth in late December. I recognized Coutts's name, of course, and wondered why *Lapwing* would list him. So I looked a bit deeper. It seems Admiral Sley discharged Coutts at Mahon for wrongful exercise of authority and sent him packing. Is that so?"

"It is. Both Mr. Harriet and I were present at Sley's finding."

"I see. Well at first, I thought Coutts had finally met his comeuppance, and I put the business to rest. But then his name came up again a few months after that."

Mr. Lau sat forward. "How is that?"

"Perhaps a mere coincidence, if there is such a thing. Either way, you may recall that before my commission in the Royal Navy I was an actor, and even now maintain relations with the actors' guild."

I recalled my first few weeks aboard *Eleanor*, when Lieutenant Rainey had hired two actors at Portsmouth dock, one to play the role of a man just pressed into the navy, and the other to play the role of an officer. At one point the pressed man went mad and charged the officer, whereupon the officer shot him. The man crashed to the deck, with blood gushing from between clutched hands held to his heart. He was hardly dead though, or even wounded. The blood was only water, dyed red, and the officer's pistol had not been loaded with shot, and with just enough powder to provide a convincing report. The thing was all a charade, devised by Rainey to put the fear of death into any man who might think of striking an officer.

Rainey tapped my forehead. "Still with us, Harriet?"

"Aye, sir."

"Good, for here's where you come in. Early in '99 a colleague in the actors' guild remarked of an unusual casting call for a young man of about your age. He was to play a midshipman hoping to claim his inheritance at some bank."

Rainey had gained my attention, certain of that. But just then Mrs. Dolan limped into the great room bearing a cloth warmed in her oven. It smelled of linseed flax, and I knew what it was for. Father had used it on horses.

"Mr. Lau, I've made a poultice. If you'll permit, I'll apply it to your neck."

"Pay before, no doubt."

"No, sir. I'll not charge you for it."

I thought he might still refuse, for Mr. Lau was the stoic one, but this time he allowed the relief. Mrs. Dolan straddled the bench, and applied her poultice with a gentle touch.

Rainey went on. "Well it turns out the man promoting this role was Coutts, and in less than a week some likely fellow answered his casting call. At the time I thought it no more than a curiosity. But no more. After FitzRoi called me to vouch for you I've come to realize what Coutts was up to. It appears his little performance at Barclays was just the opening act of some duplicitous play. Now it appears the man has fled."

Mr. Lau nodded slow. "He may be in Calais. Hopefully we are bound there in the morning."

Mrs. Dolan spoke up. "Sorry to interrupt, sir, but it may be best if you retire to your room. Scar's startin' to pulse."

Rainey and I watched Mrs. Dolan lead the Sailing Master upstairs. We sat listening to the floor creaking overhead. When all went quiet Rainey resumed the conversation.

"How was he shot?"

I couldn't tell Rainey the bare truth. Admiral Christchurch had warned never to speak of our engagement with *Hommage*. Still, I might bend the truth, at least some, so as not to catch myself in a lie.

"A marine shot him, sir. His musket discharged by accident and the round struck Mr. Lau in the neck."

A marine, yes. Not a Royal Marine, though, but a French *matelots*. And a musket, yes. Not a Brown Bess, though, but a Charleville, and never discharged by accident. I guessed Rainey knew the lie of it, or at least that it was not the full truth, but he chose not to call me out. Instead he went to a cupboard and took down a dram glass, and then another. He set them on the table before us and brought out a small flask from his waistcoat.

"You've grown since we served together."

"About one hand, sir."

"A hand? Oh, yes. Now I recall. You're a farrier's son. But what I mean is you've matured. You've learned to hold your tongue. Also to shape the truth."

He poured a measure of pale green liquid into his glass. "Have you tasted absinthe before?"

"No, sir. What is it?"

Rainey grimaced. "God's own rot. I swear it. You needn't partake."

"I'll take a small portion. But I'm on duty and must stay clear in my head."

He poured careful slow while he spoke. "On duty?"

"Well, not active duty, sir. Except I must take care of Mr. Lau."

"His wound's that bad?"

"I don't know. But while we're ashore Mr. Lau's asked me to help him never to drink. But if I drink overmuch of this absinthe, I'll do him no good."

"You're very close to Mr. Lau."

"Aye, sir."

"Your mentor."

"Yes, sir. And he's father to me now. Now that I'm gone from Newbury for so long, and …"

"And?"

"And my own father's run to the Colonies."

Rainey nodded, lost in his own thoughts, sipping his absinthe. I sipped mine, as well. It tasted vile, and I drank it down over quick just to be rid of it. Rainey raised a brow, then knocked back the last of his own measure. He wiped his mouth, then leaned in to be heard, for now he spoke low.

"There's something you should know, Harriet. Since Amiens there's been many rumors circulating at Admiralty House. Mostly gossip and rumor, but you deserve to hear one story involving *Eleanor*. Perhaps you already know it."

He waited for me to react. When I said nothing, he went on.

"The last entry in the signals log kept on *Tremendous* was Admiral Wawne's hoist signaling *Eleanor* to proceed to Portsmouth. It's common knowledge *Eleanor* did, in fact, proceed to Portsmouth. However, it appears the hoist just before that one has gone missing. Some claim the missing hoist was an order to engage the enemy. Now *Eleanor*'s undergoing a refit and the news on chandlers row's that her repairs are substantial. More in keeping with a frigate that's suffered a great deal of battle damage."

He held his hands palm up, as if disavowing the story.

"Yet in *Dispatches* there's no mention of an independent action involving *Eleanor*. Beyond that, no one at Admiralty House has located any of *Eleanor*'s logs and, more to the point, whenever anyone asks about them, including me, we're told to mind our business."

Rainey stood and made for the bank of windows. Byng Street lay empty now, and in darkness. Its denizens either tucked in for the night or in their cups at Sawyer's. Rainey turned to face me.

"I don't know what happened aboard *Eleanor* and it would

behoove me never to ask. And you, much to your credit, volunteer nothing. That's good. We should both stay far to windward of this affair. Just let me remind you to keep your own council in this matter."

Somewhere on the river a ship's bell struck two times in the first watch. Nine of the evening.

"I have an early appointment, so I'll retire. Perhaps you should go tend to Mr. Lau."

"Aye, sir. Mr. Lau and I must be at the Pool in the morning. We best make an early start."

I mounted the stairs but, when I entered our small room, Mr. Lau wasn't there.

I heard a great snoring coming from behind a closed door at the end of the hall. Likely the room belonged to Mrs. Dolan. Since it was she who last saw Mr. Lau, I thought to wake her and ask where he might be. I came to her door and raised a hand to knock but did not. The last time I'd knocked on any door in a boarding house it was Lady Elspeth who opened it. To be sure Mrs. Dolan was no Lady Elspeth, for Elspeth was beautiful to look at. And a Jezebel. But Mrs. Dolan was no Jezebel, and most discouraging to look at. So I raised a hand once more, then once more let it fall. No matter how forthright my intentions, I had no wish to be misunderstood.

I turned to go, not knowing what to do, then noticed narrow backstairs, with faint light coming from a streetlamp and pooling on the landing below. There was a door. I wondered if Mr. Lau might have taken these stairs to gain the street. Sawyer's was just around the corner and, if the Sailing Master went there, then certain I must go there too, and fetch him away. I felt my way down the stairwell most cautious, for the passage was dim and unsteady. When I paused halfway to gain my bearings, I heard a whisper.

"Sukiyama."

I'd not heard that whisper in overlong, and hardly ever while ashore. My head throbbed rapid. I lost my balance and sat on a tread to keep from falling. The high pitch of a cicada rang in my ears. I covered them and closed my eyes. I will never know if I slept then, or if what came next was some lucid vision of another time and place, for when I opened my eyes I stood in a sunlit room with an open window and a pleasant breeze bearing the scent of lilac. A young man sat at a table with a scrap of foolscap set before him. He took up a pen, not a quill though, for it was slim, and tipped with a metal nib. He drew ink into its reservoir, deliberate slow. Turquoise ink. He breathed steady, collecting his thoughts, and began to write. His nib scratched expressive on the paper until he paused, his pen waiting patient for the next thought. I sensed he knew he was not alone in the room, that someone watched him as he wrote. He set down his pen and turned my way. I gasped, for it was ...

A gentle hand touched my shoulder and I looked up to see Mr. Lau.

"Why are you sitting here on these stairs, lad?"

"There's someone I just saw, but ... not in this stairwell."

"Then where?"

"I don't know, sir. It was strange."

The floor creaked as Mrs. Dolan stepped from her room. "Strange or no, I'll not have you two jabbering on my stairs so late at night. Hush now and get you to your room."

"Of course, ma'am. Our apologies."

I lay on the floor of our room, trying for sleep. I could not, nor could Mr. Lau, for I heard him thrashing about in his cot.

"Sir?"

"What?"

"I thought you went to Sawyer's. I only meant to come looking for you. I'm sorry to have been a bother."

"Not a bother, lad. And it is I who am sorry. But thankful, as well. I am sorry to have let you down. After Mrs. Dolan left me, I snuck down the backstairs and made for the inn. I thirsted for gin."

"To ease your wound?"

"No. Just to drink it. To drown in it. But I did not go in. I did not want to put that on you. To have you come looking for me ... only to discover a pathetic half-cut. And it is for that, that I am thankful. Thankful for not wanting you to see me that way. You gave me the strength to walk away."

3. Where His Majesty's empire begins

FitzRoi was not at Barclays the next morning. But his clerk, Mr. Posey, was, and he provided us with a cache. Posey took offense when I emptied the satchel on his desk and began to count it out. Ten pounds sterling, as promised. Along with two hundred fifteen francs, all in coin, and seventeen hundred ninety-seven *assignats*, all in scrip. The clerk scoffed at the *assignats*, claiming they were near worthless.

"Stack them all in a pile and they might bring a loaf of bread. But I doubt it."

After Mr. Lau signed for our money, Posey handed over a sealed packet with Lionel David's name scribed on it, then dismissed us prompt.

We made direct for the ferry at the Isle of Dogs. While we waited, Mr. Lau pointed to a brick structure, with cupolas topping its four corners. Two stories high, set back from the river on a hill across from us.

"That building is where His Majesty's empire begins. Do you recognize it, lad?"

"The Royal Observatory, sir. The Prime Meridian passes through its doors. Both front and back doors, I should think. It's where all fleet chronometers are calibrated to the pendulum clock inside the Octagon Room."

"Incorrect."

I slumped mortified, for I thought I knew the answer correct.

Mr. Lau only clucked. "Buck up, lad. You got it mostly right, except there are two clocks within the Octagon, not just one."

The ferryman yelled for us to either board or stand clear. We gave him a copper for the two of us and went on board. We were the last on, and the bowman cast off his lines immediate. As he worked, Mr. Lau called out.

"Bowman there! Do you know where *Solitude* is moored? Her owner is Jean Dame-Marie."

"Debtford Creek. Look for a red smack with a deck cabin."

"Thank you."

Mr. Lau surprised the man by handing him a biscuit left over from Mrs. Dolan's. The man tugged his forelock and went his way.

We found *Solitude* soon enough, riding low at the stern as longshoremen carried on the last bolts of woven wool, dyed yellow and marked for Calais. A dark man, weathered from the sea, knelt in the transom reeving the tiller rope. Mr. Lau hailed him by the smack's name and the man looked up. Shaven head. A round face, coloured dark red. Eyes bulging wide. When he rose from the deck he stood tall as Ajax, and near as broad. Two deep scars, old but still livid, ran across his bare chest.

"This be *Solitude*. Who you?"

Mr. Lau shot his dentures at the man. Shocking, that, for I'd not seen him to pull that jape since the Mekong. No good first impression, I guessed, and wondered if we'd lost our best chance for transport. But yet another surprise came when the man shot his own dentures back at Mr. Lau. The clatter made an unsettling racket. Mr. Lau, though bandy of leg and no taller then me, smiled and stepped forward.

"Good on you, sir! I see we both share the morbid humour. I am Ignatius Lau, Sailing Master of the Lively Class frigate, *Eleanor*. And this is Mr. Harriet, midshipman aboard the same vessel. You are Dame-Marie?"

"I be him. You sent by dat FitzRoi mon. Last night I received dat one's message sayin' de situation of you. Now here be mine. Last week my mate, she become too much drunk at Mudchute and got herself beat down pretty bad. Can't do de work on board of here. But I got a mon and him sister bookin' passage for Calais on dis day and I hope to debark soon as dey arrive. Dey payin' in advance and I can't wish to pay it back."

Mr. Lau laughed. "Can you pay it back?"

The question seemed impolite, and I feared Dame-Marie might take offense. Instead, he only returned the laugh, his voice booming thunderous along the wharf.

"Dat I cannot! Can't pay you, neither. But if you crew for me den I afford your passage."

"That would suit us, sir."

"Mind you, though, I be in de Calais for 'bout one week. If you must return before den, den *Solitude* not for you."

"We also have business in Calais. I do not know for how long, but we will still be pleased to work our passage there, if not the return."

"Dat good. First, I make sure you know de channel, and de Calais. So den, Mr. Lau, what tide run on de Thames just now?"

"A neap tide, sir. And if we leave within the hour the current will carry us beyond the Downs before we ever need to set sail."

"You don't say. What you know of de Calais den?"

"I worked the channel for many years and called at Gaston Berthe often. That was before the French went mad with their revolution, but I am sure the roadstead at Calais is much the same as ever."

Dame-Marie nodded. "I take you." Then he pointed at a knot tied to a piling. "Now boy, what be dat knot?"

"A taut-line hitch, sir."

He smiled. "Both of you may come on board of here. Mr. Lau, finish splicing de tiller. Mr. Harriet, take your ditty bags below and commence to parcel out my cargo. Be quick about it. I expect dem passengers be here any time after now."

⚡

I went below to stow our bags and dispose of a proper ballast. I counted twelve dozen bolts of wool, each bound tight. I'd handled a great many bolts of wool in Newbury, but none ever weighed as much as these. And a bolt will fold near double when moved about, but these remained rigid. On *Eleanor*, Gleason would spread such hard labour across the crew, but a channel smack can never afford the luxury of enough hands. The hold grew stifling hot, and I became starved, as well, for I'd not yet eaten more than a biscuit this morning. My stomach complained that it might not have food again. Ever! Or at least not until Calais. I laughed at the thought of never eating until France. We'd fought the French at Aboukir Bay, and in the Mekong. But now there was a peace, and likely our next meal would be a French one. What did they eat? Aboard *Eleanor* we all feared it was only snails and frogs. Even the thought of it turned my stomach. My hunger faded. Within the hour I finished my task.

When I came on deck Dame-Marie stood with a man and a woman. The man was near thirty, with limp brown hair hanging to his shoulders. A white silk scarf. Pallid skin, except for a blush on his cheeks. I don't think he was a small man, but he looked elfin as he stood there staring up at Dame-Marie.

"I assumed that by your name you were French. The thought never occurred you would be a . . ."

"Dat I be a Maroon?"

"Well, yes. But I assure you it doesn't matter. Not one iota."

"Oh, it matter. But your money still good wiff me."

"Well, yes. Yes, of course. We are ready, then?"

"We ready." Dame-Marie made introductions. "Mr. Wordsworth dis be Mr. Lau. He be a sailing master in de Royal Navy but now he servin' for de first mate on board of *Solitude*."

Mr. Lau blanched, no doubt at being introduced as a first mate. Even so, he bowed decorous.

"Mr. Lau dis be Mr. Wordsworth. And dis here be his sister, Dorothy."

Dorothy Wordsworth was about the same age as her brother. She wore a grey bonnet, with the part of her brown hair just showing. Dark eyes, a nose much like her brother's, and a small mouth with narrow, colourless lips. Her light blue dress brushing on the deck.

"We cast off now, and wish for dis deck be clear of passengers, 'least 'til we reach Canvey Island. Please take your sister and go in de cabin, Mr. Wordsworth. Boy, stow der bags."

They'd brought much luggage aboard, with each bag marked with their last name. Wordsworth. The name came familiar. I'd heard it before, though unclear of where, or when. I finished my task and went on deck.

"Mr. Lau? How many in England are named Wordsworth?"

"I hardly know, Harriet, but for the two aboard this smack."

We had no ship's bell to mark the time, but agreed it was almost noon when *Solitude* weathered Margate. Though still not quite in the channel she began to rise on the North Sea swell. My body leaned with the motion, my lungs filling with the fresh sea air. I'd been away from the sea not overlong, but long enough, it seemed. A grand thing deep within me awoke to the wind booming on the lugsail and thrumming in the stays. Soon we raised Ramsgate, far to starboard, and stood full into the channel. I took a turn at the tiller. Dame-Marie gave me the course and bearing.

"Compass be true enough, so you be always makin' south by east. Keep a sharp eye on dat lugsail. If she luff den you let her fall off to port 'til she fill. But *Solitude*, she have a will of her own and on dis reach she be wantin' to make south by south. If dat occur den you must clew up. Call Mr. Lau if you need to sheet dem lines. If dis wind hold den we come up to de Calais in 'bout two hour. I go below now and take my meal. You have need of me den don't you hesitate none."

Soon Mr. Wordsworth and his sister stepped from the cabin. The woman carried a decanter of red wine and a basket of bread, cheese, and fruit. Pears, I think. They sat atop the cabin, chatting as they shared their repast.

"Well, Dorothy, I've no doubt Coleridge means well enough, but I think he misses the point. Pass the wine, please."

His sister passed the wine, then broke open the loaf and handed him a chunk. I gripped the tiller firm, my mouth watering and my stomach grumbling anew.

"And what point does Coleridge miss, William?"

"That *Preludes* requires the willing suspension of disbelief. Is that a Stilton?"

Dorothy crumbled the wedge, and they both nibbled silent. The wind shifted a point, and I worked the tiller to fill.

"The pears smell ripe. I'll have one, please."

Dorothy handed her brother a pear. A most edible pear.

"The willing suspension of disbelief, William? By that do you mean the childhood imagination."

"I do. The heart and sole of the young, hidden away in each of us. But a child's imagination exists far beyond a matter of belief, or mere fancy, or at least what adults think of as fancy. A child's cognition is an independent power. A dynamic force, with a life of its own. Attuned to the universe. Utterly divergent from an adult's jaded experience, and only to be perceived by a young, unadulterated mind. At thirty-two I barely catch a glimpse of what I once held true as a child. Yet I'm thrilled still to be aware that any such universe exists at all. It exists! Even as I speak, and remains the absolute reality which dominates the landscape of a child's mind. So don't you see, dear sister, that as a poet I must strive to reinvigorate those thoughts of my imagination. My thoughts first perceived as a child."

Wordsworth drew a deep breath and let out a windy sigh.

"That I may fetch invigorating thoughts from former years, might fix the wavering balance of my mind."

"*Preludes?*"

"Yes. Lines six-two-four, six-two-five and six-two-six."

The string of numbers! They sounded familiar, yet not quite right, and I recalled instanter where I'd heard them before, along with the name ... Wordsworth. A poet! My tongue wagged before I could leash it.

"Beg pardon, sir, but it's lines six-two-one, six-two-two and six-two-three."

My words caught him off guard, and he turned to stare unblinking.

"What did you just say?"

I said it again.

Without another word he went to the cabin and brought back a copy of *Preludes*.

"Extraordinary. The lad's quite right." He studied me close. "How is it you recall the exact lines?"

"It's not the lines, sir. It's the numbers. Or at least how I first came to think of numbers. I mean, when I was a boy."

"Ah! Then you developed this aptitude as a child?"

"Yes, sir."

Wordsworth raised a brow. "Pray tell more."

"I don't think so, sir. I've only told two others about the numbers."

"Then why not me?"

"Because first I told Reggie Spoon. He was loblolly aboard *Eleanor*. But then he became killed and sometimes I wonder if it was because I told him about the numbers."

"You must not blame yourself, son."

"But then I told Gottlieb, and he became killed, too."

"Gottlieb?"

"Yes, sir. He was a diplomatic passenger aboard *Eleanor*."

"An Austrian?"

"No. Egyptian."

"Gottlieb's hardly an Egyptian name."

"No, sir. But his name wasn't really Gottlieb. He said he was Ra."

"Ra? I've not heard the name."

"No matter. Gottlieb died, same as Reggie. I hope you don't die now, too, sir. I mean if I tell you."

"I promise not to die, at least not anytime soon. What about these lines from *Preludes*?"

"Well, it's just that numbers all have lives, sir. And the lines in your poem are all numbered. That's how I remember them. Six-two-one, six-two-two and six-two-three."

"Numbers have lives?" Wordsworth turned to his sister. "Do you see it, Dorothy? A perfect example of the willing suspension of disbelief. Tell me, young man, can you explain just how these numbers are alive?"

"They come that way, sir."

"What way?"

"Just the way they are, sir, and how they treat each other. In six-two-one, well ... six is a bully, and he needs to pick on the smaller numbers. And two is the number right next to him, I mean in six-two-one, so he has the chance to pick on her. Except what he really wants to do is threaten one, but two's standing between them. And two, she's sweet, and has a humble disposition and is always looking out for one, who's just a baby."

Wordsworth gaped at me.

"I'm sorry, sir. It must make no sense to you."

"It doesn't matter if it makes no sense to me. So I bid you please go on."

"I will. But then in line six-two-two the numeral two feel less threatened by six, because now there's two of her."

"Good for her. I'm pleased."

"Except then comes line six-two-three."

"Yes?"

"So now two's surrounded by six and by three."

"Is that bad?"

"Most bad. Three's a nasty one because he's not much bigger than one or two. And is always afraid of any number bigger than itself, so it tries to become important by picking on one and two."

"I see. And the larger numbers, do they have threatening personalities as well?"

"Not all of them, sir. Four and eight are most kind."

"Well I'm very relieved to know that one and two don't have to stand alone against three and six."

"Well, there's number five, sir. And also seven. They're much the same as three and six. And then there's always nine."

"Yes, of course. Always nine. We all must fear nine, I think."

I thought he was making light of me now, and I must have pulled a long face.

"Please don't take offense, young sir. I find all this quite fascinating, and very real. For you it's a sensible and complete world." Wordsworth smiled broad. "What's your name?"

I told him.

Dorothy spoke up. "Hello, Owen. You've been watching us with a hungry eye. I'm sorry we didn't think to share, for surely we have enough. Come. Sit here and tell us more while you have a bite."

"Thank you, ma'am, but I'm standing a watch."

Dame-Marie came from below. "I send for Lau. He relieve you. We still be a hour from the Calais so you spend time wiff de passengers if dey wishin' it."

I came to sit with them. Dorothy patted my shoulder with a most gentle touch. She smelled of lavender when she offered me a portion of their lunch.

"Thank you, ma'am."

"You're welcome. Make sure you eat all of it."

"I should like to save some for Mr. Lau, if I may."

"Of course."

Wordsworth took up where he left off. "I'm transfixed by your numerology, but I still don't quite understand how my *Preludes* has anything to do with it."

"It's because I remember their line numbers from when I heard them aboard *Foudroyant*. Mr. Pratt said they were part of a flag hoist."

"Who is Mr. Pratt? And how dare he plagiarize me on a flag hoist."

"Mr. Pratt was a midshipman aboard *Foudroyant*, sir, and it wasn't a flag hoist. I mean not actual. It's just that I became a bother to him so he said those words were on the hoist only to stop me from asking any more questions."

"Well I don't like for Mr. Pratt to have abused my work."

"Aye, sir. It was a bit cheeky."

The wind shifted abrupt as *Solitude* crested a steep roller. Wordsworth and Dorothy held tight on the windward shrouds.

"Cheeky? You say my *Preludes* is cheeky?"

"No, sir. Pratt only spoke those lines to quit my curiosity. That's what was cheeky. He said I had too much imagination."

"Ah! Imagination. You do seem to have a good deal of it."

"But I don't think it's imagination, sir."

Wordsworth cocked an eye. "What do you mean?"

I said nothing, only watched the gulls diving in our wake.

"Owen?" Dorothy's soft voice coaxed me from my preoccupations. "What are you thinking?"

I'd not heard any gentle woman's voice in overlong, and wished to trust the kindness in her tone.

"It's not just numbers, ma'am. There's also the whispering."

"The whispering?"

"The Sukiyama."

Her brother broke in. "Now there's a delicious sound for you. Sukiyama. The metrical foot is anapaest, though I doubt it's Indo-European. Can you describe this Sukiyama?"

"No, sir. Except it might be a tree. The old oak tree in my great nana's croft. The leaves whispered once, when me and Mum spent the night with great nana."

Wordsworth and Dorothy exchanged a look.

"What did the leaves say?"

"I can't remember, sir. I was young."

"Of course. But tell me, do you still hear the whispering?"

"Sometimes. Not too much, though. And it's always about a thing that will happen soon."

Wordsworth turned to his sister. "The Oracle at Delphi."

"I don't know what the Oracle is, sir. And I don't think I've been at Delphi."

Solitude groaned as she carried the next swell. Her rigging harped in the wind and the sea drove us on until the land breeze brought the smell of France. A fragrance not so different from England. Earth most verdant, and the bloom of wildflowers.

Dame-Marie called out, "Man dem lines, boy."

♭

The first buoy marking the outer roads of Calais flew the tricolour of the French Republic. Dame-Marie called for us to come about on the port tack, but Mr. Lau spoke up.

"I suggest we stay on the starboard tack a bit longer."

"Why dat?"

"Gaston Berthe has a strong undertow that is best negotiated on the starboard tack." Mr. Lau pointed off the bow. "That is the headland at Gris Nez." He turned again, pointing to a square tower looming over Calais, glowing amber in the late sun. "And that is the spire of Saint-Omer's. If you come about just as we intersect the line running between Gris Nez and Saint-Omar, the undertow will draw us nicely into Gaston Berthe."

Dame-Marie nodded silent, and we bore steady on, chasing the long shadow of *Solitude*'s raked mast. When her stub of a bowsprit bisected the line, we came about smart, standing handsome into

Gaston Berthe. No one met us, so we found our own slip and I hopped on to the jetty and secured our lines. I looked up as a clatter of wood knocked on the cobblestones and watched as a young man made for us. His hurried footfall had caused the racket, for his shoes were made of wood, and they rang distinctive on the stones. He wore a dark blue jerkin and white duck trousers cut wide at the bottom. When he saw me, he stopped, and spoke a few words. French, of course. I understood none of it, but for what came at the end. A name. Annette Vallon. I fetched Mr. Lau.

"Who is he, sir?"

"A *sans-cullote* ."

"Looks much like an English peasant. Except for his trousers and shoes."

"The trousers are no more than an egalitarian ploy. A ruse, so to speak. I do not wish to blather on, but long trousers and wooden shoes set the *sans-cullote* apart from the aristocracy and clergy. To some extent their attire has also kept them from the chopping block, at least until Robespierre started to guillotine everyone no matter what they wore."

Wordsworth and his sister came from their cabin. I pointed to the fellow standing on the wharf. Wordsworth addressed him in French, and the man jumped up and down.

"Dorothy, we're in luck. Annette sends this *portier* for us."

When the porter produced a cart to haul their luggage, the Wordsworths stepped ashore. Mr. Wordsworth turned to me.

"Ah, there you are. I'm very pleased to have met you, young man, and only wish we might have had more time. However, my sister and I are in Calais on family business and we must go with this man. But may I give you a word of advice?"

"Yes, sir."

"Be sure to honour your childhood imagination. You're still young and able to conjure it at will but when you become an adult that ability will diminish. So you must try to succor it, and to value it. For I assure you, your imagination is a living thing, alive as anything you will ever encounter." He nodded to his sister, and she produced a pale green ledger from under her shawl. "I wish to present you with this ledger. It's never been used. Each page is a blank, just waiting for you to fill it. I suggest you make a record. Your numbers, and such ... and surely this phenomenon you call the Sukiyama. Will you do it?"

My first ledger. Meant only for me. No one would collect it after a voyage had paid off. None would read it but me. A fine thing for me to have, and for Wordsworth to give.

"Thank you, sir! I'll be sure to write in it."

I took the thing and opened it. The binding creaked, and the cover held the slightest scent of Dorothy Wordsworth.

Wordsworth laid a hand on my shoulder. "Well then, I suppose it's goodbye."

They left the jetty just as a small dray arrived. Six men came with it. Dame-Marie called them aboard to offload the wool. He checked each bolt against his manifest. When they were arranged in the dray, he turned to Mr. Lau.

"You sent here by dat FitzRoi mon. Must be bank business."

"It is."

"Den I extend you an offer."

"What is that?"

"All dem banks be closed now so you must wait for de mornin'. But I have business onshore dat don't wait. I go wiff my cargo tonight and won't return until first light. Dere be nuffhin' of value on board of *Solitude*. But she a boat, and if left untended she likely go missin' in de night. So I askin' you to stay on board of her tonight."

"Yes, we will do that."

"Dere be a smoked herring in de larder. Share it for your dinner."

The twilight came on calm, so we slung our hammocks on deck and observed Walsingham Way filling the night sky, slow and sure. A new moon. A shooting star. Mr. Lau spread ointment on his wound ... the last of what Mrs. Dolan had sent along. It smelled of beeswax.

"No celestial navigation tonight, lad. Just stellar observation." He stiffened in resolve. "Even so, it is always best to maintain ship's discipline. We shall keep a watch. I won't sleep any time soon so I will stand first and middle watch."

"Is it your wound that keeps you awake, sir?"

Certain it must have bothered him, for the thing looked most angry. But Mr. Lau refused to admit of it. The night went full dark. *Solitude* rocked gentle as waves lapped her hull. On shore, a woman sang. I didn't know the words, but her voice sounded doleful. Mr. Lau stirred in the dark and cleared his throat. "We may live in the Enlightenment, but our past is still very dark."

"Sir?"

"Today you spoke with innermost province to Wordsworth and his sister. But some impulses are best kept to yourself, lad. Better not to tell a stranger how you come by your numbers. Or that you hear what others cannot. You are a young man now, a midshipman in His Majesty's Royal Navy. No longer a boy who can voice his reveries with the impunity of youth. And though you have seen much in your career and have learned to live with the consequence of your actions, still, there is a thing you must know. You were safe enough with Wordsworth and his sister. I believe they are both above reproach. But to some, your words ring of apostasy."

He fell silent. *Solitude* snubbed at her hawser to send a slight shudder along her hull.

"I don't know what apostasy is, sir, but it seems not a good thing to ring of."

"It is not. There is another risk, as well. More elusive. More predatory."

"Sir?"

"There are some who covet what you have and would destroy you for it."

The night watchman made his rounds, calling out. "*Minuit ... tout va bien.*"

I took the taper and went below. But, before I snuffed its light, I opened my new ledger and made my first entry.

There are some who covet what you have and would destroy you for it.

4. Sea change

In the morning we called at Nathan Mayer Bank, asking for Lionel David. A frail, clean-shaven man. Near thirty, with straw-yellow hair and a high forehead. When he finished reading our letter of introduction, he set it aside, drumming his immaculate fingers on the desk. He rang a small bell and his secretary stepped in. They spoke in French. I caught some of the words, but hardly enough. Then David addressed the Sailing Master in English.

"Mr. Lau, in the lobby I heard you speaking French. But your French is unbecoming, so we'll conduct our business in English. I've just asked my secretary to find the account Mr. FitzRoi has brought into question. But, before we go any further, I must ask you to establish your bona fides. Your commission, if you will."

"I have no commission, sir, but I believe my Master's Certificate will serve."

David examined the document.

"Ordinarily that would suffice, but this forgery entails a certain degree of sophistication, so I feel obliged to take an extra precaution. FitzRoi claims that you came to see him in his office. Please describe that office, if you will."

Mr. Lau described it.

"Very well."

The secretary brought in the ledger. David appraised it direct, his head nodding as some pigeon, then addressed us.

"This account originated on seventeen of April 1802, with an initial deposit of three hundred seventy-nine pounds, seven pence. In his letter FitzRoi counsels me to freeze this account immediately, then have the authorities find and arrest Coutts. But I see something here FitzRoi couldn't know. Since seventeen April there have been no withdrawals."

"Good."

"Good indeed, Mr. Lau. Better yet, there have been additional deposits amounting to almost three thousand francs. It seems a bit premature to restrict an account while it still accrues but, nonetheless, I'll comply with FitzRoi's suggestion. However, there's a pattern evolving here that we may well make use of. One deposit every two weeks. Always on a Thursday. If this method holds then we won't need to send someone to arrest Coutts, but only wait for him to come to us."

"You expect another deposit soon?"

"If Coutts holds to his routine, then yes, I do. This very Thursday, in fact. Only two days." He drummed once more. His face coloured resolute and he stood abrupt. "Please excuse me while I speak to my head cashier."

David returned in not overlong.

"Here's what I've done. I've just flagged this account. If Coutts or anyone else tries to access it for any reason he'll be arrested. I've also established a provisional account in Mr. Harriet's name. It contains one thousand francs, secured by his inheritance. Mr. Harriet, I suggest you make a substantial withdrawal from it before leaving here today because, for the time being, you must both avoid this bank. If Coutts were to see either you here it would tip our hand. Also, keep off the streets as best you can. Calais is small. If he sees you walking about, he's bound to suspect."

A tower clock struck ten times.

"I have another client due at any moment so we must finish our business. Leave your address with my secretary. If Coutts makes an appearance, I'll send word. Please go."

Jean Dame-Marie sat in the bow mending the leech on *Solitude*'s jib. He wore no shirt, and the noonday heat raised a sheen on his ginger-brown skin. The keloid scars crossing his chest smoldered ashen grey. When Mr. Lau hailed him from the jetty, he waved us aboard.

"Complete of dat business?"

"No, sir. It will take until this Thursday, at the soonest."

Dame-Marie nodded. "Dis mornin' I arrange for a cargo of wine. It be on Gaston Berthe dis Saturday. Den I sail for Dover. If you be willin' to work dat return passage den I must know of it soon."

"I can only tell you we are willing to work it. But, for now, is it possible for us stay on board *Solitude* while we wait on our circumstance?"

"I be no charity, mon."

"We will earn our keep. This vessel is in need of maintenance. If you permit us to stay, I am certain Mr. Harriet will undertake the work. And I will draw you a chart of Calais. Soundings and tidal flows, and the like."

"How 'bout Cape Verde? You be familiar wiff dat place?"

"Fifteen degrees north by twenty-three degrees west. Two hundred miles off Dakar."

"Can you chart dat?"

"I can chart that entire group of islands, if you wish."

"Good. Mr. Harriet, start earnin' your keep. Scrape and paint dem gunnels. Der be a paint locker in de bow. And you, Mr. Lau, you be earnin' your keep wiff chartin' Cape Verde. You may use dat desk in de cabin."

I set to my work. Mr. Lau made for the cabin. Dame-Marie laughed hearty. "Now here be a fine ting. One Maroon in command of de Royal Navy." He put on a shirt. "I goin' ashore. Won't return 'til de mornin'. Mr. Lau, you find parchment and ink in dat desk. Be a good quill, too."

Before starting his chart, Mr. Lau scribed a line to David, informing him where to find us, and hired a boy to deliver it. I scraped and painted all afternoon while the Sailing Master worked in the cabin. Twilight came on slow, and the gloaming remained overlong. We could have worked well into the night, but there was no more paint, and by then Mr. Lau had drawn an excellent set of charts.

"We have earned our keep this day, lad. I am peckish, so no doubt you are ravenous. There is an *épicier* on the jetty. A place to buy food, as I recall. They might have something we could dare eat. Their shop is closed now, but no doubt the owner lives above. Go and knock. They might reopen if you show money in hand. Ask for *baguette* and *beurre*, and *oeuf*. Bread, butter and eggs. I do not know the word for cheese but if you see any, just point to it and they will understand. Do not try to pay in sterling. They will only accept French currency. And I would not try the *assignats*. We might as well use them to start our cooking fire. Go you now."

The *épicier* was shuttered, but dim light from the dwelling above fell on the cobblestones. I knocked, then stood in the lamplight with my handful of francs. Someone inside moaned and complained, but soon a pair of wooden shoes clacked on the stairs. The door opened narrow, and an old woman holding a glim peered out. I pointed to my stomach, holding out the francs. She nodded and let me in. I asked for a *baguette*, but she had none. I saw no cheese, but noticed some eggs nestled in a wicker basket. Fourteen. Three pale-blue, and eleven speckled brown. I counted the speckles on one of the brown eggs. Twenty-four. When I laughed, the old woman scoffed, shaking her grey head. Yet I was pleased. Whenever twenty-four of anything occurred in nature it usually meant a good thing. At least Cana, the young girl in the acrobat troop, believed as much. In their skit, she played the number two, and her brother played four. He was always kind, same as Cana. Two and four. Twenty-four. I'd not thought of Cana in overlong. I liked her. We talked and laughed together at Newbury Fair. I didn't know it then, but I think her world was uncaring and overlarge, for one so frail as her.

The woman tapped on my shoulder to end my woolgathering. She mumbled in French, and from her tone I guessed she thought me the odd one. Or perhaps she believed all English lads counted the speckles on an egg. To make amends I bought every one of them, as well as the basket they were in. I remembered to ask for butter. She cut a slab, then held out her hand for payment. When I gave her all my scrip, she smiled broad and toothless.

After we ate, I lit a taper for Mr. Lau to spread his charts.

"A navigational lesson." He tapped an arthritic finger on a ring of islands. "This grouping makes up the Cape Verde archipelago. Their coordinates are noted in the upper left corner. Where are these islands in relation to the nearest point of Africa?"

I studied his drawing. The demarcations stood out vivid and true. And the marginalia flowed as an endless stream of knowledge, direct from his memory.

"How can you know all of this in your head, sir?"

"Mostly by habit. But, in this case, also by association. I first charted Cape Verde in '88, with your uncle."

"On *Zealous*?"

"Aye. We had occasion to water at Santa Maria. That is the northernmost island of Cape Verde. Your uncle was a lieutenant then, and he took me in a longboat to sound the harbour. At that time a Portuguese frigate was known to patrol off Cape Verde, protecting the slave trade. Sounding the harbour would have been a risk for a smaller war ship. *Zealous* was fifty guns, though, with a complement of four hundred, and the Portuguese stayed well clear. We watered unchallenged and then went on to chart all of Cape Verde. I remember your uncle, even now, sitting upright in the stern, glassing the coastline for runaway slaves. Your uncle never said as much, but I think he felt slavery is an abomination. I do not think there was much he could have done for them, though. Besides, rescuing slaves was not our mission. Now then, say how these islands are situated."

"In the mid-Atlantic, sir. About three hundred miles due west of Dakar."

"What is at Dakar?"

"I don't know, sir."

"It is deep water port. And about one mile offshore is the island of Gorée. That is where the House of Slaves is located, and I suspect this is why Dame-Marie asks for a chart of Cape Verde."

"Sir?"

"All slave ships departing Goreé call at Cape Verde before embarking on the middle passage."

I gazed at Mr. Lau.

"You fail to see the connection, so I will explain. Dame-Marie is a free slave, lad, and I believe he is obsessed with a great desire to free any and all slaves when their captors call at Cape Verde. He may even have been inspired by the efforts of Toussaint Louverture."

"Who is that?"

"A slave born on Saint-Domingue. He led a slave revolt on that island ten years ago. Successful, I might add, or at least for a time. Time enough to encourage others to follow on. Perhaps Dame-

Marie is one of them. Why else would he ask me to chart Cape Verde?"

"But *Solitude*'s a channel smack, sir. Certain he'd need a larger vessel for Cape Verde."

"Aye. A brig, at least. And hauling wool and wine will never earn him enough to afford such a brig."

"Except that wool, sir, I don't think the bolts were just wool."

Mr. Lau looked at me curious.

"They weighed heavy, sir. And handled too stiff."

♭

The night watchman called out as he made his rounds. Four in the morning. Mr. Lau spoke low.

"Wake up, lad. Morning watch."

I rolled from my hammock, bare feet thumping on the deck. Mr. Lau struggled into his own hammock. Still, he didn't sleep.

"You said those bolts of wool were too heavy, and they did not bend. How many bolts?"

"Twelve dozen, sir."

In the dark he massaged his wen. "Muskets."

"Sir?"

"One hundred and forty-four muskets. I suspect Dame-Marie has smuggled them into France, each one cloaked in wool. Perhaps that is how he will earn enough to buy himself a brig."

♭

On Thursday, after taking the noon line, a messenger delivered a note.

Lau,
Come at once to the corner of Rue de la Mer and Place d'Armes
—Lionel David

When we arrived, several gendarmes stood on *Rue de la Mer* keeping the crowd from gathering around a body lying motionless in the gutter. David approached us.

"An hour ago, this man called at Nathan Mayer. He tried to access your account. When *Sécureté* attempted to arrest him, he fled. They gave chase. When he failed to stop, they had no choice but to shoot him. We think it's Coutts, but we wish you to verify. Please do it now, before the coroner arrives to remove the body."

"I will tell you from here. It is Coutts. The stench remains after his death."

"Good enough for me. However, Inspector LePuy wishes for a visual confirmation. He's from *Sécureté*. Come."

David nodded for a gendarme to remove the kerchief draped across Coutts's face, his lifeless eyes staring wide, dried blood caked on his side whiskers.

"Coutts?"

"Yes."

A man caught up to David and spoke in rapid French while pointing to an apartment building. David turned to us.

"This man is the concierge of that building across the street. He claims that Coutts had recently let apartment five, on the third floor. Inspector LePuy sends word he is about to enter it and invites me to join him. Perhaps you should come, too."

LePuy looked about fifty. Overweight and sweating profuse in his twill frock. Thin strands of black hair stuck pasted to his domed pate. His right hand was missing, its stump bound in yellow suede. He lumbered as a bear as he led us to the third floor. First he tried the door to apartment five, but it was locked. No matter. He took one step back and kicked in the door, and the thing flew open as if smashed by a carronade. The room stank of Coutts, even before we entered. One room only, with a narrow cot and a desk. The desk drawer was locked, but LePuy picked it with practiced ease. He removed a bundle of French scrip, sniffing the bills as he fanned through the stack. He then produced a magnifying glass from his coat pocket and placed it on the top bill.

He growled. "*La faux monnaie.*"

"Assignets?" I asked David.

"No. Francs."

"There looks to be a great many."

"But worthless. LePuy says they're counterfeit."

That same afternoon Mr. Lau and I stood in David's office.

"Mr. Harriet, I assure you, your full inheritance is forthcoming but, unfortunately, after Coutts's original deposit, the rest may have all been counterfeit. LePuy has seized your funds until he determines the source of this forgery."

Mr. Lau spread his bowed legs over wide, as if standing on *Eleanor*'s quarterdeck. "Coutts's additional deposits into Mr. Harriet's account, counterfeit or not, have no bearing. The lad has waited patiently for you to resolve your blunders, yet you keep putting him off." He stomped his small foot. "I will speak to LePuy."

"I wouldn't do that."

"Why not? Is he not in charge of this investigation?"

"He is. But Harriet is English, as are you, and LePuy despises every one of you. He lost his right hand at Lincelles."

"The Royal Navy had nothing to do with Lincelles. And Harriet was but a child at the time."

"Do you think any of that matters to LePuy? He's a Chevelier in the Legion of Honour. If you confront him he may feel inspired to arrest you. I've barely managed to convince him not to arrest you both already for duplicity in this unfortunate affair."

"Since you have his ear, then convince him to release Harriet's money."

"I've already used any influence I have, which isn't much. LePuy despises Nathan Mayer as much as the English, for our role in financing your government in its war with Napoleon. In the past I've only kept myself from prison by reminding LePuy that Nathan Mayer has also financed the Revolution." David paused, raising a brow. "Besides, new information has surfaced. LePuy's just learned the authorities in Nantes have confiscated a set of intaglio plates used for printing the five-hundred franc note." He paused once more, examining his nails before going on. "Now it seems my cashier recalls Coutts making his deposits in five-hundred franc notes only. This complicates the matter. The inquiry will take a month to run its course. Maybe longer."

"Why so long?"

"You may not be aware of it, Mr. Lau, but Nantes is in the Vendée. Many of the authorities in that region are still Loyalist sympathizers. They're somewhat reluctant to cooperate with the Consulate. But I'm quite sure your funds will be available by this fall."

David rang the tiny bell, and his secretary stepped in. They spoke in rapid French, a sure sign we'd been dismissed.

We left Nathan Mayer and walked along Rue Leveux, making for Gaston Berthe.

"What shall we do, sir?"

We reached *Solitude* before Mr. Lau made any reply.

"As for your inheritance, it appears we have little say in how long it will take. But David says no later than this fall. That is not too distant. So, for now I suggest we continue to offer our services to Dame-Marie. But only if we know his cargo is legal."

"Sir?"

"I strongly suspect there were muskets hidden in that first shipment of wool. Did you see them for sure?"

"No, sir. I can't know for sure if they were muskets."

"Well, perhaps it is best not to know. But if they were muskets, then for sure they are contraband. And if Dame-Marie intends to haul more of them, and he is caught, then we will be implicated. And likely hanged as smugglers."

⨍

The solstice brought passable weather ... at least for the English Channel, which I learned straightaway to call *la Manche*, or at least when we called at Calais. And Mr. Lau taught me more with each crossing. Soundings. Crosscurrents and tides. The wind and the weather. While in port, Dame-Marie would spend his nights ashore, but always allowed us to stay aboard *Solitude*. We called at Calais every week, and *Sécureté* sometimes inspected our hold. While there we visited Nathan Mayer's, where Mr. Lau would be sure to badger Lionel David.

We worked the Channel all through July and August, plying the lively trade between Calais and London. *Solitude's* cargo was always bolts of wool bound for Gaston Berth, and on the return, puncheons of wine bound for Dover and London. An occasional passenger, but none like Wordsworth or his sister. And once, a spirited mare who I loved overmuch. At times *Solitude* behaved lively as a mare, too. Dame-Marie was a demanding captain, but one who recognized the worth of an English sailor, and so gave us wide leeway. And though I longed for the ocean's inscrutable pull, I grew to love the Channel, as well.

Then came a sea change, a change so far reaching that it would set a new course for my life.

5. You have your life before you

After we completed our sixth channel crossing, and Dame-Marie had gone ashore for the evening, a small coach rolled on to the wharf and stopped at *Solitude*'s berth. A young man stepped from the carriage. He wore a powdered wig, just touching on the collar of his silk, pale yellow frock. White breeches ending at the knee, fine white hose, and black, patent leather pumps with polished steel buckles. He saw us watching him and called out.

"I say, is this the *Solitude*?"

Mr. Lau made reply. "It is."

"Oh, very good. I wish to speak with Mr. Ignatius Lau. Is he here?"

"I am Lau. What do you want?"

"I am Julian Uxore, Assistant Curator with the Society of Antiquaries of London. May I come up there?"

We led Uxore to the cabin and lighted a glim.

"I will go right to it, Mr. Lau. In February of this year the Society was given the task of translating a certain stele. It is referred to as the Rosetta Stone. Just recently your name has come up, for this stele came into the Crown's possession by way of Egypt, and it appears you did work on a similar, though much smaller artifact while serving off the coast of Egypt. Is that so?"

"It is. And so did this young gentleman here. Mr. Harriet is responsible for finding that artifact in the false bottom of a chest, and then assisted me in the rubbings I took of the thing. I forwarded those rubbings to Admiralty House but, unfortunately, the artifact itself has gone missing in the desert, at Amunia."

"A pity. It appears that artifact may have been an actual piece of the Rosetta Stone that had somehow chipped away down through the millennia. So it's true that you had begun work on a translation of the artifact. Yes?"

"Yes."

"Then you may be of assistance to the Society in our attempt at deciphering the Rosetta." Uxore withdrew a fold of parchment from his waistcoat and set it before Mr. Lau. "This is a protocol. An agreement, if you will. It states you will collaborate with the Society for a fee stipulated herein, and for an undetermined length of time, in translating the glyphs inscribed on said stele." He stood. "Be so kind as to read it through. If you are amenable to the terms, then please sign at the bottom. I will return tomorrow morning. Please be ready."

We sat quiet after Uxore left. Mr Lau handed me his glasses and, as always, I polished the lenses and gave them back. He studied the agreement, mumbling now and then, but saying nothing until I finally spoke.

"Will you sign it, sir?"

"This document may read like a request but it's more of a command. I must sign it."

"But I can't crew for Dame-Marie on my own."

"Nor should you. This morning Dame-Marie spoke to a stranger, and I saw him hand over a purse. I believe he bought information from the man. Perhaps Dame-Marie deems it safe enough to haul muskets for the next crossing. But if his informant is wrong, and *Sécureté* comes aboard to discover any contraband, then anyone aboard *Solitude* will likely be hanged on Gaston Berth. I suggest you let Dame-Marie find a new crew."

"Then I should like to go with you, sir. If I may."

"I am afraid this document makes no mention of you." He groaned, if but slight, and touched his wound. "Besides. The time has come."

"Sir?"

He breathed deep and let out a sigh. "You and I, lad, we have made the long passage together. We have become more than just shipmates, and for that we should be grateful. We would never have met, if not for the navy. In return, however, the navy exacts a price. Even the best of mates must always expect the parting of ways, Owen."

"No!"

"It is inevitable."

"But you're my teacher and master, sir. When I came aboard *Eleanor* I had no one. But you took me in and it's been my honour ever since to repay your kindness. And please forgive me if I speak out of turn, sir, but you have no one except ... except me."

"Lad, you mean more to me than I could ever say, and it is a fine thing you are willing to stand by me. But can't you see it? The time has come for you to discover just who you are, and what you are made of. I suspect you are ready to strike out on your own, but there is only one way to know."

"But why haven't you said it before now? Have I made you angry, sir? To ... to make you want to become rid of me?"

"I am not angry with you. Of course not. And I will answer your question with one of my own. I told you once that someday this war would end, and the world would pipe another tune. Do you recall that?"

"Yes."

"Well, that day may have arrived, even if no one quite loves this Treaty. But, even before Amiens, I guessed that this was your time. Even more so now, since your inheritance appears to have been secured." When I tried to interrupt, Mr. Lau held up a gnarled hand. "Please hear me out. Last week I sent a note to FitzRoi explaining that in my opinion you have demonstrated sound judgement in the matter of your bequest, let alone your skill in cyphering. I told him that even though you are not yet eighteen you are ready to take responsibility for your own funds. I think he will agree." The Sailing Master gazed across the darkening Pool, as if to gather his thoughts, then went on. "You have your life before you, son, and mine is all but spent. And although I have not taught you all I might know about the sea, still, there is much you can learn from others."

"But who?"

"If offered a berth on *Eleanor*, would you stay on?"

"I don't know, sir."

"Well if you do, then you would do well to seek out Wat. No doubt he will stay on with *Eleanor*. He is a quiet old salt, but when he speaks you should listen. And if you ask him a question, he will answer. And always be sure to make note how he acts before a big sea comes on the horizon." He braced against a bulkhead. "And you are incorrect, lad, for I am not alone. I will always have the sea."

6. A perverse interpretation.

I n the morning Dame-Marie cursed most colourful when he learned we would no longer crew for him and mumbled low when Uxore came for Mr. Lau. I stood on the wharf, looking after the carriage as it departed. Neither Mr. Lau nor I waved. But certain we watched each other until the coach turned on to Clarence Road. I then wandered as any stray, until I found myself standing before Mrs. Dolan's Room & Board. She had a room. This time she didn't say I must pay before, but only asked after Mr. Lau.

"Has his wound healed, then? He masked his pain, but I knew he suffered."

And still suffers. The first great wave of longing for the Sailing Master washed over me, and I could only manage to reply with but a half-truth.

"I think the ointment you sent with him helps, ma'am, and he's taken employment with some agency."

She beamed toothless. "Ah. Good on him. Well then, you may have the same room as before. Oh! And a gentleman came looking for Mr. Lau not long ago. He didn't tell why." She fetched a card from the mantel and gave it to me. "He left this."

Matthew J. Praether

The One Body

Sixteen Monk Street, London

I stowed my ditty bag and went in search of Praether.

Sixteen Monk Street was a grim, coal-smudged building near Mulgrave Pond. In the vestibule I found a listing for The One Body, alongside Praether's name. Second floor. On the stairwell I stopped short when I heard his voice raised in argument.

"I disagree. There is no just cause for slavery, and your mother is of the same mind."

Some unseen man replied scornful.

"Along with her pious donations to The One Body."

"Not without recompense. Do you know she has asked me as a favour to take you on board *Eleanor* to serve as my sailing master?"

"So that's why you've asked me here."

"It is."

"It matters not. You and your ilk are still hypocrites."

Who was this fellow daring to speak so insolent to an officer in the Royal Navy? I wished to step in and announce my presence, if only to see his face. But, when Praether countered him hot, I knew it best to stand clear.

"Hold your tongue! We may be cousins, but I outrank you, and I will brook no insubordination."

"But the facts still remain."

"What facts?"

"The fact that you take sugar with your tea."

"Yes?"

"The fact that you offer me a tot of rum."

"Explain yourself, man."

"The sugar in your tea and the rum in your bottle. They're both products of slave labour in the West Indies."

"Yes, but . . ."

"But nothing. I grew up on my father's plantation at Nanny Town. I've seen how a slave exists in order to bring you joy."

"Then as a Christian surely you must see our point."

"I do not. As a Christian I go by what the Bible says ... for slaves to obey their masters."

"A perverse interpretation."

"The point is you're willing to consume the product of a slave's labour but you wouldn't think of forcing an Englishman to work in the cane fields."

"Not the same."

"Of course not. Only a West African can bear the heat and misery of a cane field. An Englishman wouldn't last half a season. Nor did the native Taíno."

"Nonsense. The Spanish were never interested in plantation

slaves. Only gold and silver."

"And when they found neither on Jamaica, they exterminated the Taíno. The Spaniards considered them a bad investment."

"A bad investment is not the question."

"But it is. In the Antilles a slave's worth is measured in hard labour."

"But your father's holdings on Jamaica are the reason your mother disavowed him. Now she lives alone in Hull, and you are all she has left."

"Along with her shares derived from father's sugar mills. Do you not find it ironic, Praether, that your donations come from the profits made from slave labour?"

"On the contrary. I find it poetic justice." Praether cleared his throat. "Enough. I remind you that it is in our family's best interest if you were to abide by your mother's request. I will deploy from Portsmouth later this fall and I expect you to serve as my sailing master."

"I'll think about it."

"No doubt while swilling your next vial of laudanum. You look unfit."

"As do you. Now you know how it is to be wounded."

The man stormed past me in a fit of pique. He looked about fifty, narrow built, a low brow, with his face darkened in a scowl. Only after he made down the stairwell did I knock on Praether's door.

"Come."

The man who'd just left was correct. Captain Praether did look unfit. His light blond hair had thinned and turned lighter yet. His face, though still bearing the weathered look of a sea captain, was sallow. More jowled than when I last saw him being carried off *Eleanor*, at Portsmouth. His left arm was still in a sling. It was obvious that he'd not yet fully recovered from his injuries suffered during *Eleanor*'s engagement with *Hommage*. When he looked up, I saluted. He did not return it, but only placed a yellowed sheet of parchment in a drawer and slid it shut.

"Mr. Harriet. I must say your presence here is unanticipated."

"Mrs. Dolan says you were looking for Mr. Lau, sir."

Praether squinted keen. "You have seen him?"

"Aye, sir. We crewed together on a channel smack. But now Mr. Lau's taken work with the Society of Antiquaries."

"Well, that is inconvenient."

Just then Praether's eyes opened wide and he brought up both hands to massage his head. I thought I must go to his aid, but the moment passed, and he went on.

"But in these circumstances a sailing master must find work where he can. I need an experienced navigator because I have been given an unusual opportunity. But due to the Treaty I have been left to my own devices to find a crew. So far I have signed on Gleason. And the sailmaker ... what is his name?"

"Wat, sir."

"Yes. Him."

"Has the surgeon signed on, sir?"

"No. Regrettably, Mr. Starling has declined my offer. It seems he has taken it personally that his colleague's son was killed while serving as his loblolly, and he no longer wishes to serve in the Royal Navy." Praether brightened. "But Lady Praether has acquired the service of a fellow she believes will serve well in Starling's place. We shall see." He set his desk in order and leaned back. "In any event, now that you are here, I will take the opportunity to commend you. In Lieutenant Hoyer's account of our action with *Hommage* he states, and I quote ... 'Mr. Harriet assisted me ably in putting out the fire threatening *Eleanor*'s powder magazine.'" Praether grinned. "He only wishes you hadn't doused him with a hose."

"It seemed a good thing at the time, sir, as the lieutenant was on fire."

A clock chimed twelve noon. Praether stood, donning his coat deliberate slow, then cocked an eye, looking me over.

"Have lunch with me. I know you are on half-pay so I will buy you a meal at Goddard's. A short walk." He stepped close and spoke low. "Besides, I have a situation to discuss with you, and voices carry in this place. No doubt you heard the exchange between me and the man who just left."

Monk Street thronged with the noonday trade. Carts and drays rumbling past, men rolling butts of ale meant for some inn, foot traffic swarming on the cobblestones. A friar, spare as any scarecrow, stood on a corner dispensing loaves and fishes to the poor. Praether placed a few bob in his creel as we passed by.

"*Vai con Dio, mio figlio.*"

Praether explained. "A Carmelite missionary recently arrived from Rome. Permitted to travel since the Treaty. It seems the Bishop of Rome cares for the poor somewhat better than the Bishop of London."

We moved on.

"I will tell you now that the fellow in my office is my cousin. Ezekiel Pyeweed. Only child of my mother's sister."

I made to reply, but as we neared Dial Square, a bugle heralded a procession of hussars come to exercise their mounts on the bridal path. Beautiful animals. All prime and well cared for, with hooves well shod and buffed to a sheen. Horses of Tenth Royal Hussars tricked out in their regimental colours, royal blue and white.

Praether tapped on my shoulder. "Mr. Harriet, I am no longer your commanding officer, but I still expect you to pay more attention to me than to a horse parade."

"Of course, sir."

Praether went on. "As I was saying, Pyeweed is my cousin. He served on *Culloden*, at the Glorious First of June. Three years later he was aboard *Venerable*, at Camperdown. He was wounded during that action. Deep splinter wound. Ever since, he has been dependent on opium. First to mask the pain, and now because he has become addicted. The poor devil is destroying himself."

"And now his Mum wants you to save him?"

"She wants me to offer him a berth on my next voyage ... to keep him at sea and far from the opium."

"But there's laudanum on any ship, sir."

"Yes, but kept under lock and key."

We turned a corner and walked down Francis Street, soon coming to Goddard's.

"Enough of Pyeweed. Now I want to tell you more of *Eleanor*. But first we shall eat."

As he opened the broad door, the savour of fresh baked bread filled my nose. A sea of faces, all belonging to common folk seated at long tables receding deep into a vaulted hall. A thunderous clangour rang from the beams, every customer talking while he ate.

Praether smiled. "Excellent. We will not be overheard."

A boy in a stained apron appeared from nowhere and led us through the crowd to a long table with bench space wide enough for two, still warm from the last patrons. On that day Goddard's served a thick pea soup with generous chunks of gammon, a small loaf of bread, and steaming hot tea. I was most hungry and ate as if girding for some great sea battle. It seemed Praether was hungry, as well, for we finished simultaneous. He pushed his empty bowl away.

"Now then, as you well know, *Eleanor* suffered a great deal of damage in her last engagement. Even so, a colleague has persuaded the Crown to have *Eleanor* rebuilt, rather than sold for scrap. She is the first of the Lively Class frigates, after all, and well suited for what I have proposed to The One Body." Praether leaned in. "Last week her name was expunged from the navy list. Her refit will never be mentioned in the *Gazette*. A good start. However, she lacks her full complement of officers and men, and that is why I have been trying to find Mr. Lau. I had hoped he would consider my offer. I can tell you no more." He leaned in. "However, it has just occurred to me. I want you to think about serving again under my command."

When the boy dashed by with three bowls of pea soup balanced precarious on his arms, Praether called for our chit.

"I will tell you in advance. Your duties would be far reaching and may even include serving on more than one ship."

Once more the boy rushed by, dropping off our chit and waving for the next two customers to take our place. Praether settled the bill, then tugged at his waist coat. "I cannot speak for Mr. Lau, but likely he would recommend you."

Cannot speak for Mr. Lau ... the words hung heavy. My heart

sank on a long swell, and I near broke into piteous weeping. Of course, Praether couldn't know the Sailing Master had sent me away just hours before. Even so, his casual reference caught me off guard. How could he not know of this fresh wound, a wound still so raw? It seemed yet another unfair thing ... that any man would be so unaware of my loss. But Praether only sat there waiting for my response. I gathered myself and made reply.

"I'd be honoured to serve with you, sir. But, if I may ask, what is The One Body?"

"It is a belief inherent in the vow to abolish slavery. No less than a sacred creed." Praether raised his head high and spoke proud.

"'The body is one, and has many members, but all the members, many though there are, are one body; and so it is with Christ.'"

He closed his eyes as if in prayer. "First Corinthians, Chapter Twelve, verses Twelve and Thirteen." He opened his eyes and adjusted his neckband. "This is why we call ourselves The One Body."

"I still don't understand, sir."

"Then I will explain it this way." He drew me near. "Do you recall the night we came upon that dinghy adrift off Serbro Island?"

"Aye, sir. It was from a slave ship. *Elizabeth Carton*. It went down in a storm. There was a slave in that dinghy, still shackled."

Praether nodded. "And I had the carpenter free him. And ever since, that slave has represented every slave ... the body that is all one body. To break his shackles was all I could do for him at the time. But I made a vow, that very night, to do what must be done to abolish slavery." Praether stood tall, breathing deep, and puffing his chest proud. "Now Lady Praether and I intend to honour the vow."

Not one week later, FitzRoi summoned me to his office. He stood at his window taking a pinch of snuff, then turned to me.

"It seems Mr. David has bestirred himself. He travelled to the Vendée last week, called in a debt, and now the investigation has concluded. Your account at Nathan Mayer has been released and the entire sum of your inheritance transferred to Barclays. Three hundred ninety-one pounds, seventeen pence." He paused to regard me over his pince-nez. "No doubt you've have already calculated the interest accrued."

"An additional one pound and ninety-one pence, sir, since two bells of the afternoon watch."

He smiled. "Quite right. Now then, even though you've not reached the age of eighteen, as set down in your uncle's will, I've taken the recommendation of Mr. Lau and hereby grant you full access to your funds."

"Thank you, sir."

"It's none of my business, of course, but what are your plans?"

"I wish to go home on leave, sir. Newbury Fair starts this week with the full moon. I've been gone three years."

"A long time. No doubt your family's missed you."

"I've only my brother now, Albert. He's fifteen. I know he misses me, but Albert was born slow, and he can't do much for himself. Neighbors take care of him, even though they can't afford it. I wish to repay them for their kindness, sir. That's why I want to withdraw fifty pounds, immediate."

"That's quite generous."

"It's for what they've already done, sir, and to care for Albert after I'm gone. I'm a midshipman now, and it seems I might have a berth."

"You may very well have a berth. Amiens pleases no one. Many see it as more of a truce, or a brief hiatus, only to buy time for the next coalition to gain resolve. You would do well to make use of your home leave when you can. How will you be traveling to Newbury?"

"The Bath Coach, sir."

"Then you'll be passing through Reading."

"Aye, sir."

"Well, the peace has put a good many sailors on half-pay, or no pay at all. As a result, some have become footpads, causing the roads to be more perilous than usual. It would be inadvisable for you to transport fifty pounds in cash. However, Barclays has an agent in Reading." FitzRoi scribbled a note and gave it to me. "When you come to Reading call at Barclays. Ask for Mr. Weedon. Hand him this and he'll start an account in your name."

"Thank you, sir."

"You're welcome." He took another pinch. "Now reflect on this. Should this Treaty hold, and if you wish for a career other than in the Royal Navy, I would consider your application for a position at Barclays. Good day."

7. Poor soul, gentle soul

The next morning an axle failed on the Bath coach and, since the delay caused us to arrive late in Reading, I was permitted to sleep in the carriage that night. I called at Barclays early the next day, to make an arrangement with Mr. Weedon, then began walking the fifteen miles to Newbury. At Woolhampton a carter going my way said I might ride along. When he turned at Cold Ash, I hopped off. Soon the narrow lane topped the last rise, and I stopped to look across the fields. Home. But, instead of making for the smallholding, I only stood in the ruts. Certain I was born in that place and had lived there all my life. But the smoke now rising from its chimney didn't come from any fire made by a Harriet. Sunlight washed across the fields, and the quiet air warmed my face. Yet an icy finger ran along my spine as if giving final notice ... this was no longer my home.

I walked on, wondering where to go, until I came to Mary Hare, a small paddock alongside Winterbourn Stream. For some reason known only to him, Albert had named it Mary Hare. It was his favorite place in all the world, so it came as no great wonder to see him sitting there on his bench, watching mallards landing on the stream. My heart beat full. I set free a breath held deep for three years. Albert and I would spend untold hours at Mary Hare, sitting most quiet, just watching the bright clouds. Bees collecting nectar. Birds darting through the tree line. At times, I'd teach him how to count. But we had to start new every time, for he always became muddled by any number beyond three.

I'd point to the sky. "How may clouds do you see?"

Albert would think careful, then reply. "One."

"That's right." Then I'd point to the stream. "How many swans?"

"Two."

"Good! How many willows on the far bank?"

"Three."

Then I'd pick a stem of summer snowflakes, with four showy blooms. "How many snowflakes?"

He'd think a bit, then answer. "All of them."

No matter. It was just a game. Our way of sitting together at Mary Hare. Now he sat there alone, and I called to him by the name only I used.

"Aller."

He perked up, turning my way. A round, overlarge head. Blond hair cropped short, with a low forehead and thick brows. Brown, wide-set eyes shaped in a way that made him look different from others. Smooth face and rounded cheeks, a pug nose and a small mouth. His arms were thick and powerful, but his legs were short, and his feet bare.

I hoped he might jump up and run to me, lift me clean off my feet and hug me dear. But he only sat there on his bench, quaking, and then weeping as a baby. I came to sit by him, resting my arm across his broad shoulders.

"Aller. Don't cry. I know it's been overlong, but I'm home now."

He took my hand and pressed it to his face, weeping all the more. "Owee. Owee."

Poor soul. Gentle soul. The one I loved more than any living thing, now that Mum was gone. How had these last years treated him? Albert had always been a happy giant, if simple. But in my absence, he'd somehow been reduced. He stood near fourteen hands when I'd left and weighed all of fifteen stone. But three years of lonely confusion had reduced him cruel. I felt his thick bones shift under my hand. How had he ever survived?

"Come along, Aller. Let's go find Becca. I'm hungry. Are you hungry?"

We walked along the River Kennet, where Newbury Fair was held. The fair wouldn't begin until morning but already tradesmen and crafters filled the greensward, setting up their stalls and pitching tents. The scent of roasting meat carried on the breeze. We stopped at a small stage to watch Jack Narrowneck swallow his dirk, full down to the hilt. But, unlike the Onion, when he withdrew his sword there was no black cobra writhing on its tip. I thought to ask if he could produce a cobra, same as the Onion. But that had been in another world, far up the Mekong and deep within the Valley of Reeds. Instead, I placed a copper in Jack's hat and we moved on.

The fair ran for three days, always starting on the harvest moon. As a lad, I'd spin yarn in Mum's stall while she sold her weavings. Mum always did well at Newbury Fair. People came to see her early, when they still had a full purse. All were eager to buy from her, or Joan Stanhope. They were best of friends and always set up next to each other. People said Mum and Joan were the finest weavers in all of Berkshire. Becca was Joan's daughter, and we were both proud of our Mums.

Now Albert lived with Joan and Becca in a cob hut near Bridge Street. As we approached, I heard Joan's loom working in the forecourt. When we rounded the corner, I hauled short, for the clack of her lathe sounded familiar.

"That's Mum's loom!"

Joan blocked her shuttle and looked up. "Becca! Come see who's here."

But it wasn't Becca who came to see. It was Dunstan Steep, son of Alton Steep, the squire who'd sent my father packing. All of Newbury scoffed at Dunny's blue eyes, curly red hair, and pale skin, for neither of his parents looked that way. He wasn't well set up but had learned to use his fists and was quick to lay them on anyone who dared cross him.

"Well now, will you look at this, the ne'er-do-well returns."

"Good day to you, Dunny. I trust you are good."

"I do very good. And you will call me esquire."

"I will do that. And you will address me as Mr. Harriet. I'm a midshipman now in His Majesty's Royal Navy."

Steep sneered. "Never. You're no more than the spawn of a tenant my father chased off for not paying his debts."

Joan rose from her loom. "Leave him be. His mother was my best friend and I'm pleased he's come to see us. Though I'd guess it's Becca he'd rather see."

A gentle hand touched my shoulder, and I turned to see Becca, smiling full. She'd not changed overmuch. Still taller than me, though I'd near caught up. Brown hair parted in the middle, with a thick braid falling to her broad waist.

"Hello, Owen."

"Becca."

She narrowed her deep brown eyes. "Is that a scar at your left eye?"

"Oh." I touched it. "I became shot at Otra Nova."

"I'm sorry. We'd not heard."

I only stood there, not knowing what to say next, except for something dull. "You still smell of sweet grass."

Steep's fist struck out over quick, but I ducked away.

"You'll not speak to my woman that way!"

Albert made his whimpering sound, a low moan that I'd learned as a child meant he was upset. He ran for the hut when Steep closed on me, just as a hard voice barked from behind.

"Back off, Steep."

Able Erth. Newbury's constable. "The fair's about to start and this ain't no way to begin. Make stardust, Dunny. Get you gone."

Steep said nothing, but just turned and walked away. I remembered Erth now. He'd not changed his way in all my years growing up in Newbury, and he'd not changed in my absence. He was big, with a red face and beefy jowls. Steel grey eyes that were quick to see through any lie. He'd served in Newbury a great while and had come never to expect men to shake hands and make peace. He only knew the good people of Newbury respected him and the bad ones feared him. To him it made little difference, long as he got one or the other.

"A word with you, Harriet."

"Yes, sir."

"I saw you on the sward with Albert and followed you here, just in case Dunny might be hangin' about. He's always ready to fight and you'd be a likely one. Now you hear me out. I know your family's had bad fortune, but your brother John was always a rotter, come good luck or bad. I warned him to quit stealin' 'cause I'd catch 'im sooner or later. Which I done. Now John Harriet's been shipped to Botany Bay."

"I know, sir."

"But I know you ain't no rotter. So if you stay clear of Steep then I'll stay clear of you. As for Albert, my lovely bride were the midwife who brung 'im into this world. Might a' brung you, too. She midwifed for twenty years 'til she wore thin. Now she's Newbury's apothecary, and you need to go see her. She'll tell you some things about Albert you might already know, plus some things you might not. Go see her tomorrow, before it's too late."

I meant to ask Erth why it might be too late, but someone called his name, and he moved off.

Becca led Albert from the hut. "Your brother's afraid of Dunny. He always runs away if he can because Dunny hits him. He says Albert might learn from it. But he's just a bully, and he knows poor Albert can't think to fight back."

She looked down, pawing her foot in the dirt. "Owen, I'm so glad you've come home. Albert ... he pines for you every day."

"He's lost weight since I left home. Who's living in the cottage now?"

"A baker and his wife. They moved in last spring. She's with child. They're nice, but they keep to themselves. Did you get my letter?"

"I did. It's a good one. You wrote just after I left home, but it was only this January when the letter caught up. I meant to reply, but *Eleanor* would arrive in Portsmouth before my letter. So I held off."

"Who's *Eleanor*?"

"HMS *Eleanor*. My ship."

"Oh. Well, in my letter I said that Albert ate very much, but now he ..."

"Does he still like apple pie and cheddar?"

"No. Please listen. Albert used to eat, but now he barely touches his food. Not since last winter."

"I'll take him to Speen's. He always likes their pie."

"You don't understand. There's something wrong with Albert. Mum and I know when he's hungry, but he doesn't care to eat. Besides, it's the first night of the fair. The inn will be too busy for the local trade. We'll feed you both here. Potatoes and gammon! I know you like that. And we'd offer you a place to stay tonight but it's very small inside, and Albert makes it even smaller."

"I don't mind. I'll stay with him until late, then go sleep on the sward."

"Why don't you take him with you and spend the night in our stall? The white one with green stripes, right where your Mum used to set up. You can play knucklebones. That's his favorite. And when he gets sleepy you can tell him a story. Things you do on a boat. We keep a straw pallet there. It's small for the two of you but you'll manage. Just tell the night watchman you'll be staying the night. His name's Mellwyn. I'm sure he'll be pleased to have one less stall to look after."

She sighed deep. "I'm sorry Dunny was here. He thinks he has the right."

"He said you're his woman."

She stomped her foot. "I am not his woman. He's lent us money to care for Albert and says he'll forgive the debt if I marry him."

"How much do you owe?"

"Mum says about ten pounds. It'll take forever to pay it back. But I won't ever marry him. I hate him, except without his money Albert would be doing even worse yet."

"Is that why Erth said go see his wife? He said it might be too late. What does he mean?"

She looked away. "Vivian's the one to tell you. Not me. Come inside now. We'll eat."

She took Albert's hand. Mine as well, then pulled away.

"Owen! Your little finger. It's not there!"

"The Onion shot it off in the Mekong."

"The onion? In the Mekong?"

Albert had no interest in his food. I coaxed him to eat half a potato, but then he turned away, watching the light grow dim in the forecourt.

Joan tried to explain. "He still likes his sweets and sometimes he'll eat an apple, if he doesn't give it to a horse first. We don't know what's wrong. Even with Steep's money we can't afford to bring him to a doctor. Not that we'd ever bring him to Wroxham. That one's nothing but a sot."

"Well I've some good news. I made an account for you at a bank in Reading. Fifty pounds. You can pay off your debt and use the rest to care for Albert. I mean, if you wish to stay caring for him. I'll keep him while I'm here, but I might be recalled."

"Recalled? He won't understand if you leave again."

"I know. But in some ways Albert's better off not understanding. Better off for being the way he is."

Becca frowned. "What do you mean?"

"It's just that ... that if Albert wasn't simple then it would have been him who went to sea, not me. I never dared think it before, but in the navy, he might have become killed by now. Or gone missing."

Becca murmured low. "Like father."

I looked to the floor. "I'm sorry. I spoke before I thought. You've not heard from him?"

Joan spoke up. "Not since Tournay. And don't say you're sorry for somethin' not your fault. We've all gone missing in this war."

The night fell quiet. The Kennet ran slow. Somewhere a Mum cooed, and her baby trilled. Joan stood to clear the table.

"Take your brother to the sward now. I still have much to do."

Becca tried to help clear, but her Mum said no.

"Go with them, Becca. See they have what they need."

We made to leave, but Joan stayed me. "Owen, come here."

I went to her dutiful.

"I didn't mean to be short with you. Surely it's a blessing you've made an account for Albert. But please know that we'd have taken care of him, no matter. We owe it to your mother." She took my hand. "Ten years ago, when Charles was pressed, I could only lie dumb struck. Not moving. Just sobbing until my whole body ached. Neighbors came and told me they were sorry. They said if I wanted help I just had to ask. Kind words. But words only. You were too young to remember, but it was your Mum who took care. She cooked for me. In the evening she'd come to help Becca into bed. Scraped and pounded our clothes at the mill race. So we're privileged to care for her needful child. To take care of him is to honour your Mum."

She paused then, breathing deep, and with a distant look in her eye.

"I must tell you something more, so that you might understand." She lit a rushlight and set in next to her spinning wheel. "Charles made this. He was never meant to be a soldier. He worked with wood. That's what he loved. He made my loom. Your mother's as well. And he always added a slight imperfection when he was done with a piece." She caressed the wheel. "Look here. There's a small nick in the maiden. Nothing to cause a problem. Just to remind himself that only God can make a perfect thing." She gave it a turn. "I feel his hand on it, even now."

Becca sighed. "Please, Mum, don't go on this way."

But Joan ignored her daughter's plea and went on. "Charles knew his talent was a gift from God. But for every gift there's a debt comes with it. And this debt I must repay with my life. Not knowing what happened to Charles ... it leaves a hole in my heart that will never mend. But that's not what will kill me. It's my anger. My rage, deep inside. That's what will end my days."

"Stop, Mum. Please stop."

Joan nodded silent, then dressed her distaff and began to treadle. Steady, and flawless.

⚡

The roasting pits were dampened for the night, and the last stalls lashed down. The full moon cast shadows along the sward. Mellwyn called the hour.

"Four bells of the first watch," I said.

"What?" Becca asked.

"It's how we mark ten at night. In the navy."

"Well then a boat's a very odd place. Even the time's different."

"On a ship, time starts and ends in London."

"Have you been there? To London?"

"I left there yesterday, then spent last night in Reading."

"You must be tired. I'll go now. Try to tell Albert a story. He'll not talk much but he always listens. Good night."

She drew back the flap and stepped through, but stepped back in.

"Owen?"

"Yes?"

"There's a thing I must tell you."

"Yes?"

"It's just that ... well, I didn't know it would be this way. Not until you went to sea."

"What way?"

"What way?" Becca's sweet face colored. "Have you grown dull living on that boat? Can't you see I've come to miss you? And ... and it's not just as a friend. But it seems you've not missed me, though. Not one jot. Or ... or even thought of me." She sighed deep, ringing her hands. "Well, maybe you didn't have time."

"On a warship sailors have overmuch time to think, except it's no good thing to think of home. Besides, coming home ... it seems everything's changed here." I listened to the wind falling off. "Maybe not everything, though. I'd like to visit Squire Cedric's old holdings, just to visit a place in the meadow. Does anyone live there now?"

"No. It's gone over to the Crown. Why do you want to go there?"

"To recall a certain night when I was a boy. To see if at least one thing's not changed."

A thought occurred. I'd bring my brother with me to that place, to see if it held any meaning for him, as well as me. The night deepened. Becca shifted in the shadows.

"Owen?"

"Yes?"

"The letter I wrote. I told you Mum said for me to write it. But she didn't. I wrote on my own. I wanted to tell you something. Something that's not changed, only grown stronger." She took my hand and pressed it to her heart. "In here ... inside here, that's where

I've kept you while you've been gone. And I want you to know that it's your home now." The wind died full, and the night grew still. She let go of my hand. "It's very late. Mum needs my help. Good night, Owen. Good night, Albert."

⚡

The morning sun burned off the mist to reveal a great many stalls amassed on the banks of the Kennet. Vivian Erth had pitched her booth at a busy junction, already thronged with fair goers come early to buy her potions and herbs, or to have her tend some cut or bruise. When I called out, she took me in her stall and drew the curtain shut. I stood among garlands of woad and wild garlic, with the air dusty thick in the slanting beams of morning light. Bound simples hung from every strut, each bundle labeled meticulous. Quinquefolius and Dong Quai. Fenugreek, Angelica and Neem. All overmuch for me to take in, and I stood transfixed until Vivian spoke my name.

"Owen. My good husband said you'd come to ask about Albert."

"Yes, ma'am."

"I'm very busy this morning but I'll make the time to tell you what I can. Come, sit with me." She led me to a small wicker bench. "I was midwife when your mother birthed Albert and I knew soon as he came out that he was different. Even so, and you know this better than me, he's always been a gentle soul. Happy and sweet. Never a bother. Always choosing to be out of doors, either at Mary Hare or in the village square sharing his apple with any horse led there to water."

I smiled in recollection.

"But since you left, your brother's changed. Still the gentle one, but no longer at peace." She placed her veined hands in her lap, the moonstone in her thumb ring glinting just so. "I don't know how to tell you this ... except to say it plain. Your brother has a mortal affliction. Midwives have made note of it since early as Boudicea, but just recently it's been given a name. Mongoloid."

"What is it?"

"No one knows. Except a child born mongoloid has an obvious look. Everyone in Newbury sees it in Albert, but what they don't see is that a mongoloid doesn't live very long. Most die young. Hardly any live as long as your brother. And now Albert stands at the portal."

"He's going to die?"

"Call it what you will. I choose to see it as an exit from this realm and the entrance to the next. Albert's been standing at the threshold for a long time. Just waiting for you to come home, I think."

"What can I do for him?"

"Stand by him. There's nothing more you can do."

A woman called from the lane. "Vivian! Petee Elcot's been swatted by a gander and his Mum thinks his arm's broke. Please come."

⚡

That night, as Albert and I shared the sleeping pallet, he draped his arm across me, just as when we were children. The night air brought a chill, and his warmth comforted. He slept quiet. But not me. I heard Mellwyn call out every hour. At three in the morning Albert stirred, and I guessed he might want to step outside. We stood at the Kennet, listening to it purl. Then, from beyond the sward.

"Sukiyama."

I looked to Albert. He'd not heard it. I guessed it might be meant only for me, as a warning against Dunny. If Becca told him I was paying her debt then certain he'd come for me, no matter what Able Erth said. The whisper came from above the mill, from great nana's croft tucked deep in the old family holding. I remembered the night when Mum and I stayed with her ... with Sarah Cedric. We stood under a full moon in the clearing beneath an ancient oak, listening to its leaves rustle. But that night, same as this one, the wind was down, yet the leaves stirred on their own. Only a child's imagination. Then I recalled Wordsworth's parting words.

"Be sure to honour your childhood imagination. You are still young and able to conjure it at will. Have no doubt that it's a living thing, alive as anything you will ever encounter."

His words reminded me of the pale green ledger he'd offered as a parting gift. I'd only made one entry, even though I'd kept it with me on the channel and then brought it all the way from London to Newbury. I retrieved it from my satchel, along with a pencil stub, and made a second entry. Albert had not seen me writing, ever, and he watched with interest as I scribed each line. Date and location. A few words about the Sukiyama. Guessing what it might be, and that it had now returned. Great nana's oak tree. I searched for the proper words. It seemed there were none. At least not for now, so I finished, and turned to Albert. It was time to bring him to Sarah Cedric's oak tree.

"Shall we walk, Aller?"

He nodded.

"Very well. I'll tell you a walking story." I pointed away from the river. "The story goes in that direction."

The sward led to a footpath that all of Newbury called the Hoe. Squire Cedric's holdings had run alongside, with Sarah's croft verging on a meadow just where the oak tree stood. Still there. We stopped at its base. The quiet air pressed on my ears. Albert shifted, waiting for his story.

"Did you know our great nana lived here? Her name was Sarah. I came to visit her once. A full moon, just like this one. The leaves stirred that night, even though the wind was calm. She asked if I understood what the leaves said, and I said no. But I wonder, Aller, if you might know."

I led him through the meadow and to the oak tree. We stood there a good while. I'll never understand if it was imagination, or something real, when the leaves spoke.

"Do you hear it, Aller?"

He only gazed at me, his eyes answering silent, in the way only he and I spoke. No. He'd heard nothing. A good thing. Perhaps what Albert didn't hear was a blessing.

♭

When the fair ran its course a room came available at Speen's. I arranged for a lodging tucked in one corner of their mansard, large enough for both Albert and me. He never liked change but staying in a garret seemed an adventure to him. He'd not seen Newbury from so high up, for our quarters stood some thirty feet above Northbrook Street. Truth be told, I'd not seen Newbury from this height, either. The tower gates at Donnington Castle were just visible from our small window, and we had a good view all along London Road. As the days passed, Albert settled into his old routine, spending much of each day at Mary Hare, or watching the workers build a new canal on the Kennet. At eventide he'd sit at our window, taking in all of Newbury at a glance, calling for me to come see a horse at the fountain, or some white duck waddling down a back lane.

It was then that I came to realize a certain thing. Something I'd learned, but not yet put in place since returning home. Newbury was small. The horizon began just beyond its outskirts, closing in the town to keep out what lay beyond. Unlike the sea, where all was seen for miles around.

I'd let Speen's garret for a month, both room and board. But after that, I didn't know what might come, and the lack of any clear answer haunted. Was Vivian Erth, right? Did Albert not have much longer to live? For years I'd longed to be home but, during all that time, no one ever thought to tell me home would never be the same as before. How long would it never be the same?

Not one month after the fair, the platen on Joan's loom failed. She had a great many orders to fill, all taken at the fair, so I helped her replace the platen with Mum's back beam. But that piece showed signs of wear, too. So when I volunteered to go to Basingstoke and buy a new one, Joan took my offer. She traded one of her best woven saddle blankets to the carter, Nate Woodcott, for the use of a horse and dray. Becca would come along, if only to make sure I got the right piece.

The one horse was an old piebald mare that, for some forgotten reason, had been named the Oyster. She was most unbeautiful. And Nate said she'd be disagreeable, as well, but I knew straight away that she'd accept me. In the past, I'd treated her kind whenever I'd

67

trimmed her hooves, and now she remembered my smell. I gave her an apple to crunch while I backed her in the traces. A good sound, that, of a horse crunching on her apple. At first light, we set off in the cart.

For lunch, Becca packed a shank of pork, a half loaf of bread and a flagon of mead. We stopped halfway to Basingstoke, at Ewhurst Pond, to rest the Oyster, to let her drink and give her some oats while we ate lunch. After our meal, I sat watching the waves lapping the shore. Becca rested her hand on my shoulder.

"You never say much. Is it because there's someone else? Someone in another place?"

I liked Yadra, certain of that, but she was dead. Hanged on Minorca. And at George Town there was Lady Elspeth. But I hadn't liked her. Not one bit, and it mattered little to Lady Elspeth even if I had.

"You and your Mum, and Albert … it seems you're the only ones who still know me here. Except for the Oyster."

"That's not an answer. Does it mean there's someone else?"

"No. There isn't. I liked it when you said you missed me. And I like it now. I mean you and me just sitting here."

She smiled full and gave me a kiss on the cheek. She'd not done that ever since we were ten. I'd not liked that kiss overmuch; her breath had smelled of onions then. She kissed me again. Her warm breath smelled of mead, and I this time liked it.

The sun went climbing, so we packed up and left, sharing the last of the mead as the Oyster plodded along. As we neared Basingstoke, a well-lathered steed and its rider sat astride the road. Dunny Steep. He watched quiet, scowling as we came to a stop. No one said a word, until he shifted in his saddle and spoke sharp to Becca.

"Your mother said you'd gone to Basingstoke with this one. So I took a hunter's trail to get ahead."

I tightened the reins. "Make way, Dunny, if you will."

"I will not. I intend to teach you never to go off with Becca. Remember you this, Harriet, that this is the day I beat you bloody."

He made to dismount but I stayed him with a warning.

"Not on this day. I have cold steel." I'd brought my dirk for traveling the highway, and now lifted my jerkin to reveal the hilt. "It's sharp. Be sure of it."

Dunny narrowed his eyes. "Then I'll make an example of your brother, instead. Very soon, and you'll not like it. Not at all."

He turned his horse and trotted off.

"Will he do it, Becca?"

"He will. He's been in a bad temper ever since you came home. Even more since he found out you paid our debt. He'll punish Albert to get even with you. I just hope you have a plan to deal with him."

The marine lieutenant, Tam Kyle's words came to mind, that any plan has a better chance of success if you have the good fortune of picking the time and place.

"I'm not sure. First let's fetch home your mother's new platen. After that I'll choose the moment, and the best location to deal with with Steep."

⚡

It didn't take overlong for the time and place, though it was not of my own choosing. Only a week passed before a sealed envelope arrived by messenger. I opened it prompt, for it was sent by Captain Praether.

Matthew J. Praether

Portsmouth Dockyard

Monday, Twenty-seven September 1802

Harriet,

This note finds you by way of courier who I have instructed to wait upon your reply.

Since we last spoke I have been in communication with Sailing Master Lau. As expected, he must decline my offer, but recommends you to serve as master's mate for an independent action, and I have agreed to his recommendation. I cannot go into detail at this time, but wish to know if you are willing to accept this position. Eleanor still lies in ordinary, but her refit is well under way. I expect her to be ready for ballast quite soon.

If you wish to sign on, please confirm by way of this courier and report to Eleanor on or before Sixteen October.

I remain Y. M. H. & O. S.,

Praether

I read the thing twice over yet remained puzzled as ever. An independent action meant autonomous command, much like *Eleanor*'s previous missions. But, unlike most frigate operations, *Eleanor*'s efforts had been clandestine, therefore unacknowledged by any Prize Court and never resulting in prize money. Even so, many sailors preferred serving on a frigate. There was more watch standing on a fifth rate but serving on a ship of the line while on some blockade grew tiresome. Or, as Becca might say, a dull thing.

Any frigate would be a good berth but to serve as a master's mate aboard a Lively Class frigate such as *Eleanor*, that was the rare plumb. Certain of that. The messenger coughed polite to remind me he was still waiting, and I took quill in hand to make reply.

Wednesday, Twenty-nine September 1802

At Newbury

Dear Captain Praether,

I am pleased to accept your offer and will report to Eleanor on or before Sixteen October.

I am,

Midshipman Owen Harriet

I signed and sealed my reply then handed it to the runner. Becca would not take this well. Nor would Albert. But if they had enough time to get used to me leaving again, then perhaps they'd come to accept it.

Maybe Becca. But never Albert. Not ever.

Either way, I must tell him without delay. I went in search, but stopped abrupt, shouting to no one but myself.

"No! I'll not leave him. Not this time. I will stand by him. Me and Becca."

I ran for Portsmouth Road, hoping to detain the courier. I still might catch him, then send a second note saying I must decline the offer. But he put his mount in a canter even as I closed. I'd not catch him now. I returned to Joan, preparing her loom in the forecourt.

"Where's Albert?"

"Gone to Mary Hill. It's been two hours. You best check on him."

I crossed the fields below Mary Hill and in the distance I heard my brother. Crying! I looked to see him slumping to his knees. A figure with bright red hair stood over him, punching his face. Dunny Steep. He struck Albert six times then kneed him vicious in the chest, and my brother collapsed to the ground. I ran unchecked, only to stumble on a stick, and came up gripping the thing with both hands.

"Stop it!"

I charged with the stick held high, aiming to crack hard on Dunny's skull. But he dodged away nimble, putting out a leg to trip me as I rushed by, and I fell sprawling across Albert. He lay silent, eyes open wide, unseeing.

Dunny bent down to have a look. "I only slapped the oaf."

"A lie! I saw you punching him."

"But not hard. Shake him. He'll come around."

I nudged my brother, but he didn't stir. Brought an ear to his mouth, but he didn't breathe. Laid a hand on his heart, but it didn't beat.

"He's dead!" I screamed. "You killed him!"

Dunny backed off. "Not me! It was you. You made me do it. I told you to say clear of Becca, and you didn't." He squinted shrewd.

"That means it's you who killed your brother."

He came for me, but then changed his mind and ran for the woods, just as a boat came down the Kennet. Ollie Nervet, in his coracle.

"Ollie! Hurry and fetch the constable. My brother's been killed."

When Erth arrived, I told him what happened. He took one look at Albert and sent Ollie to Newbury to bring a cart. People stopped their business when we brought Albert to Wroxham. The doctor quit drinking, but only long enough to confirm what we already knew. Albert was dead.

This was now a matter for the Crown.

✝

Newt Purdy climbed from the hole he'd just dug for my brother. Becca and Joan planted crocus bulbs around his site, the bulbs borrowed from around Mum's headstone, the next grave over. I'd not visited Mum since before I'd gone to sea, and now I stood at her marker.

MEGAN HARRIET

1762 - 1795

Be Kind

Mum always said to be kind, and then would add "and be true." I'd wanted Father to have that on her marker as well, but he said we couldn't afford it. Those few missing words reminded me of how poor we'd become after she died.

Not many came to Albert's burial, for it was a working day. A day of work for Vicar Beetly, as well, who came from Saint Nicolas to say a few words. When the service ended, Erth found me.

"Now that Albert's dead, do you intend to stay in Newbury?"

"His grave's not half filled, sir."

"It will be soon. And Alton Steep's already made it known he blames you for this matter, and the squire's a vindictive man. Wealthy. I can't order you to leave but it would be better for everyone if you did."

"I've only just come home, sir. And Becca, she says . . ."

"Rebecca Stanhope ain't my concern. But keeping the peace in Newbury is. Alton Steep will make trouble for you, just like he did with your father. We'll catch up to Dunny and he'll stand trial. But the next assizes don't convene 'til November so if you have prospects elsewhere then I suggest you pursue them."

I showed him my letter from Captain Praether.

"Did you accept?"

"At first I did, sir, but then changed my mind."

"Why?"

"I came home to take care of Albert."

"And now Albert's dead, so it would be wise if you change your mind again. Take the offer. I'll arrange for the magistrate to depose you at Speen's tonight and you can leave for Portsmouth in the morning."

"You should know a thing Dunny told me before he ran. He might say it at the assizes."

"What is it?"

"Dunny said it was me who killed Albert, and he may be right."

"What do you mean?"

"Your wife. She believed Albert was just waiting for me to come home, before he crossed over. I came home, and now he's dead. It's a fact."

"Not admissible as evidence. The fact is you witnessed Dunstan Steep strike Albert down and now Albert's dead. The fact is you stayed with your brother after he died, but Dunny run."

"Where did he run, sir?"

"Likely to Salisbury. His father has holdings there, so I've sent word for the sheriff to watch for him. If Dunny's in Salisbury the sheriff will collar him soon enough and transport him to Derby for arraignment."

"But if Dunny pleads not guilty won't I be called to give testimony?"

"Yes. But in spite of this latest peace the navy's still on a war footing and its needs take precedence in this matter. If your ship goes to sea before the trial, and you're on it, then the Crown will be allowed to enter your deposition in absentia."

Someone called out for Erth. "Now here's a thing you should know. If Steep pleads not guilty then my wife may be called to testify in his defense."

"What?"

"Albert lived longer than most mongoloids. Many of them die from a weak heart. Alton Steep's sure to hire a sharp barrister for his son. One sharp enough to raise a reasonable doubt as to why your brother died. If Dunny's charged with murder, it's likely his barrister will play on Albert's condition. He'll call Vivian and make her testify that your brother might have died of a bad heart that had nothing to do with Dunny hitting him."

"Does your wife think that?"

"She don't know, and no one ever will. But I know this. I've waited a long time for Dunny to make his own noose, and by running he's just stuck his head in it."

That evening the magistrate took my statement. I settled my account at Speen's and spent my last night in Newbury with Becca and her Mum. At eventide, I retired in Albert's cot. His scent, and the imprint of his body still remained in the tick, giving me comfort, if but small. In the middle of the night, Becca came to stand at the door. I felt her watching me, though her eyes went unseen in the dim light. And I watched her. Both of us knew there was no need to say anything. Not just yet ... only be together in the quiet night. A living bond. I'd not felt this way before. Ever. But then I stirred and broke the spell.

"Owen, please don't let Steep run you off. This is your home. People here know you. No one thinks bad of you because John stole, or because your father owed money to Steep. We've all owed money to Steep. Me and Mum ... we owed, too, until you bought our debt."

"I didn't buy your debt, Becca. I paid my own debt to you and your Mum, for taking care of Albert. And I'm not leaving just because of John, or my father."

"Then why?"

"Because it was me who saw Dunny kill Albert."

"Are you afraid of him?"

"No. But if I testify against Dunny, his father won't rest until he drives me off."

We stopped talking, only listening to the Kennet, its bank not ten feet away. It ran quiet and slow. Always steady.

"Becca?"

"Yes?"

"There's another thing. Another reason."

"What?"

"It's been three years since I left Newbury. I've learned how to become who I am. What I'm best at."

"You no longer wish to be a farrier."

"I wish to do more than be a farrier, though to look in a horse's eye is to look upon yourself."

"I saw how the Oyster loves you. You must have been kind to her once, and she remembers. Isn't that enough? To be remembered by a horse because you were kind?"

"Until there's something more."

"The sea."

"Not just the sea, but to become a sailing master. Can you understand?"

A small boat bumped on the bridge pilings. Ollie Nervet in his coracle, night fishing.

"No. I can't understand." She sighed over deep. "It's not fair. But there's no fairness in this place."

I lay silent. To say any more would only be misunderstood. By Becca, or by me.

"Will you be going a long time ... I mean this time?"

"I don't know. But ... please remember me."

She stepped in. She kissed my eyes. My scar. Her breath smelled of pears. She kissed my mouth. Her lips tasted of nectar. She slipped into bed. Her body felt soft and warm, smelling of sweet grass.

"Yes, my love. Always."

Part Two: Cape Verde

8. A Master's Mate, not a boy

Portsmouth, October 1802

I glanced sidelong at the man standing next to me in *Eleanor*'s great cabin. I recognized his angry red face. He turned my way and scowled.

"Seen you before, boy. Tell me where."

"In London. And I'm Mr. Harriet, a master's mate, not a boy."

And he was Ezekiel Pyeweed, the man who'd stormed out of Praether's office on Monk Street, not three months past. Now he was *Eleanor*'s new sailing master and made clear he saw his current posting as a demotion, having once served on a first rate. The Eleanors knew Pyeweed had mostly himself to blame, though. And when there's no one to blame but yourself, it's likely a midshipman, such as myself, who's sure to feel the rub. He said nothing more, but still glowered at me as we stood with Lieutenant Bonel, *Eleanor*'s new first officer, all of us waiting for Captain Praether to arrive. We didn't have long to wait.

"As you were, gentlemen. We have very little time so I will dispense with the formalities and begin."

He pulled a water-stained parchment from his bureau. It looked familiar, remindful of the one he'd been reading when I'd called on him at Monk Street. He cleared his throat and began reading aloud.

"Monday, Three December 1798. Manifest of Negroes, Mulattoes and Persons of Colour taken on board *Elizabeth Carton* of Charleston, South Carolina, whereof Isaiah Yates is Master, burthen 119 tons, to be transported from Dakar to the Port of Charleston for the purpose of being sold or disposed of as Slaves, or to be held to service or labour."

Praether looked up. "This is a slave manifest. It goes on to list the names of two hundred twenty-one slaves, as well as their sex, approximate age, and height. There is more, but what I have just read to you conveys the nub of our unspoken mission."

He paused to look each one of us in the eye. "Yes, you hear me right. Our mission will be unspoken. Never to be set down in orders."

He returned the manifest to its drawer.

"I do not expect any of you to have heard of *Elizabeth Carton*. That is, none of you but Midshipman Harriet. So, to put things in their proper order, I will ask him to recount a certain incident from two years ago, involving the Carton. Mr. Harriet, if you will."

His request unnerved me, for I was expected to keep my mouth shut while in the presence of superior officers. Truth be told, that would be any officer, for I was serving only as acting master's mate to Pyeweed, who now frowned at me, aghast for having been chosen to speak in his stead. I hesitated, unsure of what to do, until Praether bid me to get on with it. I adjusted my collar and stepped forward.

"If you mean the dinghy we found adrift off Dakar, sir, then this is what I can tell. There was a man in the boat. A slave, still in shackles. And the boat had *Elizabeth Carton* stenciled on her transom. There was violent weather the night before so we guessed Carton might have gone down. We searched for survivors, but none were found, nor any sign of the Carton. I mean except for the dinghy. I don't think we'll ever know how that slave came to be in it. Oh, and he played on a pipe. That's how we first came to be aware of him."

"It does not matter how we became aware of him, Mr. Harriet, only that we did. What does matter is the recent discovery of the slave manifest from which I have just read. It found its way into my possession four months ago at Monk Street, when an unseen hand passed it under my door sill, along with an unsigned note. The note stated that Carton's crew had abandoned ship during that storm off Dakar. They feared all was lost and were left with no choice but to man their boats and depart before Carton sank, leaving two hundred twenty-one souls shackled to their fate. I repeat ... leaving two hundred twenty-one souls shackled to their fate. However, it appears that Carton did not founder after all. Instead, she went aground on the lee shore of a tiny island. The note actually names it. Boa Vista, in the Cape Verde archipelago."

Praether paced behind his desk, his brass buttons glinting in the sunlight pouring through the gallery windows. Of a sudden he stopped in the light, standing stark still, as some sort of shudder coursed through is body. He brought up his hand to feel the place on his skull where a spar had crashed onto the quarterdeck and hit him. That had been in March of this year, some four days after the Treaty of Amiens had taken effect. Except no one on *Eleanor*, or *Hommage*, was aware of the signing, and so engaged unknowingly in a bloody and unnecessary battle. Several killed, and many wounded. Praether and the Sailing Master among them. The moment passed, and the captain went on.

"A grave misfortune for every soul aboard that slave ship, and a sin against all of humanity. Yet now I am blessed, for as a result of that transgression I have been offered an independent action. An action meant first to locate and then rescue those who might have survived, and then disrupt a portion of the slave trade operating at Cape Verde."

Lieutenant Bonel spoke up. "Sir, Cape Verde is a Portuguese holding, is it not?"

"You are correct, lieutenant. But it also serves as a way station for slavers in route to the Americas." The captain paused once more, as if to bring more weight to his words. "Until this moment you have performed your duties with no foreknowledge of our mission. Such are the conditions we come to expect in the Royal Navy. Even so, you may have deduced by now that, due to *Eleanor*'s unusual refit, we are no longer exactly a warship. However, our appearance is a deception. Some might consider it a ruse of war. But I think not, for we are no longer at war. Or at least not a war among nations, but a far greater conflict, the struggle between what is sacred and what is profane. The abolition of slavery."

He fell silent, closing his eyes. I supposed he might once more begin to quake, but then saw that he was praying. His prayer was disturbed, though, when a barrel broke free and went rolling across the quarterdeck direct above us. Gleason cursed expressive, as some deck hand felt the bite of his starter.

Praether continued. "My charge is to proceed by posing as a slaver. That is why we are undergoing this refit, so as to look more like a slave ship and less like a frigate. Our first task will be to search the Cape Verde archipelago in an attempt to find these people stranded on Boa Vista, as well as board any slaver we may come upon. But in order to have maximum effect we will need another vessel to sail with us. To this end my colleagues in The One Body have given me leave to search for and procure such a vessel."

Eight bells rang out. The Eleanors assembled in the waist, and soon the afternoon watch began. Praether cocked an ear, nodding his tacit approval before going on.

"In God's eyes slavery is an abomination, and its termination is His will. Of that there is no doubt. But freedom has yet to come, and the fight must go on. So even as I speak there are factions at work in the House of Commons who have joined forces to abolish the slave trade. They have tried before and have failed. But this time they are led by a man of utmost courage and desire. William Wilberforce. I doubt you have heard his name, but he is my bosom companion."

He stepped to the bulkhead cabinet, unlocked its drawer, and withdrew a single sheet of vellum. He held the vellum for all to see. Judging by its smell, it was fresh made, and the script was good fair copy.

"This document is a Letter of Marque, signed by an agent of the Crown and stamped with the great seal of His Majesty. May God bless him. It empowers me to board any ship and remove its cargo. Human or otherwise." He returned the letter to the drawer and locked it. "Be sure I will read it out again, for you and every man jack serving on *Eleanor* to hear, and to understand. Not just yet, though, but at captain's mast, and only after we have weathered Ushant."

I believe Praether had more to say, but Lieutenant Japhet, the deck officer, sent word. A lighter was approaching with more supplies. We were dismissed. All but me.

Praether massaged his head once more, then sat at his desk.

"I will inspect *Eleanor* this evening. If all is in order, I will leave for London tomorrow. While there, I intend to interview this fellow you crewed for in the Channel, Jean Dame-Marie. Mr. Lau informed me of him because he thinks the man may be of value to this mission. He owns a smack at Debtford Wharf. Correct?"

"Aye, sir. *Solitude*. Red hull, with a deck cabin. Except there's no telling when Dame-Marie might be at Debtford. He has much business ashore. Or he could be in Calais."

"I will be in London for at least a week. If he is not there when I first call, then I will call again."

"Sir?"

"Yes?"

"In London. Will you see Mr. Lau? I mean that if you see him will you greet him for me?"

Praether leaned in. "You should know something, Harriet. Mr. Lau's neck wound is not healing properly."

"I know, sir. And there's no one in London to care for him."

"There is Mrs. Dolan. He has let a room there."

"I don't think he can afford that for overlong."

"I suppose you are right. But that is none of your concern."

"Beg pardon, sir, but it is. And I should like to give Mrs. Dolan money, to care for Mr. Lau."

"That may be improvident. I understand you have already given away a portion of your bequest for the care of your brother."

"That was to pay a debt, sir. Besides, I wouldn't draw from my account."

"What then?"

"My Prélat. I wish sell it on the Hard and send the money to Mrs. Dolan. She's most keen on Mr. Lau. I know she'd use it for him."

"Your offer shows great admiration for Mr. Lau, Harriet, but your plan is ill conceived. First, you would fetch very little for your Prélat if you were to sell it on the Hard. Second, there is no guarantee that any of the money you sent Mrs. Dolan would find its way to her. Or, even if she did get it, that she would use it for Mr. Lau." He leaned back, narrowing his eyes in thought. "However, I have seen your Prélat. It is a very fine piece. I have need of a second brace of pistols for this voyage, and your Prélat could be part of a set. So if you are intent on selling it, then I am interested in buying. Bring it to me. I will pay you a fair price and deliver the proceeds to Mrs. Dolan when I'm in London, along with the proviso that the proceeds go to caring for Mr. Lau, of course. Will you agree to that?"

"I will, sir."

"Very well. Bring it."

I made to leave, but Praether stayed me once more.

"One last thing. In the morning, after the forenoon watch is set, you will take *Eleanor*'s barge with six able men to Knighton sail loft, where you will assist Wat in transferring our new set of lug sails. Dismissed."

I left the great cabin, passing by the wooden pegs I'd once used to sling my hammock. I'd needed to stand on the sentry's spittoon back then in order to sling it, but now I reached out and touched those same pegs with ease. I recalled that first night aboard *Eleanor*, swaying in my hammock and listening to her groan as if some living thing. I'd longed for my family that night, my tears welling, but refusing to let them fall. What if I'd known then? That in three years they'd all be dead, or run to the Colonies, or sent to Botany Bay? And my first encounter with the Sukiyama … it seemed but yesterday and, at the same time, a lifetime ago. I stood there, with *Eleanor* snubbing her hawser, same as on that night. All had changed since then. All but *Eleanor*'s gentle motion. But I had no more business here now … now that the captain had dismissed me. The sentry knew it as well, and sent me on my way.

I meant to inspect my uncle's Prélat. Perhaps for the last time. But first I found the pale green ledger. The one Wordsworth had given me. It still held his sister's slight scent. Only a few entries, with the last recorded in September, at Newbury. I added more now, all that I'd just been thinking. The Sukiyama. Some existence meant only for me to recognize? Some remnant of childhood imagination? Both? It made no sense, and I felt open to ridicule … my own. I closed the ledger, pushed it under my berth, and took out the Prélat.

French made, and of the finest steel, with a black walnut grip and pearl inlay. Taken from the first officer aboard *Pamone* after surrendering to *Galatea*. Uncle Cedric was a lieutenant on *Galatea* then, and had led the boarding party that forced *Pamone* to strike. For his actions that day *Galatea*'s captain had awarded my uncle with this Prélat. Now it was my honour to possess it. A keepsake. I should have loved it for the memory of James Cedric. Yet I would never love this piece.

Lieutenant Towerlight had once said a gun is a living thing. A brooding beast, with a dark sense of its own being. He was *Eleanor*'s gunnery officer. Her first, and best of them all, until he was killed by one of his own beasts. For Towerlight, it was always artillery that was the living beast. But for me, it was this Prélat, resting secure in its presentation box, its spare flintlock and frizzen nested in green velvet. The thing seemed aware of what it was, and its role in killing seaman Dilks. All who witnessed that incident believed I'd made a splendid shot, claiming that Dilks deserved to be shot dead for trying to murder his mate, Wheaton. Except I never meant to kill Dilks, but only shoot him in the leg to stop his advance. But the Prélat is a big pistol, overlarge for my hand, and as I fired it the thing kicked back hard, causing the round to throw high. High enough to blast out a portion of Dilks's brain. I'd not fired it since, and never would.

⚡

The next day Wat and I sat in the barge as we returned with the new sails. Wat was a sailmaker, the oldest tar among the *Eleanor*, and one of the first I'd met when coming aboard. Even now he wore his sailmaker's palm while taking the final stitches in the last grommet of a lug sail. We studied *Eleanor* as we drew near. She no longer cast the fierce look of a Lively Class frigate. Instead, she sat most docile in the water, with her hull and gun stripe painted dull black. All of her long guns had been removed. Only the carronades remained, and her reduced artillery unsettled the Eleanors. Just as disturbing was the queer look of her top hamper. Her foremast and main were unchanged, but only the spanker remained on her mizzen. The cross jack and mizzen yards had all been sent down, replaced by a topsail gaff and boom.

Soon as we hooked on, March, one of *Eleanor*'s two ship boys, scurried to meet me at the entry port. He reminded me of my own young self, and I only just managed to wipe my grin, for the lad was even smaller than me when I was his age.

"Beg pardon, sir, it's that gnarly one. Mr. Peachpie, I think. And don't that name make me hungry for a big slice of Mum's best pie. If I could only just …"

85

"As you were, March, and stop running your mouth before it runs you into trouble. I suspect you mean the sailing master, Mr. Pyeweed. Correct?"

"That be him."

"What about him?"

"Why it's him that wants to see you, sir. In his quarters."

"Very well. And from now you will address me as Mr. Harriet."

I made below and knocked on Pyeweed's door.

"Come."

I stepped in.

"Did you wish to see me, Mr. Pyeweed?"

He took a long pull from a narrow vial, downing its reddish-brown contents in a single gulp. Its colour was the shade of Jean Dame-Marie's dark red skin. Pyeweed wiped his mouth with the back of his hand, struggling to find me in his vacant stare.

"Just who do you think you are, the next Jack Crawford?"

"Sir?"

He squinted overlong at the empty vial in his hand before he replied. "Well, I have news for you. I was on board *Venerable* at Camperdown when Crawford nailed the admiral's pennant to that mast. And I'll tell you this. You ain't him. Nor ever could be." He set the bottle on his desk with a purpose.

"Have I upset you, Mr. Pyeweed?"

"You have, and with intent. So don't dare to apologize."

"I was told once never to apologize, only vow never to repeat my offense. So if you tell me what I've done, then I'll try not to do it again."

Pyeweed scoffed. "Not likely. Turns out my first impression of you holds true. You're a primping young strut, and today you pricked me sore in front of Praether and Bonel. But I warn you, I'm the sailing master on this vessel and you're naught but acting master's mate. Not your place to speak when I'm present."

I thought to remind him the captain had asked me a direct question, so I was bound to answer. It was also a question Pyeweed couldn't have answered, not having been aboard *Eleanor* when we found that slave adrift off Dakar. But I dared not reply, for now his face coloured deep, and he balled his fist to slam hard on the desk.

"I didn't ask for this billet or for you to be my master's mate. I don't know who you served under before me but whoever it was failed to instill proper respect in you. Either that, or he didn't deserve it. Now it falls upon me to instruct you." He leaned back, breathing onerous. "I will begin with a thorough review of your charts, and every mistake I find will cost you. From now on you will attend noon line, same as any midshipmen. And to remind you of your station, you will run any errand I see fit to hand down. Is that clear?"

"Aye, Mr. Pyeweed."

He nodded, grinning smug. "Then to begin, run this bottle to the surgery. Have it replenished and returned to me."

"Aye, Mr. Pyeweed."

"Well? Don't just stand there. Be gone!"

I spun on my heel and left over quick, pleased to be rid of his presence. On the companionway I uncorked the empty vile, breathing in the vague scent of spice. I studied the dregs, recalling such a vial clutched in the gaunt hand of Émile Coutts.

I made direct for the surgery, remembering *Eleanor*'s loblolly, Reggie Spoon. Reggie was my first best mate, and the one I'd first told of the Sukiyama. He was the only one who believed me, except for Mr. Wordsworth, though Wordsworth never claimed to know the Sukiyama. Reggie not only believed, but he claimed to have heard the whispering himself. Dear Reggie. A patient fellow, over generous with his time, answering all my raw questions. Until a round fired from a pretty brig named *Santa Isadora* ripped him in two. I shuddered at the thought, for I'd stood not one foot away from Reggie when that gun fired. For the same price it could have been me who became killed.

In the surgery a young man sat at his bench, boiling some potion. Only when I asked who he was did he look up from his work. About twenty-five, with a milky white face and green eyes, narrow set and piercing bright. Hair white as snow, unbraided, and falling well below the nape of his neck. An odd-looking fellow, and I failed in my efforts not to stare. He ignored my gape, though, and answered straight away.

"I am Elo Inari. Loblolly."

"Oh. What are you making?"

"Ginseng."

"What's it for?"

"For captain." Inari returned to his work. "You ask questions. Now I ask back. Who are you?"

"Owen Harriet, master's mate. You speak with an accent."

"Ja. Finland."

"A long way from home."

"Ja. Run to France in Gustav's War. Run again when Terror happen. Now Lady Praether take me on board to care for crew."

"Captain Praether hasn't looked over well as of late. Is he sick?"

"Weak from bloodletting. Ginseng restore strength."

I gave him Pyweed's empty vial. "Refill this, if you will."

He took the bottle and sniffed. "For you?"

"No."

"Pyeweed?"

"Yes. Not that it's any of your business."

"Ja, my business. Captain Praether says I must count how much of laudanum Pyeweed taking."

"Why?"

Elo gave a wry laugh before answering. "Now that none of your business. I give him more, though. But you tell Pyeweed no more laudanum for this month." He laughed again. "Pity. Only first day in month."

That night, Praether called once more for his officers to form in the great cabin.

"Gentlemen, upon inspection I find your work on schedule. Therefore, I will leave for London in the morning, so now is the time to see just where we stand." He turned to Lieutenant Bonel. "Lieutenant, the watch bill, if you please."

The First Officer stepped forward. "As of eight bells of the morning watch, we have aboard four lieutenants, a sailing master, one acting master's mate, three midshipmen, one hundred sixty-one ratings, one squad of marines consisting of ten men and their sergeant. Also, two ship boys. That's all, sir."

"Very well. Now then, lieutenant, since you are also serving as my gunnery officer, what is *Eleanor*'s current ordnance?"

"As of yesterday, the last of our long guns have been removed, sir, and all twelve carronades have been repositioned on the gun deck for better concealment. We're still capable of inflicting a good deal of damage, but only at close range. And, just come aboard this morning, one brass six-pound long gun to be used as a bow chaser. The shot lockers contain one hundred fifty of round shot and twenty-seven of grape. The powder magazine is full to capacity. Fifty muskets. Five pistols, with powder and shot. Thirty-nine cutlasses. Six dirks. All secured in the powder magazine."

Praether paced the stern gallery, his silhouette blotting the lights of Portsmouth harbour. He stopped of a sudden and faced us. "We are far below complement. I know you are concerned about this, but for our mission we do not require three hundred men. We have fewer guns, so we need need less crew to serve them. And I remind you, we are currently at peace. Besides, even if we were at war, I would not choose to engage any belligerent. That would be inimical to our purpose. Comments?"

None. Or at least none voiced.

"Now for provisions. Mr. Pyeweed?"

Pyeweed cleared his throat. "I've not had time, sir."

Praether scowled. "Then I must rely on your master's mate." He turned to me. "Mr. Harriet, report, if you will."

Certain I must comply with the captain's request, and certain I'd suffer Pyeweed's wrath soon thereafter. But any midshipman must learn fast how to think quick, and I found the middle course before stepping forward.

"Mr. Pyeweed's been busy, sir, but he was kind enough to share with me the following numbers. We will be fully watered by the end of the week. At present, there are seven kegs of rum, and seven casks of plug tobacco. We have sixty days at full ration of biscuit, salt beef and pork, chickpeas and beans. One hogshead of apples, one crate of limes, six cords of firewood and a full bin of coal. The officers' mess has bought a half truckle of cheddar. And we're waiting on one dozen laying hens, one stoat, and a nanny goat."

I snuck a glimpse at Pyeweed. He didn't look over vexed, which I took as a good thing.

"That's all, sir."

"Very well. I hope to depart the Solent by mid-November. Dismissed."

As we filed out, Praether called to Pyeweed. "Mr. Pyeweed, a word with you."

9. The manifest

A week passed. On the seventh night I sat on the maintop, keeping a count. Twenty-seven shooting stars since four bells of the middle watch. Mr. Lau once told me a French astronomer first observed this same meteor shower, claiming it was associated with the comet Encke. There went twenty-eight. I stopped counting, though, when a small boat came rowing out of the night, making direct for *Eleanor*. Curious, for any boat moving about on the Solent at this hour was sure to draw close attention. I watched as it pulled near, just as the anchor watch hailed it.

The deck officer stepped to the rail. Lieutenant Israel Fagen. A spare fellow, with a nap of black hair braided in a short queue. He'd come on board just one day before, and no doubt wished to assert his authority.

"What boat?"

"*Eleanor.*"

That meant Captain Praether was in the boat, and Fagen hastened to assemble his reception line. But Praether didn't wait on ceremony and came aboard prompt. A second figure followed but, in the gloom, I failed to see who it was. Except he was a big one, with a bald head reflecting in the glim. He moved agile, and with no wasted effort, and it was by that alone that I knew him. Jean Dame-Marie. The two men went below, leaving Fagen to stare after them. He turned to me.

"That maroon looked sidelong at you. He know you?"

"Aye, sir. He's Jean Dame-Marie."

"What's he doing on this ship?"

"I don't know, sir."

"Well I don't like it."

When I made no reply, he felt obliged to say more.

"Given half the chance his kind are bound to play you false. See it in their eyes."

Fagen saw caution and mistrust, to be sure, for there was much of both in Dame-Marie. But I'd worked the Channel with Dame-Marie and never knew him to play me false. I wondered why Captain Praether would sign on a man with such notions as Fagen. Not a likely choice for this operation, and I meant to ask him if he knew our mission. But I was saved from my own tongue, for just then I was called to the great cabin.

Praether wasted no time. "Mr. Harriet, name this man if you will."

Dame-Marie stood massive broad, making the great cabin seem over small. He canted his head to keep from knocking the beams, watching me direct, his eyes casting some cryptic look. I was about to name him, but then paused in my reply. What if Fagen was right? What if Dame-Marie played it false? An unwelcome thought, to be sure, and I wondered of it, but then came a whisper. Faint, yet close by. The Sukiyama. Not voiced as a warning, though, but as some remote echo dislodged in time. Then I recalled. I now stood not ten feet from where I'd first heard the Sukiyama. Dame-Marie narrowed his eyes, seeming aware of my reverie. But it was Praether who broke the spell.

"I am waiting, Mr. Harriet."

"He's Jean Dame-Marie, sir."

"You are sure?"

"Aye, sir."

"Then why do you hesitate?"

"No hesitation, sir, just to be sure of it."

"Very well. Now then, it seems Dame-Marie and I have discovered a common purpose, although when I found *Solitude* and informed him of my intentions, he was reluctant to join me."

"Still be dat."

"Yes. But at least you agreed to accompany me to Portsmouth, so I hope we may yet reach an agreement. However, and before all else, Dame-Marie wishes to review my officers. Go now, Harriet, and inform the helm to send all officers to me at once."

Seven bells of the middle watch. Three-thirty in the morning. An unlikely hour to hold a council, yet we all stood ready to hear what Praether had for us.

"Gentlemen, as previously stated, our overall mission is to aid in the abolition of slavery. But our immediate concern is the *Elizabeth Carton*. More specifically, her disappearance, and the whereabouts of the two hundred twenty-one men, women and children listed as cargo."

The captain opened his hand toward Dame-Marie. "That is why this man is here. He is Jean Dame-Marie. He has no rank or rating, and his name will never be carried on the watch bill."

He retrieved the slave manifest from his desk. "I told you this manifest came into my possession from an unseen hand passing it across my sill. As it turns out, it was Dame-Marie." He turned to the Maroon. "You have already explained it to me, but please tell my officers how you came to possess this document."

"Find dat ting inside a watertight chest floatin' off Falmouth. Dat be last year, in de spring. Chest have *Elizabeth Carton* stamped upon it, but de Carton, she leave Dakar in December of '98. Never hear from dat ship again."

"And how is it you know anything about the Carton?"

"Free slaves workin' de wharf at Debtford. Dey all talkin' in Mandinka 'bout dat ship. Dey not tink no one but dem know what dey sayin'."

"But you know Mandinka."

"*Haa. Doo.* Yes, a little. Learn it on Saint-Domingue. Dat where I be from."

"And what did they say at Debtford?"

"Say some a dem slaves on board of Carton still be alive. Be at Cape Verde. On de small island of Boa Vista."

"How would they know that?"

"You tink you people only ones who know de slave trade?"

A disrespectful reply, verging on contempt. But Praether let it pass.

"And these people stranded on Boa Vista, they also speak Mandinka?"

"If Carton take dem people from Dakar den some 'a dem bound to be speakin' it."

"And if we find them you would be able to translate for us."

"Maybe. But der be a problem wiff Mandinka. Lots 'a tribe

speakin' dat. And some 'a dem tribes be bad enemies. Mandinka speaker could be someone who kill your kin and den sell you to a Portuguese trader. And dem people on Boa Vista ... dey don't know nuffin' 'bout me. If I be findin' dem dey just might tink I just be 'nother enemy workin' for de Portuguese. Bound to kill me den."

Eight bells struck, marking the end of middle watch. Muted conversation, and light footfall on the deck as the morning watch began.

"You fear being killed by them. So you will not join us?"

"I take dat risk. If dem people be on Boa Vista, den I offer to take dem off."

"And return them to Africa?"

Dame-Marie scoffed. "Not goin' back dere. Just end up on slaver again."

"London, then. Not the best choice, or even a good one, but I am quite sure The One Body will act in their behalf if we land them there."

"Saint-Domingue be best. But *Solitude*, she too small for de Atlantic. Can't haul dat much of people, neither. I be workin' de channel trade to buy me somethin' bigger."

The cabin went quiet. Dame-Marie never looked my way, but I sensed he knew that last June I'd discovered the muskets stowed on *Solitude*, inside bolts of wool. I suspect they brought a good price in Calais. Perhaps, given time, enough to buy a larger vessel.

Praether started to pace but stopped abrupt. I thought he might be having another episode, but soon he gathered himself.

"Then here is what I propose. Sail with us to Cape Verde. If any of Carton's human cargo is there, then you will act as our interpreter and I will try to secure a large enough vessel for you to carry off these people. Will you agree to that?"

"*Haani.*"

"What?"

"I say no. Only take de risk if you find me dat vessel first. Den you makin' me de captain of it."

Later on, I sat in the midshipmen's mess sharing a stew with my new mate, Elo. I finished my portion and set down my spoon. A most excellent utensil carved from a walrus tusk and able to sway on much stew. I'd bought it on the Hard, then etched my name on it. I was fond of the thing and tucked it in my shirt before addressing Elo.

"Pyeweed's still the nasty one. He blames me for any wrongdoing. It's lucky I kept my mouth shut in the great cabin today."

Elo raised a brow. "What you say in cabin, if tongue come loose?"

"I would have mentioned *Santa Isadora*."

"Who?"

"It's the name of a brig. A Portuguese war ship we captured off Cape Finisterre. That was in '98. Its Portuguese lines may serve Captain Praether's purpose."

He jabbed me with his finger. "Then you tell captain."

"Except I don't actually know where *Santa Isadora* is, now that she's not on station at Cadiz."

☇

November came and went yet we still rode to our anchor in the Solent, waiting on some unknown passenger. The Eleanors guessed he might be a swell, or some consul or prelate. But it was neither, nor was it a he.

Ajax and I stood in the waist overseeing the watch. I breathed in the pine pitch and resin, the tobacco and the sweat, all baked hard into *Eleanor*'s seams. She may have changed her lines, but not her savour. Yet, floating above, there was a new one, a smell peculiar to any war ship.

"Ajax, do I smell lilac?"

"The captain's wife."

"What?"

"Her perfume. She came aboard last night. Captain Praether says she's to go on this voyage. Now that she's here I believe we'll deploy soon."

If Cherish Praether was aboard, then certain *Eleanor*'s crew would rush to play make-a-face soon as they laid eyes on her, with all of them keen to mimic what they called 'face of love,' and be eager to express devotion to their new angel.

"Why do you make that face, Mr. Harriet? Are you love struck? Like the rest of this crew will soon be?"

"Sorry. I'll not do it again."

"See that you don't. And I suggest you make yourself useful." He scanned the waist, then pointed to a group of tars standing idle. "Those men are on watch. Collect the lot and set them to polishing the six-pounder."

Soon thereafter, the brass six-pounder gleamed over bright, its foundry stamp shining in low relief. This gun was much the same as the artillery on *Santa Isadora*. Same carriage and slide. I'd forgotten about *Santa Isadora* since telling Elo about her. She was no good memory, too remindful of my good mate, Reggie. Still, *Santa Isadora* might be put to good use. But of no use at all if we couldn't find her. After four years, though, who aboard *Eleanor* would know where to look? By now much of *Eleanor*'s first crew had been paid off and had moved on. But not Lorca. He was a Spaniard forced to serve aboard *Santa Isadora* and, after we captured her, he was given the chance to join the Royal Navy. Once on *Eleanor* he'd cooked for our diplomatic passenger, Gottlieb, then became ship's cook.

He loved to draw, and I found him in the foretop with his sketch pad.

"Lorca."

Lorca set down his pad. "*Hola.*"

I could never expect Lorca to address me as Mr. Harriet. Not after we'd seen *le serpiente* taking our measure when we were adrift in a dinghy on the Sea of Flores. We'd shared the same fear, as that frightful thing watched us from below, eyeing us as much the same thing … its next meal. Besides, Lorca's English was mostly uncharted, and the word 'mister' was bound to come out colourful wrong.

"I should like to watch you draw, Lorca, but first I need information."

Lorca raised a brow.

"*Santa Isadora*. Do you know where she is now?"

"Plymouth *la reparación*. You say ... the Goat's Head?"

"I think you mean the dry dock at Camels Head."

"Yes. I think so.

"Thank you." I looked at his sketch. A lone shrike perched in the rigging. "That's a good one."

♭

The hens had come aboard, and all were laying prodigious. Elo and I fried a dozen eggs in the midshipmen's mess, with a wedge of plum-duff shared between us.

"I think I've located *Santa Isadora*."

Elo looked up, yolk running down his chin. "Ja?"

"Lorca says she's at Plymouth Dockyard. In dry dock."

"Tell Praether."

"Certain he should know, except I think it best if I'm not the one who tells him."

"Lorca?"

"No."

"Then who?"

"Pyeweed."

"Why not you?"

I mopped my bowl with the last of my plum-duff. "Because if it was me who told Praether then Pyeweed might think I was trying to curry favour. He'd only hate me the more."

"No matter what person does, Pyeweed always hate the more."

"But if I happen to tell Pyeweed about *Santa Isadora*, then he could tell Praether himself, and then he might hate me less."

"No more extra duty for you then. Ja?"

"At least one less duty, I hope. Noon line."

"Not good duty?"

"It's fine. And I don't mind keeping my hand in. It's just that I see Pyeweed making errors during every sighting. What's worse, he seems never to catch himself."

"What errors?"

"To begin, the index mirror of his sextant is misaligned."

Elo shrugged. "So? We are in same place every day."

"Not so. *Eleanor* may be stationary, but the earth isn't. Our stellar position changes constant, under sail or not. What's more critical, though, is that he's instilling careless habits in the midshipmen."

Elo set aside his bowl and loaded his cheek with plug tobacco. "Then tell Pyeweed he makes error."

"He'd only say for me to mind my business, then lay on some meaningless task just to punish my insolence. But I will tell him about *Santa Isadora*."

Pyeweed's door stood ajar. I knocked but he didn't answer, so I looked in. He sat slouched in a chair clutching his empty vial.

"Beg pardon, Mr. Pyeweed. May I have a word with you?"

He looked my way, eyes glassed over and unfocused, his face darkening.

"No."

"It's something I think you should know."

"I don't wish to know anything from you."

"But if I tell you and then you pass it on to Captain Praether, well, it may stand you in good stead with him."

Pyeweed shifted, cocking an ear. "Go on. But if you think it will stand you in good stead with me, you're mistaken."

I told him about *Santa Isadora*.

He sat still as any dead man, and I thought he might have breathed his last. Finally, he heaved a wet groan, and spoke ominous low.

"You play me the fool. But it's you who's the fool. My last ship paid off at Plymouth and I spent a month at Camels Head before reporting here. There's no such brig at Plymouth named *Santa Isadora*. I'll not trot off to Praether with your fanciful yarn."

He handed me his empty vile. "Replenish. Get out."

I found Elo in his surgery, stirring roots into a steaming pot. It stunk of some abysmal bog, stinging in my nose.

"What is it?"

He replied as he worked. "Thunder God. Make reduction. Store in ewer. Give to men before battle."

"Why?"

"Courage. Also make them fart." Finally, he looked up. "You tell Pyeweed?"

"He only accused me of trying to play him for a fool. He claims there's no brig in Plymouth named *Santa Isadora*."

Elo raised a brow. "Maybe Lorca tells the lie."

"He wouldn't. But he might have misunderstood."

Elo set the pot aside. "Misunderstanding. No misunderstanding. Now you tell Praether yourself. Provide information then he decide. He should know before we leave Solent. I hear we leave soon."

"Yes, I suppose I will." I made to leave, but then turned back when I felt Pyweed's empty vial in my pocket. "I forgot. Pyeweed wants his ration refilled."

Elo refilled the thing, then made note of it.

"I should like to ask you something."

"What?"

"I asked once before but you wouldn't tell."

"Go on."

"Why do you keep track of Pyeweed's laudanum?"

He raised a brow. "You know laudanum?"

"Not so much. Except that Pyeweed wants it."

"Not want it. Need."

"What do you mean?"

"Laudanum is opium. You take opium?"

"Once. The ship's surgeon gave it to me once."

"Why?"

"To quiet me. I'd been near killed and had blood all over me. Only it wasn't mine."

Elo said nothing, and I chose not to explain whose blood it was. "And I watched men smoke opium in George Town. On the Mekong, too. They become living skeletons."

He nodded. "Death wish."

"Then why's Pyeweed still permitted to serve? His mother asked Praether to take him, but in the Royal Navy a man's rank is earned, not doled out as some favour."

"*Eleanor* not navy. And now you change subject. Why you not go see Praether? Maybe you afraid of his wife? Afraid of women. Yes?"

"No. I don't fear women. It's just that I can't ever guess what they'll do."

Elo laughed. "Ja!"

I just stood there thinking of what Lady Praether might do. Befriend me, like Yadra? And then be hanged for stealing a bauble? Not likely. Or stand naked before me while sticking her tongue halfway down my throat? Such as Lady Elspeth? Hardly.

Elo went back to his work, transferring the extract into a ewer. It had thickened now and poured slow. Finally, he turned to me.

"Silence prove it."

"Proves what."

"Proves you afraid of women."

"I've not had the best of luck. Except for Becca. And I've known her since before I can remember."

"Good luck. Bad luck. Either way, go tell captain about *Santa Isadora*."

"But I can't just knock on his door and step in."

"Then write it out. Ja!"

♭

Captain Praether,

There may be a Portuguese brig in Plymouth. Santa Isadora. She was captured by Eleanor in '99 and now might be at Camels Head. She might serve your purpose.

Owen Harriet, acting Master's Mate

I sent in the note, and Praether called for me immediate. I stood before the cheval glass just outside the great cabin, adjusting my best rig. Any midshipman is bound to feel anxious when reporting to his captain, but Praether wasn't my only discomfort. Would Cherish Praether be with him? I'd not met her, but only seen her at night while walking with the captain or standing together at the taffrail. I was still smitten with her portrait hanging in the great cabin. Most splendid to look at, with her curly blond hair parted in the middle, just touching on her shoulders. Posed in a blue dress to match her eyes.

The marine sentry manning his post outside the great cabin came to attention as I approached.

"Inform the captain that Mr. Harriet is here, as ordered."

He gave a knock.

"Yes?"

"Sir, Mr. Harriet, sir."

"Send him in."

I paused, wishing for the safety of battle to forestall this encounter, or for some great storm rising in the Solent.

"I am waiting, Mr. Harriet."

The die was cast. I strode in. Praether sat at his desk. Cherish stood behind with her back turned, looking out the stern windows. She was taller than I would have guessed, with her head near touching the beams. Lilac perfume.

"Stand at ease, Harriet. Tell me what you know of *Santa Isadora*."

I spoke at length, ending with the brig's possible location.

Praether nodded, pursing his lips and weaving his fingers under his chin. He thought long, and in silence. *Eleanor* rode gentle on the tide. Muted conversation on the quarterdeck sifted through the grating. Praether finally spoke.

"It is worth pursuing this matter. If this brig is indeed in Plymouth, then we may discover that it is what we have been looking for. No doubt a Portuguese vessel would give us an advantage when operating in Portuguese waters. What is your opinion, Cherish?"

I held my breath. My missing finger twitched as she turned to address her husband. Oh. Well then, I would never say Cherish Praether was homely, but certain she was no great beauty. Homespun, with a bland face and an overlarge nose, somewhat out of joint, I think. She brought both hands to her waist, holding them in front as if about to play on a harpsichord. An odd trait, that, and made even more so when she lifted each index finger simultaneous, to point at my note still resting on the desk. Though I'd not yet heard her voice I hoped it might ring merry, like Becca's. But when she spoke, her voice came overloud for a woman, and near deep as any man.

"The brig named in this note may be our best chance yet, Matthew. It's an opportunity to redouble."

"What do you mean?"

"Our purpose is to disrupt the slave trade, and Dame-Marie wants to search for *Elizabeth Carton*, to see if it came ashore at Boa Vista. We both need a second ship, though, for us to expand our patrol and for him to return these unfortunate souls to Africa."

"Not to Africa. He says they would likely be taken as slaves again."

"Then where?"

"To a new life. If not in England, then in Saint-Domingue."

"Well, no matter where, it will be very hard for them. Hopefully they still have the strength to rise."

Praether went to his desk and pulled out the slave manifest.

"There are two hundred twenty-one names listed in this document. A brig would be just large enough. But even if we locate *Santa Isadora* the cost will be prohibitive. We must contact Wilberforce to raise the funds."

Cherish Praether came to stand with her husband. "I think not. Time presses. We must raise the funds on our own. The One Body has sponsors throughout Devon. One of them is James Wilton. He lives in Plymouth, and I happen to know he is a principal shareholder at Lloyds. I met him in Hull, last summer."

She took the manifest from Praether. "Let's present this document to Wilton. If *Santa Isadora* can be found, then we'll press him to help."

Praether beamed at his wife with great pleasure. "We shall leave for Plymouth on the tide."

10. Rame Head

Rame Head marked the entrance to Plymouth Sound. We hoisted our signal flag for the harbour pilot, and soon a lighter stood out from Drake's Island. The pilot came aboard. A stout one, missing all of his left arm. He wore an oilskin, lashed tight to shed the driving rain blown in on a sudden squall. Unlike most men, he had a full beard. When he reached the quarterdeck, he addressed Praether.

"I be Quail. Harbour pilot. Your draft, sir?"

Praether replied, "Twenty-three feet."

"You ride light. Victualing?"

"No."

"Then I'll place you in the outer roads. Easy to slip when you depart. Won't foul your anchor."

"That will serve. Now then, Mr. Quail, do you know of a captured brig of war currently berthed at Camels Head? *Santa Isadora*. She is Portuguese."

"What she look like?"

"Mr. Harriet, describe *Santa Isadora*, if you will."

"One hundred twenty-two feet, sir. With eight brass six-pound long guns. Three years ago, her hull was painted bright yellow, with a blue mainsail and a red Templar's Cross. Bevelled panes in the stern windows."

"No brig like that at Camels Head." Quale stroked his beard. "But a brig at Torpoint answers to that description. Ain't called *Santa Isadora*, though. Called *Iona*."

"Where is Torpoint?"

"Tamar estuary." Quale pointed beyond our bow. "Just there."

"Is *Iona* listed?"

"Not listed. After Amiens no one paid for her refit so now she's owned by Plymouth Dock. Up for sale."

"Is there a lien?"

"Aye."

"Who holds it?"

"Lloyds."

"Thank you for your information. Proceed to our buoy, if you will." Praether turned to March. "Fetch the bosun and Dame-Marie."

The bosun arrived. "Gleason, prepare the cutter and launch. Have them in the water immediately."

Dame-Marie made his way aft. News travels fast aboard *Eleanor,* and once again he breached protocol by speaking first.

"Gonna buy dat brig?"

Praether raised a brow but chose not to dress him down for speaking out of turn. "We shall see. Take the cutter and go have a look. Likely there's a watchman. I will send a note stamped with my seal asking permission to board. Harriet, you go with him."

Cherish Praether joined the captain. She withdrew a sovereign from her purse and handed it to me. The coin felt pleasant warm. "Mr. Harriet, if the watchman's reluctant to let you come on board you may offer him this."

The captain gave his approval. "And while you and Harriet are with *Iona*, Lady Praether and I will proceed to Milehouse."

"What dat?"

Cherish Praether made reply. "A patron of The One Body lives there. We'll begin negotiations to pay off *Iona*'s lien, then make an offer to buy a controlling share."

The squall blew out just as Dame-Marie and I approached the brig. *Iona.* Her hull was still yellow, but painted new, and with new rigging all in place. Fresh sails, furled smart. But the mainsail was no longer blue, as was *Santa Isadora*'s. I guessed it was still her, though, and my guess was confirmed when we passed under the transom. The same beveled windowpanes. The brig's old name was painted over, but the gilt lettering still showed faint beneath her new name.

"This is *Santa Isadora*, to be sure. And she's still the good one. Someday she'll pay off handsome in the Prize Court."

"What be your share?"

"Sixty-one pence." I laughed. "I was just a ship's boy when we took her. Mr. Lau's share will be near eleven pounds."

"Why he not on board of *Eleanor* no more?"

"He's in London recovering from his wound. And some agency has requested his assistance."

"Mr. Lau. He be da one who tell me go see Praether."

I'd not thought of Mr. Lau in a week. And to speak of him now brought regret, but a surprise, as well. I loved him, but the love had grown more distant now, if only some, and the hurt less painful. Less painful yet, at the same moment, bittersweet. Just then a watchman appeared at the sally port. He was old and bent, and stared chary at Dame-Marie. When Dame-Marie shot his dentures halfway out, the man jumped back from the rail.

"Bloody savage. State your business."

Dame-Marie grumbled low. "I just state my business wiff dat one. Now you tell him what we want."

I told him who we were and what we wanted, and that we had a note from the captain of HMS *Eleanor*.

"Don't read none."

I showed him my sovereign, shiny bright, and his eyes opened wide.

"Come."

He led us to the binnacle. "Brig's for sale. Don't know nothin' 'bout it. If you got a question, I can't answer it none. I'm goin' below. See yer own self off."

Dame-Marie stared at the man as he walked away, then turned to me.

"How much of a crew do it take to sail dis brig?"

"We took forty-three prisoners off this brig when it was *Santa Isadora*. But she was a war ship then and had to carry enough crew to serve the guns. If *Iona* doesn't plan to engage any ship, then certain it can make do with less."

Dame-Marie ran his hand along the aft six-pounder. "Like to shoot dis ting into a slaver."

We returned from *Iona* in a damp chill. Dame-Marie and I stood close to the galley stove, watching the steam rise from our trousers. When Praether returned from Milepoint he came into the galley for its warmth. Once again, Dame-Marie spoke out of turn.

"You buy dat brig?"

Praether raised a brow, but let it pass. "The One Body has acquired controlling interest in *Iona*, but the sale is contingent upon the brig's seaworthiness. Lloyds assures us it is. I assume you have seen it. Can you affirm their claim?"

"It seaworthy."

"And the hold?"

"Got some pig iron in it. 'Bout half of one-foot water in de hold. Got no crew."

"The last crew was paid off after the Treaty was signed. Tomorrow morning, I will hire a printshop to make up flyers advertising for volunteers. A cryer will distribute them and by afternoon we will conduct a first call at the Cornish Arms. That is on the corner of Pembroke and Clowance. I want you there to select a crew. You are lucky."

Dame-Marie scoffed. "Make de luck on my own self."

"That may be. But this crew will serve directly under you, so you are fortunate to be the one to choose them. Recruit fourteen able seamen, six top men, a bosun and a carpenter. Many of them are on half-pay and will be eager for a berth. You should have a good selection. I will send a war chest with you to offer each man a signing bonus. Lieutenant Hoyer and a marine guard will accompany you."

I spoke without forethought. "Lieutenant Hoyer? Is he well?"

Praether scowled at my impertinence, and his reply came sharp.

"He is well. I recruited him last month. Is there is anything else you wish to know, Harriet?"

"No, sir."

"Then walk with me."

We made through the officers' mess and onto the spar deck.

"Mr. Pyeweed has asked me to put you off the ship. But I will not do it."

"Oh. Thank you, sir."

"I neither request nor require your gratitude."

"Sorry, sir."

"Or your apologies."

Praether stopped abrupt when he noticed a cracked block in the deadeyes. "Who is the new carpenter?"

"Bettyhill, sir."

"When I am done with you bring Bettyhill here to have him explain why he has not replaced this block."

"Aye, sir."

"Now then, at first I was tempted to grant Pyeweed's request and send you to *Iona*. Not because you should be put off *Eleanor*, but because *Iona* will need a master's mate and I have confidence in your abilities. But I have decided to send Lieutenant Hoyer, along with Ajax, to serve on *Iona*. Hoyer will act as first officer, and he has excellent navigational skills."

The first dog watch would soon begin. Those about to go on duty roused themselves, stowing their make-and-mend and their scrimshaw. The ones who could read, and there were but few, put away their letters. Praether nodded to the men, bidding them to carry on, then told me more.

"At one point in his career Pyeweed was a good sailing master. But no longer. Not after Camperdown, when a splinter lodged in his thigh. He recovered well enough but, since then, the opium that was meant to mask the pain has inflicted its own sort of wound. He should have been cashiered by now, but I have intervened in his behalf because he is my first cousin. What is more, Pyeweed's mother is a major contributor to The One Body. Without her influence Wilberforce would not likely be a Member of Parliament. In return for her beneficence I have tacitly offered to salvage her son. Or at least try. So I gave Pyeweed one last chance in hopes that a prolonged sea voyage, along with his sense of duty, would stay him from his cravings."

Praether hauled short at the windlass, and spoke low, his words meant only for me.

"You may wonder why I would tell you any of this. That is because it involves you now. This morning I examined Pyeweed's log entries, and I find them sorely lacking. If we were on a war footing, or if *Eleanor*'s status were active, I would charge him with dereliction of duty. But, since we are neither, I have chosen instead to place him on restricted duty."

We made for the companionway and onto the gun deck, just as eight bells struck, ending the afternoon watch. The deck swarmed for muster, but all stood to attention when the captain came on deck. Praether told them to carry on, just as we passed Pyeweed's quarters.

Praether observed the closed door, shaking his head. "I do not see how we can improve upon him. But I gave my word so I must do what I can."

"I helped Mr. Lau stay away from the drink, sir. Maybe I can try to keep Mr. Pyeweed from the opium."

"Mr. Lau has the will to fight his own battles. Not so with Pyeweed. You may try, but it will take patience, a virtue you gave freely to Mr. Lau, but might not come so easily in Pyeweed's case."

We approached the great cabin. When the sentry opened the door, I stood back. But Praether had more.

"Why does Pyeweed have your logs?"

"He said he was going to examine them, sir, for any errors."

"When I examined Pyeweed's log I also went through yours. I found no errors."

"I would thank you, sir, but it seems you expect none."

"None. What I do expect is for you to continue serving as master's mate on *Eleanor*. And now you will have additional duties, as well. First, from this point on it will be your log entries that are the official record of our lambda. Second, *Iona* may be seaworthy, but she lacks provisions. So, with Pyeweed on restricted duty, you will stand in his place. Inspect all inventory marked for *Iona* and be sure to sign for each manifest. You will be, in effect, acting as sailing master. It is arduous duty, and the First Officer expects you to ask for assistance. He will assign men to you and, if all goes well, *Iona* will be fit to deploy within a week, with Dame-Marie in command. Dismissed."

11. By my own self

Except it was not within a week, but ten more days before we finally left Plymouth, departing as the smallest of fleets, with *Eleanor* disguised as a slaver and *Iona* following in her lee, and with Jean Dame-Marie standing at the helm. The wind came fair now, and it took but two days before we finally made the Atlantic, and Captain Praether called me to the quarterdeck.

"Mr. Harriet, what was our position at the noon sighting?"

"Forty-seven degrees north by seven degrees west, sir."

He turned to the First Officer. "Bonel, if you recall, I told you in Portsmouth that I would read out our letter of marque once we weathered Ushant. I am of the opinion we've just now done so. Do you concur?"

"I do concur, sir."

"Then be so kind as to assemble the men in the waist."

Bonel relayed the order to Lieutenant Strayhorne, officer of the watch. Strayhorne passed it on to Midshipman Hewitt, who sent Nary, a new ships boy, in search of the piper. Chutney scurried to the fife rail to pipe away, and the deck thundered most wondrous as one hundred nine men ran to muster by division. Captain Praether came to the main chains. He gripped a shroud with his left hand, knuckles turning white. In his right, he held a vellum scroll. He cleared his throat, then spoke loud so that all might hear.

"Men, the First Lieutenant has assembled you here at my request. That is because I have important information to make known you all. It is, in effect, the purpose of this voyage. So be you sharp and listen closely."

Praether cleared his throat and began to read from the scroll.

"Sir Harold Smethwick, Knight of the Most Honourable Order of the Bath, To The Worshipful and Honourable Matthew Praether, Captain of HMS Eleanor, a frigate:

Whereas, by His Majesty's Commission under the Great Seal of Great Britain bearing Date the 1st Day of November in the year of Our Lord 1802, and in the 42d Year of His Majesty's Reign, the Lords Commissioners for executing the Office of Lord High Admiral are required and authorized to issue forth and grant Letters of Marque and Reprisal to any and all whom we shall deem fitly qualified in that Behalf for apprehending, seizing, and taking the Ships, Vessels and Goods belonging to . . ."

Praether read for over long, and the men stood unwavering. But I saw in their expressions that they had little understanding of the decree, even if a few might guess we'd just been declared pirates, enlisted to do His Majesty's bidding.

After we were dismissed, I went below to share a slab of cold beef with Elo.

"I suspect our next landfall will be Cape Verde. I've not ever been there. Do you know it?"

Elo uncorked a squat, clay pot, dipped in his knife to scoop out some sort of green paste, and spread it on his beef.

"Come there to water at Santiago. Big island. Not much water."

"My charts say there's not much of anything there. Or on Boa Vista. The entire chain is volcanic." I watched him spreading the paste. "What is that?"

"Wasabi."

"Looks like something you'd make."

"Ja. I make it."

"May I try some?"

"Ja!"

I tasted of it, and it burned on my tongue hot as an ember. "Oh! Oh! I'm on fire!" I ran for the water butt. "You made this?"

"Ja. Boil stems from wasabi plant."

March came into the mess. "Mr Harriet, the captain wishes to see you in his cabin."

"Am I to bring anything?"

"Oh, I forgot. Charts."

"For Cape Verde?"

"I think them's the ones."

He made to leave, but I stayed him.

"March, when someone gives you an order you must be sure to remember all of what you're told. You need to improve your memory."

"But I'm just a ship's boy."

"No matter. There may be times when *Eleanor* has only her ship's boy to relay orders. One more thing, never presume you're dismissed until you are told as much."

March barely listened, for he'd seen the wasabi.

"Is that a pot of jam?"

Elo grinned once more, guessing he might now have another laugh, this one at March's expense.

He scooped a large portion of wasabi, and when March reached for it I grabbed his arm.

"It's not jam, March. And you wouldn't like it. Go you now."

March left, disappointment showing in his face.

"You were his age once. Would you like it if someone tricked you into eating that stuff?"

Elo smirked. "Someone did. Now I have courage." He pushed his bowl away. "Must go."

"To boil some more wasabi?"

"No. Snakewood."

"For courage, no doubt."

"Ja. And madness."

⚡

We bore south by west for six days, standing well into the Bay of Biscay so as to avoid other ships. We saw but two, both making for the Spanish coast, and were passed by one more. Captain Praether allowed no communication with any of them. We must have been a queer sight. From a distance we might have passed as a slaver. But why in these latitudes? And why sailing with some brig painted bright yellow, and armed with eight brass guns?

But, since the continent was no longer at war, no one challenged us, and we drove on. At thirty-seven degrees north by twenty-five degrees west, off the coast of Sao Padre, which is most easterly of the Azores, the order came to wear ship and to bear south by south. But the wind turned foul for the next week, driving us one hundred miles further into the Atlantic before, once again, making southerly. We were a full three weeks out of Plymouth before we finally raised Boa Vista. The weather held, and we began our search, with *Iona* patrolling inshore to look for the wreck of *Elizabeth Carton* or any sign of life. *Eleanor* stood out to sea, on guard for the Portuguese. The slave traffic at Cape Verde generated great wealth for Queen Maria, and she would not like it overmuch to hear of two unknown vessels loitering in the archipelago.

Boa Vista is a small island, and it didn't take long before *Iona* sent up a hoist, just off Quinta Point. I glassed it immediate. One flag only. Checkered squares, blue and yellow. A small village had been sighted.

"March, fetch the captain. Tell him *Iona*'s signaling."

Praether came on deck. "Make our acknowledgment then signal for Dame-Marie to report to *Eleanor*."

Soon all of *Eleanor*'s officers, Dame-Marie, and I stood in the great cabin waiting for the captain. Once more I gazed upon the portrait of Cherish Praether. In some curious way her portrait had once more begun to resemble her. If not in appearance, then in some unknowable quality. The woman herself had retired to the inner gallery. Through the bulkhead screen I studied her shadow as she brushed out her hair in slow, measured strokes. Her habit was to come on deck late each night, at some point during first watch, and walk with the captain, always taking the windward share of quarterdeck. The Eleanors kept their distance, for the quarterdeck belonged to officers, or to men with duties that brought them there. But, even those on the quarterdeck, there to perform some task, never dared to look full upon Cherish Praether. All were curious, though, and asked me overmuch about her, since I was approachable to the ratings, and one who'd seen her in best light. Their questions prompted me to think again about the captain's wife and caused a change in my opinion. In person, she possessed a certain presence. It may have been the grace of her footfall, more like the gliding of an albatross. If I had any reservations, the men did not, and they were always eager to hear any news of her.

"Is she beautiful, Mr. Harriet?"

"No."

And they'd cry out then, disdainful of my reply, and I'd hasten to recant.

"I mean yes, in her own way. I think so. Yes, no doubt of it."

They all would brighten then, and someone might ask, "Does she smell good?"

To be sure her flowery scent rose above that of the sea, and of *Eleanor*'s pine pitch and rigging. Certain her smell was a a good one. But not at this moment, though, for now Praether entered the great cabin.

"Dame-Marie, do you think it's them?"

The Maroon shrugged. "Can't tell. Got to go on shore and see."

"Very well. Take your cutter and have a look. Return before last light."

But Dame-Marie did not return before last light. Instead, he spent the night on Boa Vista, only returning in the morning with his cutter laden with fresh caught bluefin. It seemed the village was only a Portuguese fish camp, and Dame-Marie had traded his nanny goat for a portion of their catch.

"Were you able to communicate with them?"

"Can't talk dat Portuguese too good. Dey seen de wreck but I don't tink dey know 'bout dem slaves. I ask if dey see ships comin' by here."

"And?"

"Dey say no. But dey lie."

"But if you don't speak Portuguese then how would you know they lie?"

"Dere eyes speak de lie. Same wiff any white man. I tink plenty of ships be comin' 'round here."

It took just three days, and all of Dame-Marie's tuna, to explore the entire island and to realize that, but for the fish camp, the place was barren. Once again, we met in the great cabin.

For the last week Praether had been looking healthy and moving about *Eleanor* in proper fashion. But on this day he looked wan, with his military bearing reduced, and he spoke with a thin voice.

"I asked you this once before, Dame-Marie. Now I must ask again. How did those free slaves at Debtford Wharf ever come to be aware of *Elizabeth Carton*'s fate?"

"Dey never say."

"So you don't really know if the Carton made it to Boa Vista."

"Maybe dat ship wash up on some other island nearby of here. Got no proof 'a dat but I can believe it. You not believe dey be somewhere near of here?"

"Yes, I do. No one thought it possible for us to find a slave adrift in *Elizabeth Carton*'s dinghy. Yet we did, and I believe it was God who put that young man in the dinghy for us to find. For me it is a matter of faith, not belief." He gathered himself, and once more assumed the manner of a driven commander. "So we shall press on and investigate the next island in the archipelago. Sal."

<p>

Sal lay ten miles north of Boa Vista, and was smaller yet. While making along its shoaling coastline, *Iona* sent another hoist. Two flags. The first, a red square on a yellow field. The second, four vertical stripes, blue, white, blue, white. Wreck. On beach. Praether sent Dame-Marie to investigate, then come aboard *Eleanor* to make his report. Upon his return Praether met Dame-Marie at the entry port.

"Is it the Carton?"

"It her."

"Bodies?"

"No. All dem shackles be unlocked. I tink somebody unlock dem shackles 'fore dat ship ever come ashore."

"Salvageable?"

"Somebody carry off what dey can long time back."

"Then we will waste no more time on it. We will meet in my quarters in ten minutes. Harriet, bring the Cape Verde chart."

When we gathered, Praether had removed his bicorne and topcoat. "Until further notice, no officer will wear either hat or topcoat. We have made an effort to resemble a slaver so now we must strive to resemble ordinary seamen, as well, concerned only with minding our own business."

Bonel cleared his throat.

"You wish to say something, lieutenant?"

"We could be charged and then shot as spies for not wearing proper uniforms, sir."

"I assume you know there will be no record of this operation, lieutenant."

"I'm aware of that, sir. But as your First Officer it's my duty to advise you that we're operating in uncharted waters, so to speak."

"I will take it under advisement, lieutenant. Now we shall move on." He called for my chart. "Now then, on Sal's western approach there is a cove." Praether tapped on the chart with a well-manicured finger. "Just here. The cove was sounded several years ago, actually by Mr. Lau, I believe. He noted a depth of twenty-six feet at low tide. More than adequate for *Iona*. It provides shelter from the prevailing winds, as well as a place to remain undetected from the sea. So this is where you will anchor, Dame-Marie, and then go ashore in search of these missing people. You have two days. I will patrol the archipelago during that time. There may be other slave ships nearby, so upon our return, we will hoist a recognition code so that you know it is us. *Eleanor*'s number, four-seven-one, and below that, blue and white checkers. Say it back."

Dame-Marie scowled. "You tink I not remember dat?"

"There is more. So say it back."

Dame-Marie repeated the hoist.

"Good. Now here is your response. As of yet you have no ship designation, so now I will assign you one. Number fifty-one. When you see our hoist your response will be fifty-one, and below that, red and white checkers. Say it back."

Dame-Marie said it back.

"Good. Plan to take six marines with you."

I stood lost in thought, recalling what Lieutenant Kyle once told me. The best plan begins with being able to pick and choose your moment. But keep in mind that the only constant in a mission is to expect your plan to unravel at the first opportunity.

Dame-Marie spoke up, "No. What you tink dem people do if six of marine come on shore wiff me? Dey run and dey hide."

"It is a very small island, Dame-Marie. The marines are sure to find them."

"You mean hunt dem down like dey be criminals. Dey ain't no criminals. You people be de criminals. So I walk on to dat island by my own self. Alone. Not no marines. If dem people come to see what dis Maroon be doing on Sal, dat when I talk de Mandinka to dem all. I say '*Nto mu Dame-Marie. Baadinjyaa.*'" Dame Marie stood straight and tall, filling the cabin with his great size. "I tell dem I be Dame-Marie. Tell dem I be kin."

On deck, the stay sails luffed, and *Eleanor* fell off. The deck officer called for Gleason, and Gleason called for the port watch to sheet their lines. All went quiet, but for a small sea booming steady on our hull. I studied the men gathered in the great cabin, none of them mindful of the whisper I heard.

12. Heave, me beauties! Heave away!

We watched *Iona* clear the headland and anchor in the cove, then stood out to sea in search of any slaver bound for Cape Verde's only harbor, at Praia. The next evening, just before nautical twilight, a lookout hailed the deck.

"Deck there! Ship to starboard! Hull down. Square-rigged. Bearing due west."

Bonel sent March to fetch the captain, then turned to me. "Take a glass and go to the crosstrees. Try to determine if she's a slaver, or a Portuguese patrol."

I went aloft. The standard flying from the ship's flagstaff resolved in my telescope. A blue and gold crown centered on a white field. I hailed the deck.

"Portuguese, sir. Three-masted barque." The barque fell off another point, enough to reveal a buff gun stripe with seven ports. "Fourteen guns."

A gout of white smoke discharged from its forward gun, followed by a faint report and a hoist rising on its flag halyard.

"Two-flag hoist, sir. Green over blue."

Praether arrived. He sent a man to replace me and I came down leg over to resume my post at the binnacle, just in time to hear Praether and Bonel discussing the situation.

"Hard to know what green over blue means, sir, but I think it will do no harm if we haul our wind."

"How good is your Portuguese, Bonel?"

"Rather limited, sir. I will translate what I can."

"Very well. Be sure the officers have removed their topcoats and hats. And remind them we must all behave like ordinary seamen."

As *Eleanor* came into the wind Praether looked to Lieutenant Strayhorne standing with me at the helm. "Lieutenant, stand more at ease. Try to look less military."

Strayhorne slackened as best he could, which was not so much. The barque came within hailing distance. A tall officer called through his speaking trumpet. Portuguese, I think. Bonel cupped his hands and responded.

"*Estamos Inglês!*"

The man handed his trumpet to another officer. A squat fellow, and well rounded. He called to us in broken English.

"What is the ship?"

"Tell them we are *Eleanor*. A commercial vessel."

"*Eleanor. Navio comercial.*"

"The home port?"

"Tell them Portsmouth"

"Portsmouth."

"Where going?"

"What should I tell them, sir?"

"I don't think it would be an absolute lie if you told them Praia."

"Praia."

"Off course."

When Bonel made no reply, the Portuguese conferred. An excited debate, with the tall officer bending low and the squat one flailing his arms. Finally, they came to an agreement, and the tall one called to us.

"*Procedentia.*"

Praether gave a nod to Bonel. "Bear away."

But before Bonel relayed the order a man stepped onto *Eleanor*'s quarterdeck. Pyeweed! I'd not seen him as of late, for he'd taken ill. Elo was dosing him with his snakewood potion and had confined him to quarters. Pyeweed's face drained when he saw me at the binnacle, standing the post that used to be his. He wore his bicorne, and a blue frock coat. No officer's rig, yet looking much the same at a distance, and sure to alert the Portuguese that *Eleanor* was no slaver.

Praether reacted instanter. "Pyeweed, remove yourself from my quarterdeck."

"Beg pardon, sir, but I would like to resume my . . ."

Praether ordered Ajax to take Pyeweed below. Too late. The tall officer screamed frantic.

"*Navio de guerra!*"

Bonel translated. "I think he's just accused us of being a fleet of war, sir. Or some such thing."

Another man with a white plume rising from his tricorne joined the tall one.

"That's their captain, sir. White plume gives him away."

After a short conversation, the barque's captain reached for the trumpet.

"*Acompanhar. Agora!*"

"I guess that would mean for us to follow them, sir, and right now. I think we had better do it."

So we came about, which seemed the right thing, for the barque's captain made no more demands. They set a course for Praia, and we followed in their lee.

⸸

Two bells in the first watch. Nine at night. Light air, north by east. Scudding clouds. Not uncommon in this latitude, but the Eleanors had turned restive, and went about their work with little chatter. Not a good sign. Wat came onto the quarterdeck to make use of its wide space for cutting a sail pattern. I felt uneasy, same as the others, but watching the sailmaker's measured pace soothed me. The same steady rhythm of a farrier, until he paused to gaze overlong upon a wakeful sea. I recalled Mr. Lau telling me to trust Wat to know whenever a big sea might come over the horizon. That advice, along with the Sukiyama, heard not two days past, led me to ask the sailmaker what he saw.

"What's out there, Wat?"

Wat made a final cut, then replied, "The feel of it." He said no more, but only groaned, with both knees creaking as he stood up.

The Portuguese fired another signal gun. It seemed they were fond of firing the thing. I looked to see a lantern, now hanging in their stern. In its glow, the letters on the barque's transom. *Villa Real.* Just then a voice carried on the water. It came from *Villa Real*, telling us to light our bow lantern. Night fell complete, consuming any last trace of the gloaming. *Eleanor's* officers joined Praether on the quarterdeck. Bonel spoke first.

"The men blame Pyeweed for this incident, sir. They will speak in guarded tones if nothing's done about him."

Praether thought overlong before replying. "For the last week the loblolly has been reducing the potency of Pyeweed's laudanum, gradually replacing the opium with some potion he concocted."

"Elo says it's snakewood, sir. To cure Pyeweed's madness."

Bonel raised a hand. "As you were, Harriet. If the captain wants to hear from you then he will address you."

Praether went on. "No doubt it will take a great deal of time and patience to improve upon Pyeweed. But the man has run out of time. And I have run out of patience."

Lieutenant Japhet, the deck officer, stepped forward. "Beg pardon, sir, but in order to stay in *Villa Real's* lee we need to go on the starboard tack."

"Do so."

Japhet called the watch and we fell off to leeward as the men hauled away.

"As for Pyeweed, it was my Christian duty to do the right thing by him. Or at least try."

"And so you did, sir."

Praether dismissed the compliment. "An odd thing, Bonel ... doing the right thing. I have tried to save Pyeweed from himself. Yet by doing so I may have imperiled our mission."

Eleanor's topsails luffed, then boomed loud as she stood into the wind. The sound of topsails filling always brought joy, and Praether smiled, if but slight, before going on.

"The men do not need to know any of what I just told you. But you may tell them this. As of now Mr. Pyeweed has been relieved of all duties. He will be confined to his quarters until further notice. The men can expect to see a marine sentry posted at his door."

"Aye, sir."

Praether set his jaw. "Now then, on to the matter at hand. I have my own intentions regarding *Villa Real* but will now hear my officers' thoughts."

Lieutenant Fagen spoke up. "The Portuguese might not believe we're a slaver, sir, but they don't know we carry twelve carronades. I say close to fifty yards and give her a broadside." He balled a fist and smacked it in his palm. "Then board her."

Praether mulled it over, then shook his head "I commend your aggressive attitude, Fagen, and if we were at war with the Portuguese then I might consider your suggestion. However, we are not at war with the Portuguese, or with anyone. We are in the Cape Verde islands posing as a slaver on return from the colonies. *Villa Real*'s captain chose not to engage us, only escort us to Praia. So, as of yet, I think we remain no more than a curiosity to him. No more than an errant vessel requiring further investigation."

The wind increased to a fresh breeze. Praether turned to face it, studying the sky before going on.

"I remind you. Our purpose for being in these waters is to disrupt the slave trade and to assist Dame-Marie in returning however many people survived *Elizabeth Carton*. If we engage *Villa Real*, it would defeat that purpose and might cause her captain to react in a way no one can predict. Portugal is a neutral country, and the Treaty of Amiens is fragile. Any provocation could eventually lead to renewed hostilities."

The wind shifted a point, blowing stronger yet. Praether looked beyond our stern and across a gathering sea. "Bonel, I feel it now. I swear it." He raised a brow. "And you?"

"I do, sir."

Praether observed the night sky once more. "I can assure you, gentlemen, that we will part ways with *Villa Real* before dawn. There is a sea change coming. And very soon."

♭

We stayed in *Villa Real*'s lee half the night, tacking as she tacked, always struggling to hold our position. The wind strengthened to a fresh gale, holding steady from the north and bringing heavy weather, lightning and rain. *Villa Real*'s stern lantern grew distant and faint, at times going unseen, until finally we saw no more of it.

By morning watch we'd reduced sail, and by two bells carried just our flying jib and reefed spanker. The wind came a strong gale now, with hail drumming along the deck. At three bells Praether sent men aloft to take another reef. It took overlong, and the top men finished just in time, just as lightning struck the mizzen royal mast. Men went diving away from a halyard crashing to the deck. One jeer crashed on the binnacle, smashing the compass. Praether sent March to the great cabin to fetch another one. Not our best instrument, for at times it swung wild. But at least this one's casement was undamaged, and its needle swung free.

The wind harped in the rigging. A sheave failed in the main top. Two men went on to the shrouds to reeve it anew. *Eleanor* drove on, shipping it green, until Bettyhill came to report a foot of water in the hold. Praether sent the carpenter and a dozen men to the pumps. But they couldn't keep up, and the water kept rising.

Finally, Praether ordered the helm to heave to, and ride it out. I checked the compass. The needle spun wild, but this time it may have been true, for *Eleanor*'s bow swung in a great arc, plunging deep into every swell and barely rising in time to meet the next sea. Two monstrous waves, one to port and one to starboard, slammed together beneath *Eleanor*. She rose high on the swell, her keel wrenching in the strain. The wind shrieked as a banshee. Another sea broke heavy on the stern, and as it crashed on the quarterdeck, we all braced and held tight. March as well, but his grip on the cross rail was that of a boy, and a waist-high surge swept him into the lee. He caught in the scuppers and I ran for him, seizing his free hand. Yet another sea broke on the stern, pinning us to the gunnel, and I fought to save my own self. The next wave flooded the deck. My grip on March weakened and then broke. He slipped away, thrashing frantic and screaming, but his cry went unheard in the din.

In that instant he was no longer a boy named March. He was Tate, *Eleanor*'s stowaway child. And no longer was *Eleanor* in the straits of Cape Verde, but weathering Ushant in another great storm, where Tate had gone overboard, though never by accident, but stuffed in a sack and pitched overboard. I made one last effort, but another surge jammed me on the rail, heaving March over ...

swallowed by the indifferent sea, gone to join Tate. God have mercy on them. On me, as well.

$\maltese$

By first light the wind had died away. The men finished pumping the hold. We rode becalmed on the Atlantic rollers, with a copper vault of sky merged with a molten copper sea. A specter I'd not seen before, and so thought to ask Wat how long it might last.

"A day. A week."

"A week? We'll become over lost by then. Even now I can't find the horizon in my sextant."

Wat dismissed my concern. "Once, off Leeuwin, the sextant were no good for ten days."

The compass was no good, either. At first it pointed west by west, but when I tapped on its casement the needle came free, pointing south by east. Fagen stood with me, observing the variance.

"Worse than no compass at all."

"I have a lodestone, sir."

"Crude instrument."

"Aye, sir. But it serves when the compass is unreliable."

"Where you get the thing?"

"From Mr. Lau. Shall I bring it?"

"Do that. And bring your Cape Verde log. The captain's being rowed around the hull inspecting the damage and he'll want to set a course once he's back on board."

"Will we look for March?"

"Gone to the bottom by now, or in a serpent's belly."

Nary came to report. "Captain Praether's at the entry port, sir."

Fagen turned to me. "Go now. Have that lodestone and your log available when Praether arrives on the quarterdeck."

Pyeweed still had my charts and ledgers. But they were mine, with my name written on each cover, and with all entries filled out in my own hand. No matter if Pyeweed liked it or not, I performed his duties now, and went to his quarters to fetch my property. A marine sentry stood a post at the cabin door. When he let me in Pyeweed lay sprawled in his berth. Sleeping, I think, until he stirred. I froze. If he awoke and found me in his quarters, he'd make a scene. Certain of that. But he settled once more, and with a steady, if shallow breath. I found my logs, then went to the midshipmen's mess and stowed them under my berth. The lodestone rested in its cradle, secured from a beam. I brought it on deck, along with the Cape Verde charts. Captain Praether already stood on the quarterdeck, listening to Bonel's report.

"No sign of *Villa Real*, sir. No doubt she was blown off course, same as us. Bettyhill just spliced the mizzen royal and if we had any wind we could get under way."

"Very well. Set the gallants and we will wait on the wind. We shall return to Sal as soon as possible, though I suspect Dame-Marie does not quite miss us. At least not yet. Mr. Harriet, is that your Cape Verde chart?"

"Aye, sir. And I've brought a lodestone."

"Set it up."

The sea was quiet calm. *Eleanor* lay motionless in the swells, permitting the lodestone to swing free. The stone was leaden gray, the size and texture of a walnut. We stood silent, observing the stone rotate in the magnetic field.

"Watch that brown smudge, sir. When it stops turning that smudge will be tending north."

The magnetite held little power and took its own time to find its way. Finally, the smudge came to rest, leading off our starboard bow.

"Is it dependable, Harriet?"

"A bit off, sir, but consistent. Mr. Lau measured it against a fleet compass whenever he had the chance. It always came to rest five degrees east of north. Two weeks ago I checked it in the calm off Costa da Morte. Still five degrees east of north."

"Very well. Show me your charts."

I spread them on the chart table, and gasped. My entries! Most had been struck and written over with marginalia scribed in Pyeweed's hand. At first his notes angered me. Pyeweed had no right to alter my work. He was only trying to spite me for being

126

assigned his own duties. But then I saw him for what he was, saw him as nothing more than a pitiful man. One who didn't realize that striking over my work would never erase it from my head. I smiled at the thought, just as Praether leaned in to read one entry aloud ... some reference to a sounding off Santa Marie, Cape Verde.

Praether read it out. Inaccurate. *See Admiralty log from HMS Stout—April nineteen, 1790*. He turned to me. "These notes are very sloppy, Harriet. Outdated. I expect better of you."

"Those aren't my notes, sir."

"Oh?"

"They're Mr. Pyeweed's, sir. He's scratched mine out. All my entries are transcribed direct from Mr. Lau's findings. And the ones for Cape Verde are more recent. Dating from February of '97."

"How many of your entries has Pyeweed scratched out?"

"I don't know, sir. But it doesn't matter. I have them all in my head."

Praether looked at me dubious. "Do you stretch the truth?"

"I don't think so, sir."

"We shall see." He took the chart and turned to another page. "Now then, tell me what you have entered for Mona Island."

I thought a moment, then told what I knew. "Mona Island. Eighteen degrees north by sixty-seven degrees west, sir. Situated in the Mona Passage, midway between the Greater Antilles and Puerto Rico. The threshold depth is unknown. There's always a strong current running through the strait and into the Atlantic. The island itself is about seven miles long, and four wide. Shoaling water along south and west coasts. Possible holding ground at a small inlet on the southwest quadrant. Last charted by *Gull* on 19 April 1794. The island's called Amona by the Táino Indians. The name means ..."

"That will do, Harriet. Your response is verbatim. How do you do that?"

"The numbers, sir. They tumble out. The rest of it's done the way Mr. Lau taught me, sir, by association."

Praether stared at me, unblinking. "What do you mean by tumble out?"

I thought to tell Praether about the acrobats playing on the sward at Newbury Fair, and of my friend Cana, a kind girl with her left hand malformed in the shape of a crow's foot, and that she played the number two in her family's troupe. Except no one ever believed how the acrobats' strange little play could ever lead me to see numbers the way I did. No captain of a frigate would believe me, either. Certain of that.

"No sir. I can't explain. It's been that way since before I remember."

Praether turned to Bonel. "Uncanny."

I think Bonel meant to reply, but just then Lady Praether came on deck. Unusual, that, it being the first time she'd appeared before nightfall. Yet it soon became obvious why she was there, with her blue eyes staring wild, her face waxen and pale.

"Matthew, I'm very ill."

"Go below, my dearest. The sea is mirror flat now. Your nausea will soon abate."

"I'm not seasick, Matthew."

As was her habit, she extended the index finger of each hand, pointing them both at her waist. Then she took hold of her cloak, raising it slow. We drew back, gaping at her gown, drenched in fresh blood while she stood there barefoot on the deck, with blood dripping onto her feet.

"The storm, Matthew. It's caused me to miscarry."

Praether cried out. "Dear God!" He lifted his wife off the deck and carried her below, calling for someone to fetch Elo. When no one responded I ran for him myself.

"Grab your kit and go to the great cabin. Lady Praether's had a miscarriage."

Elo ran to collect his instruments, stuffing them in a box. "Can't bring it all on my own. Take a can of alum. All of the duck cloth. And whiskey. Fast!"

He took off running, and I caught up on the companionway. "She just came on deck bleeding awful. I didn't know she was with child."

"She didn't either. Not 'til last month. She tell me she miss her time before leaving Plymouth. Then one more. Last week ask for nettle tea."

The cabin door stood wide, with every glim lighted and their wicks turned high. The marine sentry, looking horrified, stood aside as we entered. The look on Praether's face reminded me of my own father's when I was but nine, and Mum bled to death giving birth to sister Peg. Father had told me not to go in, not to look at Mum as she lay dead. But Vivian Erth was midwife and said I must see for myself that Mum was gone. And now I saw for myself that Cherish Praether was gone, as well.

$$\natural$$

"Surely goodness and mercy shall follow me all the days of my life: and I will dwell in the house of the Lord forever."

Captain Praether closed his Bible, and then his eyes. We all stood remorseful, knowing he was saying a last good-bye to his cherished wife. He stood rigid, as any captain must stand before his men. Still, a great sadness weighed heavy on his shoulders. It came to me then. Few captains would ever find need to conduct a sea burial for their own wife. Finally, he nodded to the bosun. Gleason tipped the board and Cherish Praether, wrapped in a white shroud, entered the sea, with a twenty-four-pound lead shot tied to the sail cloth taking her down. The wind harped in the rigging. *Eleanor* rose and fell, and the men stood silent and still, until Lieutenant Bonel dismissed them, his commands uttered low and respectful. Captain Praether stood alone at the entry port, then made his way to the taffrail. The last time he stood there, he'd been there with his beloved wife.

The rain came not long after, and in torrents I'd not seen since the Mekong. Every hatch secured, and all water butts gushing overfull. It came pouring steady until first light, if such a thing can be called light, with its pale green sky, and a dull sheen lying flat upon the water. A dead calm, with no horizon. The leadsman leaned away from the mizzen chains as his chip log floated alongside, with never a knot slipping through his hand to mark our progress. Praether ordered all boats in the water, with strong backs at every oar, all straining to tow us northerly, or as northerly as my lodestone would point. It seemed we'd not been blown off course, or at least not by much. Some guessed we might raise the main island of

Santiago before long, if we only kept rowing. Others guessed we might raise Maio instead, more easterly, and with Mount Penoso rising a thousand feet. White sand beach, and a large forest.

That night Elo and I sat in the mess, eating salt fish and pulse. When Elo finished, he stuffed his left cheek with plug tobacco and spoke through the right side of his mouth.

"We find Maio, then maybe Praether let me go ashore."

"No one will be allowed off *Eleanor*, I don't think."

"Maio have losna."

"Don't tell me. Losna's good for courage."

"Ja. For stomach, too."

I wiped my best spoon and stowed it. "I don't think we'll raise Maio. Or Santiago, either. There's a steady current bearing us westerly. If we keep rowing that current might take us past Pico da Fogo. That's the westernmost island in the group, and with the highest peak."

"Pico da Fogo. Funny name for island."

"It means peak of fire in Portuguese. They named it for the volcano rising nine thousand feet."

"Volcano? Ja! I see Katla. That in Iceland. See glow from ten mile. If we pass Pico da Fogo in dark then I think maybe we see glow."

"Probably not. It's not erupted since 1675. But any volcano stinks of sulphur, so if we pass near then we're sure to smell it."

Six bells in the first watch. Eleven at night. I made for my berth, but Elo stayed me.

"I listening when you tell captain how numeral tumble out for you. You have gift."

"I don't know if it's a gift. It just happens."

"Come to surgery. I show you something."

The orlop was pitch black. Elo lit a taper and invited me to sit while he went for a ledger.

"This left by Starling." He tapped on the cover. "He say strange thing about you. Page thirty-seven."

Owen Harriet—Twelve June 1799, off Fisterra. During a hostile action I found Harriet covered in blood. It wasn't his blood, but he suffered greatly from genus filum. To relieve his condition I gave him a lozenge treated with opium. But the dose was meant for a man, not a small boy, and he lapsed into delirium lasting about twelve hours. During this period he mumbled incoherently, repeating several words and phrases. One of them was Sukiyama. I do not know what this means, but it would appear the boy has some sort of premonition.

I closed the thing and gave it back. "I keep a ledger now, too. A record, of sorts, though not so good as Starling's. But I don't leave the thing behind for others to read. I keep it tucked away."

"Where?"

"I can't tell you. At least not right now. Except I moved it from under my berth to a more secure place. How long have you known about the Sukiyama?"

"Portsmouth."

"Then why bring it up now?"

"Captain Praether in command of *Eleanor*. But mission belong to Lady Praether. She think mission must have strong faith. But must pray for miracle, too. Slave trade big business. Very big for people to fight alone. Must have holy war. Must have miracle. Pray to end agony."

It fell silent in the orlop, with both of us lost in our own thoughts, until I spoke out.

"God have mercy on him."

"On who?"

"The slave we found adrift in Carton's dinghy. If ever there was agony, it was him. Mr. Starling asked God to have mercy on him."

"Did God have mercy?"

"I don't know. But the captain did what he could."

"Lady Praether said was miracle when husband join One Body. Miracle you join, too. Sukiyama is miracle? Ja? Sacred thing. Pray for it in holy war."

The recurrence of childhood imagination. An oracle stirring the leaves of an oak tree. Could either be considered a miracle? Or sacred? I held up my left hand for Elo to see my missing little finger.

"See before. What happen?"

"The Onion shot it away."

"Onion?"

"Théophile Oignon. A French privateer. He questioned me about the Sukiyama, then shot away my finger because I told him I didn't know."

Elo smiled grim. "I won't shoot finger."

"Of course not. Still, I'm not certain I should tell you anymore."

"Why not?"

"Because anyone I tell about the Sukiyama ... they all die. I don't want you to become dead."

"Suomeksi."

"What?"

"Nonsense. All who live, is all who die. So I think okay if you tell me about Sukiyama."

"Except I don't know what to tell you. Only that it comes in a whisper. And always brings some warning."

He arched a brow. "When last time you hear?"

"Two weeks past, when Praether explained our mission. I knew to pay heed but didn't know why. Now it seems the whisper came as a warning, first for March, then Lady Praether."

Elo nodded. "Before that?"

"Dog Island, coming down the back stairs of an inn. It was night, and the stairs were dark. I heard the whisper and stopped, closing my eyes. When I opened them I stood in a sunlit room. A young man sat writing at a table. He sensed my presence, and he turned to look. And I ... I've never told this to anyone."

"Tell."

"I knew him."

"Who?"

"It was me. Except it wasn't. I mean ... not me, at least not right now."

"He from past?"

"No. I had the queer feeling he lives in my future."

"Ja?"

132

"And that I live in his past."

"You?" Elo narrowed his green eyes. "But not you?"

"Not me. But I think I know him."

Eleanor creaked and groaned. Out upon the dead calm her oarsmen rowed into the night. In the lead boat the piper played a steady tune, with Gleason calling out. "Heave, me beauties! Heave away!"

13. Women are always the sharpest traders

Three bells in the morning watch. Five o'clock. The wind came at last. Light air, variable, and bearing the hint of sulphur. I rose from my berth straight away and made for the helm, just as the lookout hailed the deck. He'd spotted a lone peak, rising three points off the port bow. I went aloft. A rounded summit with a shallow caldera resolved in my scope, caught in the first rays of morning light. I returned to the quarterdeck, where Captain Praether already stood waiting for my report.

"Pico da Fogo, sir. Bows on. About five miles."

"Inhabited?"

"My charts show two villages on the island. One is Sao Filipe, in a shallow bay on the west coast. And the other one is Mosteiros, on the northeast coast. It's a small island, sir. Only four miles across, and shaped annular round. That's because when the lava flows it …"

"That will do, Harriet. Is either of these villages large enough to accommodate a chandler? We need to replace at least one of our compasses before we go on to join Dame-Marie."

"There's not much demand for a chandler on Pico da Fogo, sir. But whalers used to call there, so there may still be one or two left."

"When was the bay at Sao Filipe last sounded?"

"Last charted by *Syon* in April of '94, sir. Depth of only twenty-two feet at low tide. Foul bottom. Not a good anchorage, sir."

"And Mosteiros?"

"Much the same, sir. About seven miles farther up the coast."

"Then we will try Sao Filipe." He turned to the deck officer. "I wish *Eleanor* to remain unidentified for as long as possible, so I intend to stay well out to sea. Have Gleason put the jolly boat in the water and step its mast. Assign four blue jackets. Once ashore, they will set a watch." Then to Lieutenant Bonel. "You will go ashore at Sao Filipe. If there is a chandler or any mercantile that sells compasses, buy their best." Praether handed over a coin purse. "Three pounds, all in shillings. Since Amiens it is likely a merchant will accept these. If not . . ." Praether dug in his waistcoat for a guinea, "use this. Either way, be sure to make your best deal. And be quick about it. I told Dame-Marie we'd return to Sal long before now."

Bonel took the purse and tucked it in his waistcoat, along with the guinea. "May I suggest taking along the compass we are currently using, sir? If I were to show it to them, they will better understand what I want, and perhaps they can repair it. I can transport it in a sack readily enough, sir."

"Yes, do that. And this evening look for *Eleanor*. I will bring us close inshore and you be ready to return by then." Praether turned to me, handing over another coin purse. "Twenty shillings. Go with the First Officer. If there is a market at Sao Filipe, see if they have limes. Buy as many as you can."

The dock at Sao Filipe stood two hundred feet into the bay. The fishing fleet, if there was one, had not yet returned. A young boy stepped from a small cabana and secured our lines. Lieutenant Bonel gave him a copper and asked if there was a chandler or a market nearby. I don't think the boy understood. He only stared vacant, then returned to the shade. The blue jackets we'd brought with us rigged the jolly boat's sail to provide their own shade, then rested on the thwarts to watch and wait for our return. We went ashore to a small plaza. The sun was high, baking on the cobblestones. Some unseen bird called out, its voice ringing empty in the plaza, now deserted for siesta. Bonel and I were on our own, sweating prodigious and standing in the heat risers with nothing but a failed compass between us.

"Look for a chandler, Harriet, or a market. Whichever we see first is where we start."

We both scanned the waterfront. Bonel pointed to a faded yellow sign, with blue lettering.

"*Mercado*. That's the word for market. Come. It's very hot standing here in the sun."

We wasted no time but made straight for the market, with still not the first person seen. Except for an old woman nodding in her produce stall. Bonel rapped on the counter.

At first, she carped at being disturbed, but finally made reply. "*O que?*"

"*Limas. Você limas?*"

"*No limas.*"

I walked behind the stall, then called for Bonel to come see a cart loaded with fruit.

"That may be shaddock, sir. Or something like it. It can serve in place of limes."

Bonel pointed at the shaddock. "*Quanto?*"

They haggled overlong, finally agreeing on a price. Bonel turned to me. "Give her twenty shillings for the whole cart. It should fill the jolly boat handsomely."

I handed her my purse and she dumped all twenty coins on her counter. I thought she might bite on one but, instead, she counted them out careful slow, licking each one. Not one tooth in all of her black mouth. I took a shaddock and sniffed, recalling the smell coming from the dark green fruit, round as any six-pound shot, and rolling about in my sampan as I sculled down the Mekong.

"They're fresh, sir. You've made a good bargain."

"Likely I paid too much. Women are always the sharpest traders, especially an old one. But at least she charged nothing for information. When I asked her where to find a chandler, she said there's none here in Sao Filipe."

"That's discouraging, sir."

"Buck up, midshipman. When I pressed her she said there may still be one in Mosteiros. It's two miles on the cart path but there's a foot trail at the base of the volcano that cuts the distance in half. We will inform the blue jackets to come wheel this shaddock back to the jolly boat, then you and I will pay a visit to Mosteiros."

The trail provided little shade. The quiet air reeked of sulphur, with grey slag from the volcano scraping at our shoes as if we were treading upon some unending holystone. After rounding yet another bend we spotted *Eleanor* far out to sea. To an unknowing eye she might have been any ship. But she was our ship and we knew her well and couldn't help but pause for a moment to admire the set of her sails.

"Enough, Harriet. Come along."

It took forever on the trail, or so it seemed, yet in just half an hour we arrived in Mosteiros. The place was even smaller than Sao Filipe, and we found the chandler immediate, but with a note nailed to the door. Bonel read the note aloud.

"*De falência. Cai fora.*"

"Sir?"

"I believe *de falência* is some sort of financial failure. I'm not sure how to translate *cai fora*."

We heard a wet cough and turned to see a man padding toward us, barefoot. A narrow fellow, all of forty, with bushy white hair, a high brow and bulging blue eyes. He spoke the King's English.

"It means go away."

"Oh, yes. Now I see it. And who are you?"

"Daniel Goodhoney. You must be from that ship out there."

"Correct. I am Bonel, and this is Harriet. We're in Mosteiros to replace a compass. This shop appears to be out of business. Is there anywhere else I might buy one?"

"None for sale on the entire island. What's in the sack?"

"A failed compass."

Goodhoney brightened. "Let me look. Maybe I can repair it."

Bonel removed the thing and handed it to Goodhoney. He took out a magnifying glass and examined the instrument.

"I can fix this."

"How much will you charge?"

"Come to my hut. It's not far. You can get out of the sun while we discuss terms."

Goodhoney's dwelling was barely a hut. Open sided, with palm leaves thatched over to make a low roof. An orange cat sat perched on his workbench watching Goodhoney's nimble fingers as he took the compass apart.

"This is a copy of a Lynch patent model, probably made around 1800, in Dublin. It's inferior to the Lynch because there's an impurity in the brass."

"Impurity?"

"Yes. Brass is an alloy of copper and zinc but there's a trace of iron in this casing that distorts the magnetic field. However, the workmanship is adequate, so I can correct the error."

"How much will it cost?"

Goodhoney slid the compass aside. He sat back, stroking the cat, both of them eyeing Bonel and me.

"I don't know who you are, but your military bearing leads me to believe you're not John Company. And certainly, you're not off a slaver. Neither of you carries the stench of a slave ship. So I think you're Royal Navy, even if you're not in uniform, and I suspect that ship out there belongs to His Majesty."

Bonel made no reply.

"If such is the case then here's what I ask in exchange. I wish to sign on for your ship."

Bonel shifted his stance. "You're no sailor."

"No. I'm a metallurgic and a tool maker. But all ships have chronometers, sextants, and optics." He tapped on the workbench. "Not to mention a compass. I can keep them all accurate, and in good repair. Besides, I'm an Englishman. And I wish be taken off of this place."

"First repair the compass, if you will. Then we'll take you to see our captain. He'll decide what to do with you."

Goodhoney said the repair would take a few hours so Bonel sent me back to Sao Filipe, to be sure of our shaddock and wait for *Eleanor* to come fetch us off. If she arrived before Bonel returned to the jolly boat, then I'd deliver the fruit to *Eleanor* on my own. Bonel would remain onshore for the night, and I'd come back to Sao Filipe in the morning. I thought it a forthright revision of our plan, and guessed Lieutenant Kyle, who always warned that any plan will fail at the first opportunity, would approve. But, by late afternoon, Bonel still hadn't shown, and when *Eleanor* stood into the bay I chose to leave without him.

Captain Praether wasn't over pleased with my choice, and of a sudden it seemed not a good thing for me to be standing in the great cabin trying to explain the First Officer's absence. Praether sat fuming at his desk, his brow flushing every shade of red. I feared he might be having another spell but, even so, I muddled on, ending my report by reminding the captain I'd returned with a boat full of shaddock.

He stood and paced, then turned to me. "You begin to repeat yourself, Harriet, so you may as well repeat to me what you said about Goodhoney."

I told again what I knew.

"What do you think of him?"

"Mr. Lau taught me to maintain a sextant and telescope, sir. They're not over difficult. But for a chronometer and a compass, it might be best luck if Mr. Goodhoney's on board."

Praether scoffed. "Only if what he claims is the truth." He thought for a moment, then went on. "Very well. At first light you will fetch Lieutenant Bonel. I wish to get under way for Sal, so be sure there are no more delays. If Goodhoney has repaired our compass then you may bring him along, and I will interview him. Take Inari with you to examine Goodhoney for disease."

⚡

At first light I found Lieutenant Bonel and Goodhoney waiting on the dock at Sao Filipe. Bonel held the compass sack, and Goodhoney sat on a trunk with the orange cat hunched at his feet. When we came alongside, I hailed the lieutenant.

"Sir, the captain wishes to get under way instanter, but first he must know if Goodhoney's made the repair."

Bonel confirmed as much, and as the lieutenant stepped aboard, Goodhoney tried to follow. But I stayed him.

"No. First the loblolly must examine you."

Elo's inspection took not overlong, looking only for lice, or any sign of typhus. When he pronounced him free of disease, I told the oarsmen to bring the trunk on board. Goodhoney followed on, then turned to the cat.

"So is it goodbye, then?"

A moment of decision, and with all of us hoping the cat would choose to come along, for a cat is a welcome mate aboard any ship. In spite of our haste, we watched attentive as it felt its way on board,

140

most cautious, and found a tolerable place next to Goodhoney. In not half an hour Bonel and I stood with Goodhoney in the great cabin. Captain Praether wasted no time.

"Why have you asked to sign on with this ship?"

Goodhoney raised his chin prideful. "As I told Lieutenant Bonel, a tool bin filled with well-maintained and calibrated instruments is essential for navigation. I know these mechanisms very well and can make sure of them all."

Bonel spoke up. "The man also speaks Portuguese, sir. Far better than me. He could be of considerable value."

Goodhoney slumped. "I must tell you that I no longer have an interest in communicating in Portuguese. I am a metallurgic. And a tool maker."

"And there are not many instruments aboard *Eleanor*."

"You make my point, sir. If one were to fail it would be very good to have it back in service as soon as possible."

"You would remain idle for much of the time."

"Would it not be better, sir, for you to have my abilities and not need them, rather than need my abilities, and not have them? Besides, I do not wish to be paid for my services, only provided sustenance and transportation to some place where there are Englishmen."

"Hardly the case on Pico da Fogo. Which begs the question. Why are you even here?"

"I've been on this island nearly six months, sir, and never wanting to be here at all."

A quick rap on the door, and Hewitt stepped in.

"Beg pardon, sir, but Lieutenant Japhet says we're ready to set the topsails."

"Tell the lieutenant to call the watch. Go on deck, Bonel. I will join you shortly."

When Bonel left, Praether came to stand in front of Goodhoney. "Now then, Goodhoney, I believe you were about to enlighten us as to how you came to be on this island."

He took a deep breath and began. "Well, I suppose I must start with when I worked for Lloyds, at Dale End. Mostly assaying gold and silver. Steady work, but none too stimulating. I was no longer young, mind you, but not old by any stretch, and began to experience what the French call ... *ennui*. Over time I came to realize that if I did nothing to change my circumstance then I might languor in Birmingham until it became too late to change anything at all. So I wrote letters of inquiry to the firms that knew my name well. All of them far removed from England."

Goodhoney stopped when Japhet's voice filtered down through the grating, barking an order for Gleason. The bosun relayed the command for the men to stand by their lines, and the evolution began. Two hundred bare feet stamped on the spar deck, giving rise to a thunderous din. Yet taking not overlong, and when all stood in place, Goodhoney went on.

"I waited six months, but not one firm replied. Not until three years ago, when I was offered a metallurgic position with Vila Prudentea, a Portuguese venture doing business in São Paulo. They would pay me well, along with providing a cook and a small bungalow with a sweeping view of Santos Bay. A fine offer. And I accepted. The crossing took just two months, and upon arrival in São Paulo my only task was to develop an inexpensive alloy, highly resistant to salt corrosion yet still quite strong. I set about my work with relish. However, after eight months I was quite shocked to discover how my services would be put to use."

He paused, as if searching for what to say next.

Praether tapped his foot impatient. "I have no time for your haverings, man. Get on with it."

"It seems the alloy I designed was to be forged into shackles, sir."

Praether stopped fussing and raised a brow. "For use in the slave trade?"

"Yes. Thousands upon thousands of shackles ... that I helped produce. Be assured I would have nothing more to do with the enterprise and gave notice."

"A Christian act."

"I suppose it was. Except by then I'd been gone from Birmingham nearly a year, don't you see, and hadn't known when I took the job how terribly much I'd miss home. I longed for my snug rooms in Handsworth Wood, the reassuring smell of bangers and mash, and the tight purl of English spoken freely in the streets. So I was very anxious to return to England, and not just to quit Vila Prudentea. But it seems there was a complication, so I asked my overseer what was the delay. Only then did he point out a certain clause in my contract that I'd failed to fully appreciate."

Praether crossed the great cabin and stood before the cheval glass, adjusting his epaulette while addressing Goodhoney's reflection.

"I must go on deck. I will take you off Pico da Fogo, but only if you agree to the following provisos. First, you will see to our navigational instruments. Second, you will agree to communicate with the Portuguese whenever the need may arise. Do you agree?"

Goodhoney sighed, nodding his consent.

"Good. There is one more thing to discuss. I am collecting intelligence, so I expect you to tell me all you know of the slave trade operating at São Paulo."

"I'm only a metallurgist, sir. I know very little of how the slave trade functions."

"Only a metallurgist, perhaps, but one who has worked for Vila Prudentea. I am sure you have specific knowledge of how they conduct their enterprise. So think you hard."

"I will indeed, sir."

"See that you do. Now then, I do not know when or where you will next go ashore. But on this vessel, even though it is a mix of nations, you will mostly be among Englishmen."

"I am grateful, sir."

"I neither request nor require your gratitude, Goodhoney. Just do as you are told and stay out of my way. However, I am not yet done with you, but for now it would be more expedient for you to write out the rest of your statement."

"Why?"

Goodhoney's question was an affront to Praether's authority and, even though Goodhoney was not in the Royal Navy, I thought the captain might charge him with insubordination. Instead, he only replied in his nasal whine.

"Because I am interested in all dimensions of the slave trade, starting with just how these slaves are stolen from their villages. Be

143

sure to include all you know, even if you think it is of no consequence. You may use my desk." Praether turned to me. "A word with you, Harriet."

We stepped out.

"Stay with him. Likely he is hungry so when he is finished with his statement take him to Lorca and have him fed. Find a berth for him in the midshipmen's mess, then report to the surgery. Inari has asked for assistance in brewing another of his vile decoctions."

14. Grain Coast of Africa

After installing Goodhoney in the midshipmen's mess I beat feet to the surgery and reported to Elo. He sat at his work bench stirring a small crucible. A foul stench hung in the close air, remindful of some bog. He muttered low, never looking up, but instead kept his eyes focused on his work, watching heedful as a muddy blue potion came to a rolling boil. I stepped to the work bench.

"Ja, Harriet. Feed flame. Keep small."

"What is it this time?"

"Aconitum."

"Smells like blue rocket."

Elo shrugged. "Some call blue rocket. Some call wolf bane. Deadly poison. Don't get near mouth."

"I know you wouldn't give anyone poison to drink."

"Not to drink. Unguent. Knead into body. Good for big muscle. This for Ajax. He come get treatment after his watch."

Elo turned his sandglass and went on stirring. After five minutes he gave the pot one last fold, then told me to snuff the flame. He poured the brew into a saucer and set it aside to cool.

When his watch ended Ajax came to the surgery. Elo told him to remove his shirt and sit on a stool. He took a firm stance behind Ajax and began working the aconitum into the giant's broad shoulders. Ajax breathed steady slow. Never the one for words. But Elo talked constant as he worked, asking how Captain Praether was feeling.

Ajax replied over sharp, "That's none of your concern."

"Captain just lose wife. Bury at sea. Very bad thing. Don't like way he look."

"And how should he look?"

"Should look of grief."

"Who says?"

"I say."

"The captain has no time for it. And even if he did, no commander would allow his personal feelings to be seen by his men."

"Captain stand alone at taffrail. Same place with Lady Praether, every night."

Ajax stood abrupt, looming over Elo and giving him a look meant to forestall any more talk.

Elo knew the look and quit the subject. He sealed the aconitum in a ewer, then washed his hands in soap and water while giving Ajax instructions.

"Leave shirt off. Go to deck pump. Hose down five minutes. This unguent good for sore muscle, but strong poison."

Ajax nodded, making to leave, but stopped at the bulkhead. "I will tell you this one time only. Neither of you is to repeat it or you will answer to me. The Captain does mourn, but only when he's alone in the great cabin."

It's no great distance from Pico da Fogo to the island of Sal. But the approach still took all the next day, with the wind blowing steady, east by east, putting us in irons at every chance. I was anxious for us to raise Sal on the leeward tack. Best thing, that, for the marginalia scribed in my ledger made note of rapid shoaling all along the island's southern reach. And we were bearing on just that reach when, one hour before the noon sighting, Lieutenant Fagen pointed at the lookout perched on the mizzen top.

"Who is that?"

"Groats, sir. Able Seaman."

"He's spotted something."

Just then Groats hailed the deck. "Smoke rising about five miles off the starboard beam. I see land. Same bearing."

Fagen sent for the captain, then turned to me.

"Our recognition code?"

"Four-seven-one, sir, over blue and white checkers."

"Tell Shawhead to run that hoist. Then go you aloft and join Groats."

Once on the mizzen top I glassed the rising column of smoke. A big fire, to be sure, coming from near on shore. Certain this smoke came from a ship, for Sal was a barren place, volcanic, and providing little on its own that might burn so furious. It billowed thick and black, no doubt fueled by tar and resin. When *Eleanor* rose on the swell, I saw not just the smoke, but flames running eager on the deck of some ship. I dared not think that inferno burned on board *Iona*.

I called to Groats. "Keep a sharp eye on that brig. I'll look to windward."

Only soon enough, just as a square-rigged vessel rounded a headland bearing south by east. Still distant, but making straight for us, and with a bone in her teeth. I hailed the deck.

"I see a ship. Square-rigged. Making south by east and bearing on us direct. I can't tell how many masts."

"Distance?"

"About four miles."

Just then her sails luffed, and when she filled, I saw much of her hull. A white gun stripe gleaming bright along her hull. When she came onto a broad reach, she revealed three masts.

"A three-masted barque. It may be *Villa Real*."

Fagen called back. "Ensign?"

I watched careful for an ensign, but saw none. No flag at all, until a hoist ran on the staff. Five-one, and below that, red and white checkers.

"No ensign, sir. But she's just sent up the proper response to our hoist."

Praether arrived on deck.

"Mr. Harriet, what is burning."

"It may be *Iona*, sir. The fire's coming from the cove where she was at anchor."

"And that barque making for us. *Villa Real*?"

"I can't know for sure, sir, except it has a black hull and a white gun stripe. Same as *Villa Real*."

Praether paced the quarterdeck before returning to the binnacle and addressing Bonel. "Smoke rising from *Iona*'s last known position, and now the correct hoist, but on the wrong ship."

"If it's *Villa Real* they'll know us from before, sir. And this time know us for what we are."

"I do not like it, Bonel. Beat to quarters."

♭

Before leaving Portsmouth Captain Praether had ordered the carpenter to make a small sandglass to fit in a gimbal, and then to secure it on the mizzen. The white sand ran out in ten minutes and was used only for timing how long it took us to clear for action. Our best effort took one turn, and then half a turn more. That's how long the sand had already run for this evolution, but with divisions only just starting to report. All bulkheads stowed. All hammocks lashed in place along the top rail. Gun deck strewn with wet sand. But still no guns ready to run out, and with just the port battery primed. A poor showing, certain of that. When Shawhead turned the glass yet once more, Bonel spoke his displeasure.

"If that ship chooses to close on us, they'll engage before we can return fire."

Praether agreed. "We must assume it is *Villa Real* and that she intends to fight. Her long guns are no more than brass nine-pounders, though, and *Eleanor*'s hull is built stout enough to shed nine-pound shot. We can withstand their fire until we are within range of our carronades."

In a frightful short time, the barque came within range of her artillery. I thought she might bear up and present a broadside. But she luffed, instead, swaying out her davits and lowering a boat. I watched, to be sure, then called down once more.

"She's hauled her wind, sir."

"Coming about?"

"No, sir. She's sending a boat."

Wells ran from the gun deck. "Lieutenant Strayhorne reports all guns ready to run out, sir."

"Inform the gunnery officer he comes late to the battle, then tell him to hold off until we see who is in that boat." And to Bonel. "You may heave to, lieutenant."

We lost way immediate, wallowing in the deep troughs, with the mizzen top swinging in precarious arcs. To brace up, I wrapped one leg on a deadeye before training my scope on the approaching boat. A small cutter rowing for us direct, and I needed no scope to know the figure standing in the prow. Not some Portuguese officer wearing a plumed hat and an epaulette shining bright. Instead, the sun gleamed off a bare head, most bald, and with skin coloured dark red. I called down.

"Dame-Marie's in that boat, sir."

"Bonel, send Sergeant Moran to meet Dame-Marie at the entry port and bring him to my cabin. You will join us there, Mr. Harriet."

I wished to know why but thought better than to ask. No midshipman would be so foolish. Even so, Praether deemed to provide a reason.

"The man is unpredictable, and I am as chary of him as he is of me. But since you served with him in the Channel, your presence might ease his suspicions."

The sea ran heavy, with the wind shrieking in the rigging. Between each swell the cutter dropped away unseen, only to reappear. They made slow progress. Made slower yet by oarsmen rowing no better than lubbers. As they topped another long swell I saw why they fared so poor. Lubbers indeed, with each oar pulling independent, and with every oar manned by Negroes, all unsure of their task. It took an hour for them to hook on, and Dame-Marie turned to wave off *Villa Real*. The barque wore ship immediate, bearing for Sal. When Dame-Marie went below, I followed on.

He didn't wait for Praether to speak first. "You late. What you tink happen if you not come here before now?"

No doubt Praether would have reacted to Dame-Marie's impudence, but once more the captain wore a pale expression, and stood with a diminished posture. He only replied with questions of his own. "Why were you on *Villa Real*, and where have you sent her?"

"I be on dat ship 'cause I be in command of it. And now I send her to back side of Sal."

"You have much to explain. But first. . . is that *Iona* burning in the cove?"

"Dat right. Captain of Real ... he take *Iona* dis mornin' but den we cut her hawser and she run aground. When dey fight I take all twenty of dem prisoner. Not before dey burn *Iona*, though."

"Where was Lieutenant Hoyer during all this?"

"Dis mornin' he first to see Real on horizon. He tink maybe they come lookin' in here so he make a plan."

"What plan?"

"Hoyer tink dey not come by sea. Tink dey come overland. Come from backside of Sal to bring de fight. Dis a small little island. Only take five minute to come across of it."

"And did they?"

"Dat so. But dat captain ... he leave half his crew wiff Real. Send only ten sailor to *Iona*. Keep ten at Real. Dat a big mistake, cuttin' his force in two like dat. Hoyer take advantage. Lead boarding party on to Real. Dat when he wounded."

"Wounded? How bad?"

"Cutlass slash him on de right of shoulder. Ain't too deep."

"And all this happened while the Portuguese were taking *Iona*?"

Dame-Marie nodded, smiling. "Dat so. And dey burn her before we take her back."

"Where is *Iona*'s crew?"

"All on Real now."

"And *Villa Real*'s captain and his men?"

"On shore. All prisoner of me."

"They are not your prisoners. We are not at war with the Portuguese."

"I be at war wiff dem 'cause dey be runnin' slaves."

A quick rap on the door, and Shawhead stepped in. "Beg pardon, sir, but the loblolly says Mr. Pyeweed's not in his quarters, and he can't find him."

Praether tightened, scowling severe. "The man tries me beyond limit. Very well, tell Sergeant Moran to conduct a search."

"Aye, sir."

"Now then, Dame-Marie, I need not remind you. The One Body is heavily invested in *Iona*. An expensive outlay. And now, while under your command, you have allowed her to be taken and burned."

"Not under command of me. When we find dem people on Sal, dat when I tell Hoyer he be in command of *Iona*."

"Why?"

"I can't be comin' on dis island here actin' like some chief mon. Let Hoyer be de chief mon and stay on board of *Iona*. I be de one come onshore and earn de respect. Eat same food. Sleep on same ground. Den maybe dey trust me. Maybe."

Praether fixed Dame-Marie with a critical eye. "All well and good. But lives were at stake and property has been destroyed. Even though The One Body owns controlling interest in *Iona* they will still need to defend its loss to the other shareholders."

Dame-Marie shrugged. "Always be a gamble ... ownin' part of some ship. But dem two ships ... dey much of same value, I tink. 'cept Real, she got sixty day of water and ration on board of her." He smiled, looking pleased. "But *Iona*, she be runnin' low."

The captain paced behind his desk, then pulled up short. "I suspect you found survivors from *Elizabeth Carton*. How many?"

"'Bout fifty make it on to Sal."

"Praise be to God."

"No praise be to dat one. Over two hundred leave Dakar but only twenty-three be here now. Eight men. Two boy. Three girl. Rest be women. One wiff life inside of her."

"What happened to the others?"

"Drown. Starve. Get sick. Die of sorrow. One woman ... she beg of sea to be takin' her on de rip tide. Go join her baby ... baby who die on Carton. Sea oblige her and she drownded. Dese people need to get off dis island, mon, 'fore dey all die."

"But not transporting them to London. Is that so?"

"That so. Djéli tink so, too. He say des people not go to London."

"Who is Djeli? Their chief?"

Dame-Marie laughed scornful. "Not chief. He be djéli."

"Explain."

"In Mandinka dat word mean blood. Djéli know in de blood what no one else know. Djéli know in de blood dese people die at London. Got to make new home."

A knock. Moran stepped in. "We found Pyeweed, sir."

"Where?"

"In the chain locker, sir."

"March him to his quarters. Use force if necessary."

Moran smiled grim. "I will, sir."

Elo stepped in. "Beg pardon, sir, but Pyeweed holds knife to his own throat. Threatens to kill himself if you don't return him to duty."

"If Pyeweed kills himself then so be it. Regrettable, but I will not have him at large in my ship."

"Then best if I stay with Pyeweed. Ja?"

"No. I am sending you ashore to tend Lieutenant Hoyer's wound." Praether turned to Dame-Marie. "And you will go with the loblolly and fetch this djéli fellow off Sal. I will interview him here in my quarters."

"Why you want to speak wiff him?"

"I would be amiss if I did not talk to this man. The One Body expects a full report of our mission. An individual's personal account would be invaluable. Does he speak English?"

"No. I stand between. But djéli never step inside of no cabin. Too prideful to go inside of place like dis. You come to him."

"Very well. Harriet, you will come along and take notes. Be sure to bring a fresh ledger."

Just as one bell rang in the first dog watch Gleason lowered two of *Eleanor*'s boats. First the cutter, then the longboat. Eight oarsmen and the coxsun all went into the cutter. I came next bearing a small ledger, a pot of ink, and two good quills. Elo brought his kit, to look after Hoyer, and Dame-Marie came along to translate. We sat together on a thwart, watching as six marines climbed down into the longboat. Soon Captain Praether came aboard, followed by Sergeant Moran and two more marines bearing a wooden chest. Not an overlarge chest, but the marines struggled with its weight. Praether took his place in the stern and ordered the thing set next to him. The longboat cast off first, then our coxsun took firm hold of the tiller and the bowman gaffed us clear. We rowed into the cove, all watching silent as we made past *Iona*. A fine brig, once named *Santa Isadora*. Now, a smoldering ruin.

As we approached Sal a glitter of gold from their uniforms revealed just where three Portuguese officers reclined in the shade. Twenty Portuguese sailors hunched together in the open, ringed by a dozen Negroes. Farther along, a knot of men stood apart on the beach. One taller than the rest, though he was no more than fourteen hand. Skin black as pitch. He wore a black bicorne topped with a white plume, and a pale-yellow frock. He paced the beach in white leather boots. A Portuguese uniform, no doubt taken from *Villa Real*'s captain. I nudged Dame-Marie.

"The one in uniform. He must be the djéli."

"Be wrong if you tink dat."

Dame-Marie pointed to four men sitting in a tight circle just inside the tree line. All of them young, except for the one speaking. He was older. Near forty, I think, though it was hard to know. Bushy white hair, a high sloping forehead and thick brows. The top of his left ear notched deep.

"Him?"

"Dat right."

Praether overheard. "His name?"

"No name. People call him djéli."

"Bring him to me once we land."

"Djéli stay where he at. He tellin' de story now and dem others ... dey listenin' close. Gonna say it back exact same way he tell it."

"What story?"

"Be only one story, mon. Start of time. Take time to say it all."

"How much time?"

"All dere is of it."

"Nonsense. I am pressed. Can you interrupt him?"

"What you tink?" Dame-Marie spat in the sand. "But he stoppin' soon now. 'Bout to come 'round tellin' what happen on board of *Elizabeth Carton*. Say it many time before now 'cause dat what a djéli do. Say it all. Den start over and say it again. Come."

Our party struggled through the deep sand. Baking hot, black volcanic, and reluctant to let us pass. Elo bore away through the trees, heading for *Villa Real* to tend Hoyer. Soon we approached the djéli sitting on a woven mat, with the men gathered around him. A small, frail-boned man. Large eyes, dark and protruding, calm, fixed and unblinking, yellowed whites. A string of cowrie shells hung from his thin neck. No hat or shirt, only a threadbare madras skirt, likely some remnant taken off *Elizabeth Carton*. Thin legs stretched out. Splayed bare feet. Overlarge, with pink soles. He spoke high and clear, almost a song. Dame-Marie translated. I sat in the sand and opened my ledger.

"Fatou Ceesay. She be first to die. Throw her into da sea."

The djéli went on, speaking the name of every person who died on *Elizabeth Carton*. The three men told back all of what the djéli said. He sat alert while they spoke each name. The list was long, and the djéli cocked his notched ear listening for mistakes. Certain his students had recited these names many times before, and it seemed they made no errors, for the djéli went on.

"Come storm. Sailor all leave in small boats. Last to go give Ebrima Dabo one key. Key unlock shackles on right side of boat. Right side free to go on deck. The boy, Musa Turay, he on deck, still shackled. No key for to unlock him. One small boat left on deck. Musa Turay climb in dat small boat. He still shackled. He play his flute. People hear him. They find drum. All dance in circle. Storm tossin' dem all about."

The djéli leaned in, raising a brow as the men said it all back. Then he continued.

"Drum and dance make storm die. People give praise to drum. Give praise to dance. Give praise to Musa Turay still wearin' dat shackle and playing dat flute. Still in dat small boat. People set dat boat adrift. Musa Turay play his flute 'till he be out of sight."

He stopped of a sudden and spoke to Dame-Marie.

"Djéli want to know what you people want."

Praether stepped forward. "Please tell him he has already given us much of what we want. Now we know what happened to the people on board *Elizabeth Carton*. I am quite sure we came upon Musa Turay. He was alive. Adrift some twenty miles off Dakar. Tell him."

"Djéli want to know where Musa Turay be now."

"I decided it was best to return him to the coast. Same as I now must decide what is best for all of you."

Dame-Marie spat. "Why you be da one decide what best for dees people? You just some rich mon blinded by de light. Be you one to know dere agony? Some rich mon never lament of nuffin' in dis life?"

Praether stood silent, bowing his head. A slumping figure, breathing long and slow, his boots buried in the sand. Ajax was right ... Captain Praeher did lament, but no longer in the privacy of the great cabin. But here in the open, and for all to see. Even so, he soon composed himself and went on.

"You know nothing of my circumstance, Dame-Marie. Think what you will, but the fact remains. I will not abandon these people. We must get them off this island."

"Den you give me Real and I take dem off dis place."

"To where? Saint-Domingue."

"Dat right."

"*Villa Real* is undermanned for such a long voyage."

"You be wrong. I teachin' dese people how to sail. Dey green, but dey eager. Know dey can't stay here. Time run out on dis place."

Praether raised a brow. "I doubt you have been in command of any ship that has made a crossing."

"Always be a first time." Dame-Marie shrugged. "All captain make a first crossing. Same for you."

"True. But no captain would risk such a voyage with no experienced hands."

"Oh, I got de experienced hands. Be seven who sign on back in Plymouth dat be willin' to come on to Real. Got me a manifest of names."

"And you say there are enough rations?"

"'Nough to make de Leeward Islands."

The captain paced the beach, working his hands behind his back until he stopped, looking to the sky.

"No. I cannot allow it."

"Damn you, mon! You jus' wantin' to bring dese people back to London your own self. Jus' savin' your soul for when time come to atone."

Praether glared at Dame-Marie, barely able to control his rancor. "Is it not one's duty to save his own soul? Besides, what would be the fate of these people if The One Body had not sought them out?"

Dame-Marie made no reply.

"You choose to withhold an answer and that is wise, because we all know what their fate would be. However, my decision is not based on feathering my own hat or saving my own soul. Rather, it is a matter of navigation. Lieutenant Hoyer has been serving as your sailing master, as well as your first lieutenant, but I will not send him on. Therefore, you would have no navigator to undertake any such journey."

"Den you give me Harriet. He be tolerable fair at navigation."

"Mr. Harriet does not know enough about navigation."

"But he know other tings. I hear him talk on *Solitude*. Talkin' wiff dat mon and de sister of him." Dame-Marie turned to me. "Say dat mon's name, boy."

"Mr. Wordsworth."

"Dat be da one. I listen when you say 'bout dat voice in de oak tree. You bring dat knowledge wiff you if you sail on to Saint-Domingue."

Praether narrowed his eyes. I felt relieved. Certain he'd never send me on. Not without supervision. Not with but half a crew. And not on some captain's first crossing. And what after that? Find my own way home on board some Royal Navy ship? I'd not do it! And was about to voice my opinion on the matter ... asked for or not. But before Praether could reply Dame-Marie marched off to squat in the sand with the djéli. They talked overmuch, then of a sudden Dame-Marie stood, nodding respectful to the djéli, and came to speak once more with Praether.

"Djéli say never go back. We goin' to de Leewards and I lead dem. Djéli say I take place of Bréda."

"Bréda?"

"De one you people call Louverture."

Praether raised a brow. "Toussaint Louverture? How would the djéli know of Louverture?"

"'Cause he a seer."

"A seer?"

"Like Harriet. Know tings you can't know. You tink you de only ones who know 'bout Louverture? Dat he rise up all dem slaves on Saint-Domingue? Tell dem slaves dere be ten of dem for every one of you?"

"Yes. But does the djeli also know that Louverture eventually changed his mind and went over to the planters? In the end he brought thousands of slaves into the French camp."

"I ain't Louverture. I bringin' free slaves wiff me to Saint-Domingue." Dame-Marie set his feet in the stand. "You stoppin' me? Den you got to shoot me. Gonna do dat?"

"No. Of course not."

"Den at first light we leave dis place for Saint-Domingue, on board of Real. Navigator or not."

Certain I wished to become a navigator. But never at sixteen, for the sea is vast and unfathomable, demanding a lifetime to understand what little we know of it. I smiled grim, recalling what McFerron once told. Never fear, boy, land is never more than five miles away. Five miles down! Just then, Praether turned to me. I hoped he meant to ask if I thought it a good thing for me to navigate some barque across the Atlantic. Piteous of me to hope any such thing for, instead, he only told me to fetch Sergeant Moran.

Moran arrived double quick.

"Have your men offload the chest and bring it here."

The marines struggled to haul it across the deep sand. Praether took a key from his waistcoat and handed it to Dame-Marie.

"Open it."

A chest, near half-filled with sovereigns.

"From Lady Praether's endowment. Two hundred fifty pounds, sterling. She hoped to use it in our effort to abolish slavery. I have brought it ashore, in case I could not talk sense into you."

Dame-Marie glanced sideways at the chest. "You payin' me for not tryin' for Saint-Domingue."

"No. You are a free slave and will try for Saint-Domingue no matter what I say or do. But free slave or not, when you arrive there, that is to say, if you arrive there, then you and these people will need money. I can think of no better use for Lady Praether's legacy than to provide you with a chance to thrive. I know she would approve."

"Den I take it. And give you de name a place for you to land any slaves you find from here on of now. Place called de Pepper Coast."

"Where is that?"

"Grain Coast of Africa. Dem free slaves working on Debtford Wharf ... dey talk 'bout dat place. Say maybe dey try for it someday."

"Then why don't you try for it? Or, as a last resort, Freetown."

"No. Freetown be no good. I know de Marroons in dat place. Dey make a war dere once. Bound to do dat again. And I not be from Africa. Grow to a man on Saint-Domingue. I know Saint-Domingue. Best chance for dem people. Africa behind dem now."

"I will keep the Grain Coast in mind." Praether adjusted his bicorne, just so, then went on. "Now then, the Portuguese. Mr. Harriet, return to *Eleanor* and fetch Goodhoney. I shall need him to interpret when I interview *Villa Real*'s disposed commander."

"Shall I gather my kit, sir?"

"No. First bring Goodhoney to me. Have Lorca collect your kit."

♭

When I found Lorca in the galley, a thought occurred. This day might be the last I see him. Ever. A good mate. And a steady one. I stood in the shadows watching him stoke the firebox. A sack of dry beans rested nearby, ready to be boiled and served at evening mess, along with a cask of salt pork. I smiled, recalling when Lorca had drawn a cask of salt pork. A common enough thing, yet I thought it a most wondrous drawing. He drew all things, and made them look real. He loved to draw birds. They came to perch next to him, as if posing for their portrait. He'd drawn my face as well. Three times. Always looking full on, and with a certain look I never saw in any mirror. It may have been what Dame-Marie saw, as well, when I said those things to Wordsworth. I guessed it might be a good thing to record these notions in my ledger, hidden now behind the bulkhead in the purser's quarters. Except I had no time for it.

A slight tremor ran through *Eleanor*'s hull. Only the sea running beneath. Yet it brought a chill, for it was remindful of the Sukiyama. But, instead of a whisper, I thought of what Mr. Lau told me once while plying the channel on board Solitaire. That I must be careful of what I say, for my words may come back to haunt. Just then Lorca sensed I was watching and turned to face me.

"Lorca, Captain Praether says for you to collect my kit while I find Goodhoney and bring him ashore. I ... I might be leaving the ship."

When I returned with Goodhoney, Praether called for the Portuguese officers. *Villa Real*'s commander stepped forward, displaying much contempt.

"Ask his name."

Goodhoney asked, then waited for an overlong reply.

"A windy name, sir, so with your permission I'll just refer to him as Tenente João da Gloria, captain of *Villa Real*. He wishes to know by what authority you have taken him prisoner, and why you have commandeered his ship."

"Be so kind as to remind the Tenente that Portugal and England are not at war, and if he had not sent a raiding party onto this island there would have been no need for this audience. And as for why we have claimed *Villa Real*, please tell him it was he who boarded *Iona* and burned her to the waterline. His actions left us no choice."

Goodhoney translated, and da Gloria replied.

"*Porto privateer.*"

"He says *Iona* was manned by pirates."

"*Você são enviadas pelo diabo.*"

"He says you are in league with the devil."

"Hardly." Praether removed a document from his frock and handed it to Goodhoney. "This is a copy of my Letter of Marque.

Translate it for the Tenente, if you will. Be sure he understands this mandate was issued by the High Court of Admiralty of England. I act in full accordance with its moral compass, that being the abolition of slavery, of which the Tenente is bound to protect and insure against reprisal."

Da Gloria scoffed as Goodhoney interpreted the fiat, then replied expansive, ending with what sounded like a demand.

"The Tenente blusters away, sir. I will pare it down, if you wish."

"Proceed."

"Stated more simply then, he demands you release him at once and return his ship immediately."

"Tell him that will not be possible. However, I shall be departing Sal very soon and will do my utmost to send word of his predicament to the Portuguese Consulate in Praia."

We heard footsteps plodding through the deep sand and turned to see Lieutenant Hoyer and Elo coming from *Villa Real*. Elo stopped next to me but Hoyer went on to Praether. He came to attention, saluting smart. Praether returned it.

"You are fit for duty, lieutenant?"

"I am, sir. And we've just spotted a square-rigged vessel bearing south along the coast. It seems their bowsprit's been damaged and they sail poorly."

"Slave ship?"

"I think so, sir. No other reason for a vessel that size to be in these coordinates. I believe they're trying for Cape Verde, sir, and if this wind holds then I'm sure we'd catch them up soon enough."

"Very well. Take the cutter and return to *Eleanor*. Tell Bonel what you just told me and have him prepare to get under way. Have him fire a signal gun when he is ready. I will come aboard shortly but first Dame-Marie and I must come to an understanding. Dame-Marie, you say you have a crew manifest?"

Dame-Marie produced his list, and Praether read it out for all to hear.

"Enoch Brill, Able Seaman. Leopold Sharp, Francis Casper, Junie Temple, Derby Thomas, Ordinary Seamen. Antoine Mason, Carpenter's Mate. Xerxes Finch, Sailmaker's Mate." Praether paused to study the men, then went on. "I have just called out your

160

names because Dame-Marie claims each one of you has volunteered to serve on *Villa Real*. He further states you all understand that very soon *Villa Real* may depart for Saint-Domingue. Be advised. It is over three thousand miles from Sal to Saint-Domingue and even with seven additional hands *Villa Real* will remain far below complement. No doubt you will all stand watch-and-watch for the duration. Questions?"

None.

I waited patient, still hoping to hear Praether deny Dame-Marie's request for my service. He did not.

"Then step forward, all who still wish to join *Villa Real*."

All seven came forward. But not me.

The sharp report of *Eleanor*'s signal gun echoed around the bay.

Praether went on. "Very well. Now for navigation. In Portsmouth Mr. Harriet signed aboard *Eleanor* with the full knowledge that I may find need to assign him to some other ship under my command. That need has now arisen."

He turned to me. "Mr. Harriet, return to *Eleanor*. Fetch your charts and belongings and join Dame-Marie aboard *Villa Real*. You will serve as sailing master, with all rights and duties accruing."

Elo whispered in my ear. "Maybe Praether should . . ."

Praether heard his name and glared at Elo.

"Inari, if you have something to say to me then come forward and say it."

Elo complied. "Pyeweed, he fit to resume his duties, sir."

Praether only scowled, grumbling low. "Never."

"And I think maybe . . ."

"Think you what, Inari?"

"I think send him with *Villa Real*. Ja?"

At first Praether made no reply, but then raised a brow, grinning full.

15. *Black Joke*

We departed Cape Verde the next morning and set a course for the Banana Islands, just off the west African coast, in Yawri Bay. We called there to take on water and supplies. A stoat for the officers' mess. And a peacock that kept following Lorca.

Soon we were underway once again, with our white pennant cracking smart in the freshening breeze, west by west, and the Atlantic swell running steady under our keel. I checked our bearing once more, still making south by east, and still most grateful to be standing a watch aboard *Eleanor*. Far better than serving on *Villa Real*, only to be sent on to the Leewards as sailing master on some not half-baked voyage. Better for Pyeweed to have been sent instead, both for him and for *Eleanor*. Yet I still served only as master's mate, now standing Lieutenant Hoyer's post while Elo dressed his cutlass wound. So it was my responsibility to react when, as the last dog watch began, our lookout hailed the deck.

"Sail off the port bow."

I called to the crosstrees. "Distance?"

"On the horizon, Mr. Harriet. I think they're signaling with a mirror."

I ordered Nary to fetch the captain and made ready for some officer to send me aloft to investigate. I stepped to the mizzen chains, but then stayed my progress. As a deck officer I belonged on the quarterdeck, not skylarking through the rigging. I called for Hewitt, the signal midshipman.

"Mr. Hewitt take your glass and go aloft. That may be the ship Lieutenant Hoyer saw earlier."

Hewitt turned ashen. He was no top man and feared going aloft. But he went onto the shrouds smart enough, holding the rail over tight as he called from the mizzen top.

"A three-masted ship. Square-rigged. Bearing south, and we're closing."

The wind shifted another point.

"I can read her name on the transom now. *Black Joke*. Out of Recife."

Praether came to the helm. "Recife is on the Brazilian coast. No doubt with a hold full of human cargo. They signal with a mirror, Mr. Hewitt?"

"Aye, sir. Winking three times. A pause, then repeating. Five times in the last few minutes."

"Any other sail?"

"I can't see any, sir."

The captain turned to me. "Mr. Harriet, your midshipman must go farther aloft to confirm if there are any other sails in sight. It was your responsibility to send him higher, not just to the mizzen top. Send him now."

"Aye, sir."

Hewitt struggled precarious on the narrowing shrouds, taking overlong to gain the crosstrees. After scanning the horizon, his voice came drifting feeble on the wind.

"No other ships in sight, sir."

"Very well. Harriet, send for Goodhoney. His Portuguese will be needed shortly. And since that ship is from Brazil he might know what the signal means."

Goodhoney came on deck. "A light blinking three times?"

"Not a light. A mirror. What do you make of it?"

"I don't know. Why not send the same thing?"

"No. The sun is behind us so we cannot make use of a mirror. Besides, we will overtake them soon enough. Then I shall send a signal of my own. Harriet, inform Japhet to load the bow chaser and stand by to fire a warning shot. Inform Sergeant Moran to assemble a boarding party."

Goodhoney cleared his throat. "What if they resist?"

"A well-placed shot across their bow and a squad of marines forming on our bow will likely discourage that inclination."

"May I ask a favour, sir?"

"What?"

"Permit me to go aboard that ship."

"You consider it a favour to go on a slave ship?"

"No. An act of atonement."

"Why?"

"I need to know if any of those slaves are bound by the shackles I designed."

$\maltese$

"A splendid shot, Japhet. Not so close as to do any harm yet near enough for *Black Joke* to understand its meaning."

Black Joke understood well enough. She spilled her wind and lay hove to. When we closed to within fifty yards Lieutenant Bonel, Sergeant Moran and nine marines made for them in our longboat. A thickset figure wearing a black tricorne and frock coat stood at the entry port. A pistol in each hand, and a dragoon nearby. He called down loud and thunderous. In English!

"Keep your distance or I'll shoot. I am Shotwick, out of Cape Breton. Captain and owner of this vessel and its cargo. I've just killed my driver for signaling you. The fool guessed you were another slaver that would help him take *Black Joke.* but you're naught but a war ship disguised as something else."

Bonel waisted no time. "Sergeant Moran, direct a volley over that man's head."

"Aye, sir. First rank, make ready. Take aim above the man's head. On my mark ... fire!"

Three muskets rang out simultaneous but Shotwick never flinched, even as one round parted a stay not three feet from where he stood.

Bonel called out. "Drop your pistols or the next volley will be aimed at you."

Certain the man would back down now but, instead, he raised a pistol and shot Bonel full in the chest, knocking him overboard. Moran ordered the second rank to return fire. But, just as they fired, a wave took the longboat broadside and every round went low, splintering the rail. Shotwick fired his second pistol but hit no one. The marines heaved their grappling line and hooked on to *Black Joke*. Moran scrambled on the tumblehome and went straight on through the entry port wielding his cutlass. He slashed on Shotwick's wrist to dislodge yet another pistol. Shotwick howled in pain, but still he reached for the dragoon. Another marine charged with his bayonet, meaning to plunge it deep. But Shotwick jumped aside and the bayonet bounced off in a glancing blow. He grabbed the dragoon and shot the marine in the face. Three more marines closed in, each one slamming his musket on Shotwick's head. The first strike only knocked away his tricorne. But the second cracked open his skull, and Shotwick buckled to the deck. A third for good measure.

Praether put his gig in the water to search for Bonel, but by then the first lieutenant had gone under, and taken by the current. When the lookout spotted a school of sharks frothing the water, Praether called off the search.

Goodhoney came to stand with the captain. "Awful. He was a decent chap. I'm so sorry for his fate. Here one moment and gone the very next. To be shot and then eaten by sharks is a . . ."

Praether slammed his fist on the rail. "Damn your eyes, man. If you have nothing to report, then bloody shut your mouth. And if you are going aboard *Black Joke* then make yourself ready. Harriet, fetch the loblolly. Tell him to bring his kit and he will go aboard, too. You, as well, Harriet. Stay with Goodhoney. Make sure he stands clear and is prepared to translate the Portuguese."

Goodhoney stepped forward. "If I may speak, sir, I actually do have something to report."

"Be quick about it."

"Translation might not be necessary. A slave ship will have a driver on board, to brutalize the cargo and such. A slave himself ... usually owned by the captain. So in order to serve his master this one will need to speak English, as well as some African tongue."

"I still want you to go aboard and assure the Portuguese crew we mean them no harm. I will send Fagen to *Black Joke* when he returns with the gig. Go now."

♭

I held my breath as I sat in the cutter with Elo and Goodhoney. Goodhoney turned to me.

"What's the matter?"

I released my breath and replied. "I'm trying not to breathe too much air of a slaver. They stink overmuch."

"Well you can't hold your breath forever. Besides *Black Joke* doesn't stink. Not quite yet. Not like it would after completing the middle passage. When a slaver finally calls at Valongo Pier it's soaked in shit and piss, blood and vomit. And if it can no longer be swabbed out well enough to transport plantation crops to Europe, the owners would likely have the thing towed out to sea and burned."

"A ship's an expensive thing to burn."

Goodhoney shrugged. "The cost of a slave ship counts for little when compared to the value of its human cargo."

The cutter hooked on, and we came aboard. Elo hurried to the marine, looking most dead lying there on the deck, not far from Shotwick, who also looked most dead. Moran marched an unshackled Negro from the waist.

"This one speaks English, Mr. Harriet. Wants to speak to an officer."

"I'm not an officer."

"But I am." Lieutenant Fagen stepped forward. "I've just come aboard. I relieve you, Mr. Harriet."

"Did you find Lieutenant Bonel, sir?"

Fagen gave me a dark look. "What do you think?" He turned to the Negro. "Who are you?"

"Kofi. I not kill him."

"Not kill who?"

"Ismaela."

"Who is that?"

"Driver for Shotwick."

"Are you a member of his crew?"

"Cook for him." Kofi looked to the deck. "Dead?"

The lieutenant turned to Elo. "Well?"

Elo nodded. "So is Private Thirst."

Fagen grabbed the cook by his long hair and twisted painful. "Tell me what happened here or I'll rip out your stinkin' hair."

Kofi stiffened, balling his fists. But he kept them both at his side, resigned to obey Fagen's demand.

"Ismaela take slaves on deck to shit. He unlock some. Try to take ship."

Fagen glanced along the deck. "Where's the crew now?"

"Below. They try helping captain for taking back ship but then Ismaela ... but he damaging bowsprit and shooting at crew. They running and locking inside fo'c's'le. Ismael ... he see you on horizon and make signal. But Shotwick ... he coming on deck to shoots Ismaela dead. Taking back ship then. But crew stay hiding. Still afraid."

"Afraid of Shotwick?"

"Yes. Afraid of slaves, too."

The cry of children rose from below decks. A marine opened the forward hatch and a grim fug rose from the hold.

"Unshackle them."

"Cannot."

Once more Fagen twisted Kofi's hair. He shut his eyes tight in pain but said nothing. Fagen twisted harder yet.

"I said unshackle them!"

Kofi screamed. "Shotwick throwing away key in ocean."

"Good for him. No matter. Hewitt, send for the carpenter. Have him bring his cold chisel and maul."

Goodhoney joined us. "That won't be necessary, sir. I've had a look at these shackles. I didn't make them, but I know who did. They're made with a warded lock, and I can fashion a new key to align with the wards. Besides, these shackles are tempered steel. It would take longer to break just one of them than to make a new key to fit them all."

"How long?"

"Not long. I've found the workshop, but I'll need assistance."

"Take Harriet."

The shop was no more than a cubbyhole shared with the tiller. Goodhoney cleared the work bench while I lit three glims.

"You know who made these shackles?"

"I do."

"That's fortunate."

"Not fortune, Harriet. Preordained. These shackles were made by Nino Silva. We were the only ones at Vila Prudentea who knew how to design them. Our overseer kept demanding more, so to increase production we shared ward pattens for certain models, and the model on board *Black Joke* is one we shared." He pulled a flat metal slug from his waistcoat, a quarter inch thick, one inch wide, and six long. He pointed to a vise. "Open the jaws. Not much, just enough to accept this. About one quarter inch."

I opened the vise, and Goodhoney fit the slug.

"Now tighten the spindle hard as you can."

"What is that?"

"A brass ingot. Alloys have shape memory. They'll eventually break if you work it back and forth. We'll break this ingot in two, then use one piece to shape a lever lock key. Brass is stubborn, though. It takes two people."

I worked the ingot back and forth while Goodhoney ran a file along the edge. When it finally snapped in two I thought we'd done a proper job of it, but Goodhoney only wiped his brow and shifted his stance.

"Now for the difficult part. Filing the notches to fit each ward."

"Only be careful where you stand." I pointed at the tiller. "This thing's sure to knock you about if the helm turns on the wheel."

The moan coming from the hold grew louder. A low call, heard as one voice, crying mournful. Goodhoney and I exchanged a look.

"Listen to them, Harriet. Human agony. Some people think they're barely human. Or a race of low intelligence. Others know different, but don't care."

"Pyeweed said we're all hypocrites."

Goodhoney nodded. "Some more than others." He spoke in a voice meant only for me to hear. "Jesus says the truth shall set you free. But the truth is ... I'm making these keys to set me free."

He worked methodic. File held just so, shaping the wards with every pass. I stood entranced, watching his fingers move across the ingot.

"Nino's the one who told me our shackles were designed for the slave trade. He didn't like it any more than me. Said our knowledge and skill deserves better use. Loosen the spindle and slide the ingot forward another quarter inch."

"You told Captain Praether that you quit Vila Prudentea. Did Silva quit, too?"

"He was of a mind. But he was old, with not much longer before he could retire."

"And go home to Portugal?"

"He no longer considered Portugal his home."

The ship slid down the steep side of a comber. The rogue wave caught the rudder and swung the tiller on its post, catching Goodhoney by surprise. He dodged away, then went back to work.

"You should know a thing. I didn't actually quit. More like escaped." He switched to a smaller file. "I explained how, in my report. Did you read it?"

"No. You wrote it for Praether."

"Do you wish to know?"

"Yes."

"Very well. Last year I was sent to Ilhabela. An island not far from São Paulo where Vila Prudentea was building a new foundry. I was to join Nino there, to assist him in its design. By then I'd found out that if I quit Vila Prudentea I'd have to pay a year's back rent on my bungalow, plus my cook's wages. I didn't have it. Worse yet, if I refused to go work at Ilhabela they threatened to put me in prison. I had no choice but to go."

A rapid footfall rang heavy on the deck. The Eleanors had come on board *Black Joke*, with Gleason bawling out commands to haul the main yard.

"When I joined Nino on Ilhabela I told him my situation. I wanted to run but he said it was too dangerous. Still, he looked the other way when I crossed the strait to Cabelo and booked passage on a commercial vessel. *Dona Catrina*, waiting on a cargo of rosewood bound for Lisbon. I paid the captain under a false name. Half in advance, half upon arriving in Lisbon. But torrential rains washed out the timber road. It took four months to rebuild the road and fill *Catrina's* hold. By then Nino had left Ilhabela. There was a new mail packet in service. A fast one, and Nina wrote to me, inviting me to join him at a certain place along the grain coast of West Africa. At Cape Mesurado." Goodhoney set down his file and searched through the shop. "Have you seen a grease pot?"

"No."

"Sperm oil, then. Take it from a glim. I must coat this new key to ease it past the wards."

The topsails boomed overloud, the hawser strained, and the tiller swung once more. *Black Joke* was under way.

Goodhoney went on with his story. "After the final consignment of rosewood, *Catrina* departed Cabelo. It seemed I'd made an escape. But just a day into the Atlantic the captain called me to his cabin. He knew who I really was, and who I'd worked for, but if I paid the rest of my passage now, plus an extra five pounds, he'd not put me off the ship at Cape Verde. I was reluctant, but what could I do? So I paid. But then he took all of my money and put me off the ship at Cape Verde, anyway. That was at Boa Vista, where you found me. I'm lucky that man didn't throw me to the sharks."

The clang of metal sounded in the waist.

"What was that?"

"A cold chisel. I think Fagen couldn't wait any longer. He's sent for Bettyhill to break the shackles."

A colourful round of swearing followed on, with Bettyhill carping overloud that the whole thing was no use. Soon Hewitt came to find us.

"The lieutenant wants to know how much longer."

Goodhoney loosened the vice and held his work to the light. "Done. There may be final modifications but there's only one way to know. Come with me to the hold. Bring a glim."

The hold reeked of bilge and human waste, along with some ungodly stench lurking in the gloom.

"Do you recognize that smell, Harriet?"

"No. What is it?"

"It has no name. A rational man might consider me unhinged, but I call it agony and despair ... brought together in a cauldron of fear. Raise the light."

I held the glim high to reveal a long bank of shackled slaves. Men, women and children, all lying on their sides in narrow shelves and curled tight as a row of spoons. Goodhoney bent low to the nearest slave, a young man, and tried to insert his key into the lock. It went in but halfway. Goodhoney withdrew it, studied the wards, then produced a file to remove a final burr. He tried once more. This time the key passed through, and he prized it open, careful slow. When the shackle released, I thought the young man would rise and be grateful. But he did neither, for he was dead.

But the rest were alive, though none seemed over grateful for their release, for they still cowered in the hold.

Goodhoney looked at me. "They don't understandd what any of this means. It will take time. I can only hope I've given them enough."

A Christian service for Private Dilly Thirst, *Eleanor*'s marine, followed by a splash. Soon followed by another splash, but with no words spoken over Shotwick.

We made smart to leave Sal, bearing south by east. Goodhoney, along with every available officer and my own self, as well, stood in the great cabin, each of us taking heed of Praether's nasal whine, a clear sign of his displeasure.

"I have never considered returning slaves to the Dakar coast as a viable solution. It was meant only as a temporary measure, at best.

But, since relieving the survivors at Sal, I begin to agree with Dame-Marie. Dakar is entirely out of the question, and bringing them to London is not practical, either."

Goodhoney stiffened. "Them? You make it sound as if these people are some sort of theoretical equation. No more than chattel."

Praether countered. "Untrue. They are as much God's creation as we are. However, their plight still remains a challenge best considered with forethought and diligence, as well as compassion. So here is . . ."

Hewitt knocked on the cabin door and stepped in. "Beg pardon, sir. The wind backs in our favour and Lieutenant Japhet wishes to lay on top gallants."

"No. We must be sure not to outdistance *Black Joke*. And remind him, I want two reliable men to keep a steady watch. We may have freed those people held prisoner in *Black Joke*'s hold, but no one can know how they will react."

Praether waited for Hewitt to leave, then shot his cuffs. "So here is what I have in mind. Three years ago Lady Praether and I were sent as missionaries to the Colonies. Our mission field was Loudoun County, in the Commonwealth of Virginia. We had little success there, but did meet with several gentlemen who shared a similar belief with The One Body. One of them was a young solicitor named Charles Mercer who, for reasons of his own, supported the concept of returning free slaves to Africa. Not to Dakar, but to some more suitable location. He was kind enough to provide me with the chart for a particular location."

Praether withdrew a ledger from his desk drawer. Africa and the Gulf of Guinea. "Mercer was interested in this particular settlement." He tapped on the map. "Here, at Freeport. Are you familiar with it, Mr. Harriet?"

"No, sir. Mr. Lau had me review the Ephemeris for all suitable harbours along the west coast of Africa, but there was no sounding taken at Freeport."

"I see. Well it would present a major problem if there is no good harbour at Freeport."

Goodhoney spoke out. "There may be a better place, sir."

"Where?"

"The Grain Coast."

Praether raised a brow. "Ah, yes. The Grain Coast."

"You've heard of it, then?"

"You are the second person to mention that very coast. Why might it be better?"

"Nino Silva."

"Your companion at São Paulo?"

"Yes, sir. We stayed in communication after he left Vila Prudentea. In one letter he said he'd retired along the Grain Coast. He'd overheard a number of free slaves in São Paulo talking of a particular location. A place for them to go if they get a chance to run. Certainly not their home village, but at least a return to Africa."

"Where is this place?"

"At Cape Mesurado. A small outpost established by the Portuguese."

"Go on."

"I believe Silva would be of a mind to help us land these people there."

"Why?"

"Because that's where Nino has chosen to begin life anew."

The captain scoffed. "As atonement for his hand in the slave trade, no doubt."

"Not atonement, sir. In his letters he calls it *asilo*."

"Some ... Portuguese word?"

"Yes."

"See here, Goodhoney, I brought you on board to translate Portuguese, not speak it."

"In that case, the translation would be asylum. But for Nino I must interpret it more broadly. His sanctuary. His last attempt for eternal life."

"Likely a specious attempt. But, either way, I must consider your suggestion."

Praether turned to me. "Do you have a recent chart for the Grain Coast? Specifically for this Cape Mesurado?"

"Yes, sir. It's in Index Nine—Ledgers . . ."

"Spare the particulars, Harriet. Just fetch it."

In the chart room, which had once served as Mr. Lau's quarters, I stood on a milk stool to pull down . . .

Index Nine—Ledgers Eighty-One Through Ninety

Grain Coast at Cape Mesurado

Charted for The Nautical Almanac and Astronomical Ephemeris

J. Detwiler, Sailing Master, HMS Pilgrim

September 1793

Revised December 1797

by I. C. Lau, Admiralty House

I had the volume in hand but hauled short when a strong recollection came over me ... of Mr. Lau standing on this same stool reaching for some chart. I'd not had much time to think of him, not since departing Portsmouth, and the onrush of neglected questions unsettled me. What was Mr. Lau doing this very moment? Did he still let a room at Mrs. Dolan's? No doubt the money Praether gave her for my Prélat would stand him in good stead. But would I see him again? I dared not consider that last question. Instead, I opened the Cape Mesurado ledger. His tight cursive ran methodic on every page, with any manner of eccentricities scratched in the margins ...

Two, November 1794—4°W x 12°N

four bells of the afternoon watch, vague apparition observed on the eastern horizon

lookout claims it was a chimera

not out of the question.

Nineteen, June 1796—2°W x 8°N

evening nautical twilight

unexplained sound coming from astern

Remindful of a banshee. I was the only one to hear it.

Dear Mr. Lau, always the first to hear any sound upon the water. Sometimes the only one. I spoke his name under my breath. "Mr. Lau. I hope all goes well for you, sir."

All goes well ... but for the gin. He swore off it while at sea. But in London I feared for him, recalling a certain night when, in a weakened condition, he vowed never to quit the gin, never until the last bottle was drunk down. On that same night I'd provided the strength he lacked. But what now? Who provided?

If he was with Mrs. Dolan then certain she'd look after him. She liked him some, and would be sure to dote, if in her own brusque manner. But he was fierce independent. He'd complain, telling her not to fuss about. He might even shoot out his dentures at her. I grinned at that, for there's no doubt Mrs. Dolan would shoot her own dentures back at him in response. I laughed gleeful at the thought of it, just as a knock sounded at the door, and Nary stepped through.

"Beg pardon, Mr. Harriet, and I don't mean to interrupt your joy, but the captain ... he wonders if you will ever find the time to bring him the chart."

I returned double quick to Praether's quarters and set the ledger before him, placing my finger on the cape.

"There's a deep water bay here, sir, in the lee of Cape Mesurado."

Praether glowered, upset with my delay, but then leaned in to study the chart, eyes squinting, and taking overlong before announcing his decision.

"This site is surely foreign to what these people know, but far more familiar than London. However, such an undertaking has never been tried at Cape Mesurado." He turned abrupt, facing us. "At least not until now. What is more, I am convinced the time has come for us to initiate contact with a certain, like-minded faction."

16. A band of warring tribes

It took but a week to raise Cape Mesurado, and on the seventh day Captain Praether stood at the davits, along with Fagen and Hoyer, all three of them observing as I called for Gleason to step the mast on the barge, already in the water. The lines drew taught and the mast eased onto its step. When Gleason lashed it tight Praether gave his approval, then turned to Fagen.

"Lieutenant Fagen, for these last few weeks you have kept *Black Joke* under steady sail. You have maintained good order."

Fagen grinned, if only slight, for any praise coming from Praether usually carried a condition.

"Even so, you have not made best use of your translator, and I wish to know why not. Kofi speaks English. Mandinka, as well."

"I don't trust him, sir. He lies when he tells me what the others say."

"How do you know this?"

"Because the little monkey won't look at me. I think he should be taken off *Black Joke* and sent here. Treat him like a slave, just like the others."

"He is not a slave, Fagen. You will treat him as a free man."

"I treat him fair, sir, just as you ordered."

"But none too kindly, nor any of the others on *Black Joke*."

Fagen jut his jaw. "They may not be slaves, sir, but they're still of a low order. They understand nothing. I must always show force to keep them in place. No mistreatment, sir. You may be sure of it."

Praether gazed out to sea, taking overlong before he replied. "I am recalling you. Since Lieutenant Bonel was killed you are my acting First Officer and I want you back on board *Eleanor*. I will be going ashore at Cape Mesurado and will need you to take command in my absence. Go you now. Submit your watch bill by this afternoon."

Praether watched him go below, then turned to Hoyer. "I am giving you command of *Black Joke*. You are well qualified, and you have spent time on Sal, so you are more familiar with the inherent

177

risk. There are nearly two hundred newly freed slaves on *Black Joke*. Their reaction to a newly won freedom will likely be unpredictable, so I will send Ajax with you. His size alone may discourage any thoughts of rising up."

Praether began to pace the quarterdeck, then returned to Hoyer. "Is it not ironic? I have promised these people their freedom yet have placed them under house arrest, in a manner of speaking."

"I did take note of the situation, sir."

"And in your opinion, just what is the situation?"

Hoyer paused, as if wondering just how to reply, then spoke his mind, "I believe the free slaves on board *Black Joke* are no more predictable than the rest of us. And no less."

Praether raised a brow. "A discreet response. However, this operation may take a while, and I will not put them ashore at Cape Mesurado until I have determined if the place is suitable. To do anything less would only prolong their agony. Therefore, you must maintain order on board *Black Joke* while I make the attempt. Africans taken as slaves have risen in ship's rebellion on several occasions, and who can blame them? But I rely on you to avert such an occurrence." Praether frowned in thought. "It may be too expensive, and they might not understand my intent, but what if I were to buy their complicity?"

"You mean to buy them off, sir?"

"After a fashion. With funds from Lady Praether's war chest."

"Very generous, sir."

"Hardly. The assets come from her inheritance. From shares derived in part from the slave trade. Lady Praether felt that such money must be returned to those who were sold into slavery. I know she would expect me to do just that."

"Is this money in scrip?"

"Some of it."

"Silver, as well?"

"A limited amount."

"Then may I make a suggestion, sir?"

"Yes.

"Offer them silver. While on Sal I watched these people conduct their business. Very little of it, to be sure, but all goods and services were bartered. No exchange of money, for they had none. Somewhat remindful of how the men exchange sips of grog. Very confusing to an outsider, but it all seems to work out well enough."

"What are you driving at, lieutenant?"

"Only that these people are not familiar with scrip, sir. Their economy isn't based on paper. But silver ... that they know. If you wish to buy them off, then silver is the way."

On the quarterdeck, one bell rang. The afternoon watch manned their stations and the ones off duty took to the shade. Praether and Hoyer watched the changeover. When both were satisfied, Hoyer went on.

"Another way is to restore their dignity, sir."

"A Christian act."

"I hope so. And to help relieve their circumstance, I have a request."

"What is it?"

"I would like to bring Cuxhaven with me, sir. Able Seaman. He plays a handäoline."

"The instrument I hear playing on Sundays?"

"Aye, sir. I think the free slaves on *Black Joke* would feel more at ease if he played for them."

"You think them simple minded, Hoyer? Easily won over by someone playing on a handäoline?"

"I suppose some of them are simple minded, sir. As are some of the men on board *Eleanor*. Nevertheless, the Eleanors enjoy the break in routine. And so might the free slaves on board *Black Joke*."

"Very well, take him." Praether withdrew a sealed packet from his waistcoat. "Your orders. To reduce the chance of any misunderstanding I will read them aloud." Praether cleared his throat. "While at Cape Mesurado you will keep *Black Joke* out to sea and hull down. Send down your top hamper so as to reduce the chance of being sighted. Post two lookouts on the crosstrees during each watch. One to watch for all flag hoists originating from *Eleanor*. The other to watch for ships approaching from seaward. Hoist one flag on the mizzen at first light each morning, meant to signal that all is well. Always on the mizzen. Always a certain colour, depending on the day. Mr. Hewitt will provide you with a code book."

Gleason stepped forward. "Beg pardon, sir, but the barge is squared away."

"Very well. Hoyer, take the barge to *Black Joke*, then tow it astern. I expect you to instruct these people in the rudiments of seamanship. Make it clear that if they work the ship and obey your commands as best they can, then they have nothing to fear, and will begin to earn pounds sterling. Surely I intend to set them free, and for that they will need all the silver they can earn. Not just cowrie shells and whatnot."

Praether handed the packet to Hoyer. "The next stage of our mission is critical. Soon I will take *Eleanor* into the bay at Cape Mesurado and try to make contact with Nino Silva. Go you now."

♭

Cape Mesurado still lay unseen in the mist when Captain Praether called me to the great cabin. All glims burning bright, and Lady Praether's likeness gazing serene, though I must admit not looking so radiant as when I first saw her portrait. Praether looked not so radiant, either, the colour drained from his face, replaced by a thin wash. A blank sheet of parchment lay on his desk, alongside a quill and a pot of ink.

"Mr. Harriet, I have taken note of your steady cursive. That is why I have summoned you here, to act as my recording secretary. Since my injuries off Ushant my hand is erratic, at times verging on illegible. Lady Praether would write out my correspondence for me, until she . . ." He paused before her portrait, standing silent, rocking with *Eleanor*'s motion.

"Sir?"

"Just dress your quill and take this down." He said no more of Lady Praether, but only commenced his habitual pace, speaking deliberate slow.

Cape Mesurado

20th February 1803

To The Right Honorable Charles Fenton Mercer

Nine, Sophia Street

Fredericksburg, Commonwealth of Virginia

Dear Sir,

I am Post Captain Matthew Praether, in command of His Majesty's Frigate, Eleanor.

In May of 1795, as mission agents for The One Body, of which I hope you recall with partiality, my wife and I had the pleasure of meeting with you, and a select group of your colleagues, at your holdings in Louden County. Upon that occasion, you spoke of your incipient belief in returning free slaves to the African continent. To wit: at Freetown, in Sierra Leone.

However, if you are still considering Freetown for any such venture, then may I suggest another location? I have in my possession recent information describing a certain anchorage offering far more promise in regard to the returning of free slaves upon the soil of Africa. Namely: Cape Mesurado; situated along the Grain Coast, also referred to as the Pepper Coast.

I should like to add that the Grain Coast has been suggested to me as a possible relocation by two stedfast individuals, and on two separate occasions.

Therefore, I pray that by the time you receive this letter, The One Body's efforts at Cape Mesurado are well under way, and will have met with a measurable degree of success. Perhaps what The One Body tries to enact here will serve as an inspiration to advance your own worthy cause.

You may be sure I intend to keep you apprised of our progress, and I anticipate with earnest resolve any future communication you may wish to address to me.

For, Dear Sir, all Comfort and all Satisfaction is truly wished upon you, by Your Most Obliged, Most Obedient, and Most Humble Servant,

Matthew James Praether, Captain, HMS Eleanor

He didn't sign it but, instead, withdrew a sheet of vellum from his top drawer.

"Make fair copy on this vellum. Include the coordinates for Cape Mesurado, if you will. Have it ready for me to sign by the forenoon watch and I will seal it with my stamp. In these waters it is not likely we will meet another Royal Navy ship bound for home. But I would be remiss if I did not have this letter ready to forward, just in case."

⚡

At first light, *Eleanor* weathered Cape Mesurado and stood into the estuary of the Saint Paul River.

Captain Praether had regained his strength, and now stood at the helm. "Tide and depth, Mr. Harriet."

"We're entering the estuary on a neap tide of no more than one foot, sir. Mr. Lau's chart indicates a depth of forty-one feet in the middle. And there's shale bottom with fair holding ground off Mamba Point." I pointed beyond our bow. "Just there."

Praether studied *Black Joke*, hull down on the horizon, going full and by, and under the command of Lieutenant Hoyer. After one last scan he swung his scope to glass a small village at the mouth of the river, then addressed Lieutenant Fagen.

"All is in order, lieutenant?"

"Aye, sir. Anchor detail standing by at the catheads."

"Then send the following hoist to *Black Joke*. I am about to anchor. Maintain station."

Praether watched for *Black Joke*'s repeater, then snapped shut his telescope. "Have Sergeant Moran form his men to repel boarders."

Goodhoney stepped forward. "If I may make an observation, sir?"

"What?"

"We are here in search of Nino Silva, and Silva is a vigilant man. If he sees marines forming on this vessel he may decide to retreat into the jungle and wait us out until we leave."

"Very well. Fagen, have Sergeant Moran keep his men out of sight." Praether glassed the shoreline one last time, then gave the order to drop anchor. "Set the watch. Have Gleason step the cutter. Be sure he rigs the mast with a flag staff and stows a flag locker on board. I do not know at this point if we will need to signal by flag, but once ashore, I will fire my pistol in preparation of any hoist. Be sure to listen for it. Goodhoney and I will get underway shortly."

Soon thereafter Praether and Goodhoney departed in search of Silva. On board *Eleanor*, an equatorial pall clung to every shroud, and to every man. In his absence, Praether had allowed for make-and-mend. The men chatted on the spar deck, patching their worn slops, or just sprawled at ease, doing not overmuch. I counted eleven tars sitting around the main mast in tight a circle, each with his back turned to the man behind him, in order to braid the queue of the man in front. I sat, as well, listening to our fiddler, Soapwirth, who'd gained his perch on the capstan to saw away at some jig, though in this day's swelter no Eleanor was eager to dance it. Nary sat beside me at the fife rail, reeving a frayed line. Since coming on board at Portsmouth the lad had proven keen to learn his duties, and to find his way on a man-of-war. I'd been assigned to teach him his knots, and a thought occurred.

"Nary, since Portsmouth I've shown you a great many knots. Look in the rigging and call one out."

He studied the rigging, then pointed to a knot close at hand. "Bowline."

"Yes. The first knot I showed you. How's it made?"

"Make the rabbit hole. Out come the rabbit. Run around the tree and hop back into its hole."

"Tell me one of its uses."

"Makes a fixed loop at the end of a line."

He went on to identify two more knots, beaming prideful of what he knew.

"Good on you, Nary. But I wonder, do you know the best way to know a thing is to teach it? Too bad for that, since there's no one on board who you might teach."

"'Cept I might teach you the knots I learn from Binta."

"Binta?"

"That small Mandinka girl. The one who come over from *Black Joke*. She helps Lorca in the galley."

"Show me these knots."

Nary withdrew a tight ball of string from his purse and unravelled it methodic, laying out a tangle of cord, dyed light blue. Some sort of loose weaving, or a lacework spread upon the deck to form a necklace.

"What is that?"

"Binta call it *Suutoo aro*. I think she call it that. She can't talk too good, though. Got a big ugly hole in her face right under her nose. Kofi said she's cursed."

"Cursed?"

"Some bad spirit made her born with that hole right where her top lip should be. Her Mum died last week and when they threw her body over some wanted to throw Binta in, too."

Remindful of Tate. I said nothing, though, just told Nary to go on.

"But Lieutenant Hoyer, he was on deck. He seen what was happening and stopped it. Then he sent the girl here, to be safe. Lorca said she could help in the galley. Guess he don't think she's cursed."

"Do you, Nary?"

"Don't know. Ugly to look at, though."

"How old is she?"

"Ten, maybe. She can't speak English. Don't matter, though. No one can understand what she says, anyway. Hole makes it so she can only mumble. But she can say *Suutoo aro*, except I don't know what it means."

"*Suutoo* means night." We looked up to see Lorca standing close. "In Mandinka tongue. I don't know second knot ... *aro*."

"Unusual name for a knot," I replied. "How is it used?"

"Not used for a knot. Used for naming." Lorca grinned broad. "Quipus."

"What did you say?"

"Quipus knot. Peru. Where Inca people live. I learn. Now teach Binta. Now Binta tells her story with knots. That way not having to talk much." Lorca reached out with a callused hand. "May I see?"

As he examined the knots, eight bells of the afternoon watch rang out. The men bestirred themselves, preparing for the first dog watch.

"These knots speak. Tell the night of strangers who sneak into village." Lorca touched the first knot. "Look ... that is Mandinka. *Yoolee*. That mean . . ."

A pistol shot rang out from shore, echoing along the shoreline. We looked to see a flag hoist on the cutter's mast. Hewitt hailed us from the maintop.

"Signal from the captain. First hoist. Solid blue field. They've found Silva! Second hoist. White X on red field. Surgeon stand-by."

Nary was quick to point out that we have no surgeon.

"No. Just Elo. Go you and fetch him"

He left me me standing at the fife rail with Lorca. I asked him to explain more about Binta's knots.

"That knot, just there ... that is *yoolee*. Means someone sneaks. And the next. . . the one Binta calls *aro*. I do not know it. But *muta* ..."

Nary returned with Elo.

"Someone injured?"

"We don't know. The cutter's signaled for you to stand by."

I turned to Lorca. "Now then, this knot ... what did you call it?"

"*Muta*. That is abduct."

"Abduct?"

"Do you mean ... capture?"

"Think so."

"Say no more. We'll wait for the captain. I'm sure he'll want to hear this. Wells, where's the girl now?"

"Below decks, Mr. Harriet."

"Bring her here."

We waited overlong, and I was about to send someone looking for Wells. Finally, he returned, but only with a sorrowful look, and not with the girl.

I'm sorry, Mr. Harriet, but I can't find her and no one seems to know where she's got to."

I thought to tell him never to apologize, but only try to do better. Instead, I just asked where he'd looked.

"Everywhere. Even the chain locker."

"I doubt you've looked everywhere so keep looking. I'll look, as well."

I went below, not knowing where to start. She could be anywhere. Nary said she was small, and might hide in any narrow space. I began at the head timbers, working my way aft along the gun deck. It seemed a pointless effort, for there were many places to remain unseen. Then, as I approached the galley I heard it ... the Sukiyama.

I wondered if the sound was true. I sensed no danger, or any threat, but then it came once more. Insistent, and leading me to Lorca's cook stove. I stared at the thing, recalling my first night aboard *Eleanor*, some four years past. I was most fearful on that night, alone, in an unknown place, and among strangers ... the night Émile Coutts came for me. I'd hidden behind that same stove, tucked between the wood bin and the firebox and hoping never to be found, for my hidey-hole was a good one, and easily overlooked. Same as now, if one didn't know where to look.

I edged toward the stove, but again sensed no danger. Not danger, but fear, though coming not from me. And then I knew. It came from Binta. And why not? She was young, younger than me when I'd hidden myself in that same space. Did this strange foreboding also warn of another one's fright, as well as some danger to me? I couldn't guess but, just then, Goodhoney's orange cat darted from behind the stove. I came close. There she crouched, tucked small and looking terrified.

"Binta?"

The sound of some foreign voice calling her name shrunk her tight to the deck. She stared up at me, eyes opened wide in panic. Nary was right. Something was wrong with her mouth. Swollen and misshapen. It hurt to look.

"Binta. Come with me."

I reached down to help her, but she shot away from the far side quick as a hare. And she ran. Not far, though, for some tar reached out and grabbed her as she dashed by. I led her to the spar deck, to Lorca, who soothed her with his kind smile.

Within the hour Praether returned with Goodwin, and with some fellow sitting alongside. I thought it might be Nino Silva, and made to observe him through my glass. An old man, wearing no hat. Bald on top. A weathered pate, white hair falling limp to his shoulders. Grey frock, worn thin. He sat erect, eyes fixed straight ahead. Eyes most queer, never blinking. Sunken and dull, as if made of pewter. It took overlong for the cutter to hook on, and when they finally came through the entry port Goodhoney took great care in guiding the man. Certain this man needed it, for when he finally came to stand firm on the deck his vacant eyes bespoke a grave misfortune. The man was blind. Goodhoney took his hand and addressed him in Portuguese, but the man stayed him.

"No, Daniel, speak English ... for the benefit of your captain."

"Of course. But first I place your hand on the main mast so you may gain your bearings. Now I will lead you to the galley. The cook has made a savoury flan. Just for you!"

When they went below I brought Binta and Lorca to Praether.

"I am very busy, Harriet. This had better be important."

"I think it is, sir. This girl's telling about her people. In language knots."

I motioned for Lorca to show Praether the string of knots.

Praether studied them, looking puzzled. "Do you mean to tell me this string of knots actually says something? Some sort of language?"

"Aye, sir. At least that's what Lorca says."

Praether eyed Lorca. "Explain what this is all about, starting with how you happen to know these knots."

Lorca explained. Once, some ten years past, he signed on with a Spanish merchant vessel, *Antigua*, a sloop of some sort, that plied the coastal trade between Peru and Chile. But the Pacific coast all along South America is treacherous, with strong westerlies driving ships onto the rocks in every season. Among them *Antigua*, with all but seven of her crew drowning in the surf.

Lorca survived, washing ashore at a fishing village. The villagers were kind in that place, and an old woman offered him a pallet. She fed him, dressed the gash in his forehead and set his broken arm. She spoke Spanish, if only some, but enough to explain the knots she tied.

"Lorca says the first knot she taught him was for a dove, sir. See a bird. Tie the knot. And so bird was the first knot Lorca tied for Binta. Then cat. Goodhoney's cat, I would guess. Eat came next. Then drink. And when her . . ."

"Yes, Harriet, I begin to understand." Praether stopped his pacing and turned to Lorca. "So you learned these knots in Peru and now you teach the girl. Why?"

Lorca grinned. "Why not?"

"See here, man. When I ask a question, I expect an answer, not another question."

I spoke up once more. "It's the hole above her mouth, sir. She can't say much."

Praether bent down to consider Binta for the first time, wincing at the sight of her gruesome face. She cried out, likely frightened by yet one more stranger repulsed by the sight of her. She spun around and ran for Lorca.

When Praether backed away, I went on, "She talks with those knots, sir. To tell her story ... telling what happened to her. To her people. The killing. How they were captured."

Praether cocked an ear. "Captured?"

"I think so, sir."

"And she has tied several strings of these knots in order to tell a story?"

"Aye, sir."

"Very well. I will question the girl at length. Bring her and Lorca to my cabin. Then fetch Goodhoney and Silva. Elo, as well. Perhaps he can do something for her."

The captain paced behind his desk, waiting for the sentry to close the cabin door. Only after it latched smart did he stop and level his glare at Goodhoney.

"I am of a mind to put you off this ship, here and now. There was no excuse for never telling me Silva was blind."

Goodhoney made to respond, but Silva spoke first.

"No excuse, sir, but a reason. Daniel didn't know my vision has failed. I saw good when he departed São Paulo."

"When did this happen?"

"Six months. My eyes, they begin the itch. Very bad itch. Very painful. A matter of days before the light starts to go dim. I still see the shapes, if only a little. And for this I am thankful."

"You may also be thankful for me permitting you to come on board now that I realize your condition. I am sorry for your malady, Silva, but I have no use for a blind man. I will allow you to remain on *Eleanor* only long enough to have my loblolly see what he can do."

Elo stepped forward. "Already examine, sir. Too late. Nothing I can do. See this before. In tropic. Tiny insect."

"Some bite ... or a sting?"

"No. Insect crawl under eyelid. Sometime one eye. Sometime maybe both. For Silva, both. Insect lay many eggs."

"Unlikely that an insect's eggs would cause blindness."

"Eggs hatch. Larvae born hungry. Eat eyeball."

"Good Christ!"

Once more Praether began pacing, his shadow passing silent through the cabin as he crossed the gallery windows. Then, of a sudden, he stopped, turning again to address Elo.

"And the girl? Can you do anything for her?"

"No. Ja. Maybe."

"Well you must try. But first I need to question her about these knots. Harriet, take all this down."

One bell sounded, marking the last dog watch. The men assembled for their ration of grog. Their banter drifted down through the gratings, along with Gleason calling cheery as he measured out shares.

"Favourable portions tonight, me beauties. Short on water, so more bite in your rum. If you have sips comin' then now's the time to call 'em in!"

Praether raised a brow, always leery of serving strong rum, but this evening there was more on his mind than the grog ration. He stepped from behind his desk to offer Binta a chair set in the middle of the cabin. She cowered small, still hiding behind Lorca. Praether motioned to him.

"You have her trust. Tell her no one will hurt her."

Lorca said nothing, but only sat in the chair himself, cooing as some dove. Binta smiled, if but weak, and came to stand by him. He showed her a length of cord. "Please talk to us." She took the cord and tied three small knots. Each one different. All strange to look at.

Lorca began. "They say who take her people."

Praether moved in once more, and Binta cried out. He looked to Elo. "She is in pain."

"Afraid of you. Maybe you step away."

"Of course."

Only then did Binta go on, tying another knot. Lorca examined it. "This the Aro knot. The one I do not know."

Silva moaned. "*Santa Mãe.*"

Praether looked his way. "Holy Mother?"

"The Aro. A band of warring tribes. Very strong on the Grain Coast. They attack the small villages, from the land of lagoons to the Gambia. Raid. Kill. Take prisoners and sell them as slaves."

Part Three: Letter of Marque

17. The Onion's hair burst into flames

aku paha. The evil palate. Elo said in Finland that's what they called Binta's mouth. And, just like on *Black Joke*, many of them believed it was a curse, and would have nothing to do with anyone who had the *Maku paha.* No doubt the people of Newbury would behave much the same, even though they'd come to accept Albert. To be sure Albert looked different, not that much, though, and the difference was one that the town could overlook. Not so with Binta, but Elo said he'd try an old Muslim remedy that might work ... some sort of incision filled with a clove of garlic that was left in place for half a day before removing it and sewing the gap shut.

A most painful procedure, and I felt relieved that when on the day of the procedure I was assigned the task of overseeing a punishment detail and ordered to swab out the chain locker. A dark hole crammed to the carlins with oakum, frayed hawsers, and a drowned rat floating in the bilge. Even so, it was better to be in the chain locker and far removed from the surgery, though even in the chain locker we still heard Binta's muffled screams.

For the next few days Lorca stayed with her at all times, cooing low, speaking her name and sponging her feverish face with fresh water. Elo came to see her whenever she slept, applying a salve to mend her cut and soothe her battered mouth. I went with him once, for I was most curious to see what he'd done. She looked shrunken and discoloured. I thought she might die.

But she did not. And within ten days Captain Praether ordered me to sit with her on the spar deck, along with Lorca and Kofi. Lorca was there to calm her, for she was still terrified, and Kofi, sent from *Black Joke* to speak in Mandinka. I would take down all she might relate, striving to make written sense of the strange knots she tied. It still pained her to speak, but she was mending, and anxious to be with Lorca. The girl breathed deep as she stood with him, taking in the freshening wind coming off the Atlantic. She wore a curious expression. I don't think she'd smelled much of the sea in her young life.

She tied her first knot. Small, nimble quick hands working the cord ... over two times, under once, then through and back around to make a small loop. Complicated, yet she made good progress, and soon gave the cord to Lorca.

"This is *suutoo*. Yes, Binta?"

She shook her head no. Kofi said that meant yes, so I asked him what *suutoo* meant.

"Mandinka word for night."

She tied the next knot.

Lorca examined it. "*Yoolee*?"

Once more she shook her head.

I looked to Kofi.

"Mean someone sneak in."

Together they went on. Binta tying a knot. Lorca naming it, then Kofi saying what it meant.

"*Saatee*, that one is village. And the next, *moofallaa*, that is kill. And ..."

"Belay. Let me take all this down."

I wrote most deliberate, with the wind shifting now, and increasing to a moderate breeze. *Eleanor* swung to her anchor and shuddered as if a living thing when she snubbed her hawser. The sand ran once through the half-hourglass, and Hewitt rang six bells of the watch, just as I finished writing. When satisfied, I cleared my throat and read it out.

"She says someone snuck into her village during the night. They killed people. They killed *babbaa*. Who, or what, is *babbaa*? And they took prisoners." I turned to Kofi. "Ask her if that's right."

He spoke but one short word, and once more she shook her head. Yes.

"Very well. Please tell more."

Another string of knots. Lorca explained them. "I see now. *Babbaa*, is father. Her father. And *muta*. That is capture."

I wrote again, careful slow, and was about to ask for more when a lookout hailed from the crosstree.

"Deck there. *Black Joke*'s raising a lengthy hoist."

Hewitt went dutiful onto the shrouds, signal book in hand, to record the hoist. When he returned to the deck, I asked him what it said.

"*Black Joke* has sighted a two-masted vessel. Hoyer thinks it's Dutch. Still hull down, but under full sail. Bearing on Cape Mesurado."

Silva came to join us on the spar deck. "Maybe calling to trade with the Aro."

I asked how he might know such a thing.

"Aro headman. He tells me."

Praether joined us. "What is his name?"

"He will not say."

"But you have met him?"

"One time. Come to coast looking for Duarte."

"Duarte?"

"Portuguese trader. But Duarte is dead."

"This head man. Describe him, if you will."

"How can I describe him? I am almost blind. Except his voice. He speaks Mandinka, but it sounds different."

"What do you mean?"

"Not his mother's tongue. But he knows I speak Mandinka, so he speaks it. He thinks I am a trader."

"Are you a trader, Silva?"

"No. But it's best if he thinks so. Otherwise he would kill me."

"Yet he does not."

"No. He needs a broker. Three days before you came here he sent word of holding prisoners. At Gbowees."

Praether turned to me. "Where is that?"

"It's a rapids, sir. On the Saint Paul River. About one mile upstream."

Silva went on. "Waiting at Gbowees for next ship to arrive."

"Does he always wait there?"

"Yes. Wait there for exchange."

"Exchange for what?"

"Strong spirit. Tobacco. Maybe *fábrica*. Always asking for muskets. Wants me to arrange."

Praether paced on the gangway, each tar standing to attention as he passed. He came full circle, then stopped to address Silva once more, "Then maybe you should arrange it."

"No. I will never again partake in the buying or selling of another human being."

"Of course not. But I wish you to participate in a scheme."

"What scheme?"

"A ruse of war, Silva, meant to undermine the Aro."

"But your country is no longer at war."

"Not with the French Republic. I grant you that, and am grateful for it, though I suspect the peace will not hold much longer."

Goodhoney stepped into the dispute. "A good excuse to wage war on the Aro, I suppose. No doubt one war's good as the next."

Praether flushed red. "You mock me for attempting to free those captured and sold into slavery? Even when they might wear the very shackles you and Silva have fashioned?"

Goodhoney countered the charge. "All the more reason, sir, to lay blame on English and Portuguese holdings. We may not have invented the slave trade, but our enterprise surely drives the industry."

"That may be so. But I remind you," Praether tapped his waistcoat. "In the pocket of this vest I bear a Letter of Marque enjoining me to wage war on slavery. If the Aro are involved in the slave trade, then I will act against them. The French may pose a threat to England's sovereignty, but I remind you, slavery is a curse upon all of humanity."

Praether bowed his head, praying, I think. Soon he went on. "Now then, where is my signals midshipman?"

Hewitt arrived double quick.

"Mr. Hewitt prepare the following hoists to *Black Joke*. Engage vessel just sighted then remain on station. Say it back, Mr. Hewitt."

Hewitt said it back.

"Very well. Send it. Someone fetch Sergeant Moran and have him report to my quarters. Harriet, tell me once more. What is the name of those rapids?"

"Gbowees, sir. On the Saint Paul River."

"Find the chart. Bring it to me."

$\maltese$

Sergeant Peachy Moran braced rigid, looking mortified of being called to the great cabin, no doubt expecting to be yelled at for committing some grievous error. Captain Praether did not raise his voice, though, but only told Moran to step to the chart table.

"Examine this chart, sergeant. It is the mouth and lower reaches of the Saint Paul River. You can see the river from my gallery." Praether pointed out the stern windows. "Just there. Become familiar with the lay of it, for tonight you and one of your men will accompany Mr. Harriet and go upstream until you reach the rapids at Gbowees." Praether tapped on the chart. "Here, at this bend."

"Aye, sir."

"This is a reconnaissance mission You must remain undetected, so move smartly, and in silence. Your objective is to confirm the presence of a prison compound. It will likely be situated downstream of the rapids. Do not engage. Just make a count of how many guard the compound. Mr. Harriet will command a cutter and will land you below the rapids. Return at first light. Questions?"

"No, sir."

"Then go you now. Select your best man. And you, Mr. Harriet, for this mission I offer the use of your uncle's pistol. I suggest you accept it. Then inform Gleason to prepare a cutter."

$\maltese$

I stood at the port davits watching as Gleason prepared *Eleanor*'s second cutter, a boat not used so far on this voyage. I recalled the last time I was put in command of a ship's boat. Not a cutter though, but only a small sampan in the Mekong Delta, and I was not in charge of a landing party, just one other man. A small command, no doubt of that, and worthy of no more than a midshipmen's experience and skill. Even so, the sampan had sunk instanter, sore in need of a fresh caulk. I vowed never to let that happen again.

"Gleason, when was the last time this boat was caulked?"

"Portsmouth, Mr. Harriet."

"Then before you sway it out, I want you to pump the thing full of sea water. I must know if it leaks."

Gleason pumped the boat full to the gunnels, and we observed for five minutes.

"She's sound, Mr. Harriet. Permission to pump it dry?"

"Yes. Who have you chosen for oarsmen?"

He named eight men.

"The captain says I may have an extra four oarsmen."

"No room for a squad of marines then."

"No squad. Only Sergeant Moran and Corporal Dobbs. We'll be headed upstream against a strong current and the men will need to rest, but I can't rest them all at once. I'll need the extra oarsmen to rotate turns. So give me four more of your best."

"Aye, Mr. Harriet."

"Have Lorca feed them. We depart with the morning watch."

I went below. The midshipmen's mess was deserted. I lay in my berth, resting up for the mission. Goodhoney's orange cat came to see me, to see if I might have something for him. I didn't, so he went off. Five bells of the middle watch. Two thirty in the morning. I snuffed my taper, trying for sleep. But sleep would never come, and I knew as much, so I lay there trying not to think of previous missions. Trying not to think of them, and so recalling them clear.

The first ... a cutting out action on Minorca, and with no good outcome. I reached instinctive for the scar above my left eye. The graze of pistol shot fired in the night. And, later that same night, in the hill country above Port Mahon, captured by the resistance. And though I escaped, the mission was deemed a failure.

The second mission ... a reconnaissance on the Mekong River, sent to discover the whereabouts of a French corsair. Théophile Oignon. The Onion. I rubbed the stub of my missing finger. Shot away by the Onion soon after he captured our river junk. One more escape. And one more dismal effort.

Twice failed. So why would Captain Praether send me on a third? It's a given that every man is expendable in the Royal Navy, and I was no more than a lowly midshipman, so therefore more expendable than most. Perhaps it mattered not overmuch if I returned. Who would miss me? Who would care? Becca. She would care. I'd not thought of her in a while. But now I recalled our last night together. In Newbury. In her home. In her bed. That night she'd promised never to forget me. But if I became killed, or went missing, how would she ever know?

One bell of the morning watch. Time to make ready.

⚡

No moon. A dead calm on the water but, direct above, storm clouds raced on a high wind, at times cloaking the stars, at times revealing them. There, Rigel. And there, Betelgeuse. Brightest stars of Orion. Low in the sky now, just off our prow. We passed soundless on the river, thole pins well-greased, oars muffled and plying the water in measured silence. Some night animal splashing heavy as it entered the river. Unknown smells, a malodorous fug stinking of rot, but with one smell standing out, if only for its fragrance. Likely some night-blooming flower. All proof of a shifting, though unseen terrain, and affirming our steady progress. Time to check our bearings.

I whispered a command. "Unsheathe your knife, sergeant."

The muffled snick of a blade drawn smart. I held forth my compass. "Reflect the starlight off your blade and onto my compass."

A good thing Moran kept his kit in order, with his knife honed razor sharp and glinting in the night. A dim glow, but enough to take a bearing.

"South by southwest."

Moran growled low. "None easterly?" He spat his quid overboard. "Bloody lost."

"I think not. The river doubles back twice below the rapids. When we reach the bend, that's when Orion will come astern. I'll keep us in the channel. You listen for the rapids."

Just at the bend, but still below the rapids, we heard the hollow beat of a drum, with voices raised in a chant.

Moran whispered under his breath. "Don't sound like no prison compound."

The drum beat steady as we made upriver, until we caught sight of a small fire, set back from the bank, with figures standing around it. The oarsmen struggled overmuch now, making little headway against the increasing current. No matter, for we heard the rapids now, and I steered for the near shore, not ten yards to port. Close by, yet no more than a deeper shadow standing out from the rest. The bowman cast his line, missing with his first try, but grappling on a tree with the next. He pulled us in taut and secured his line. I withdrew my pistol, placed it nearby, and gave final word.

"Go. We'll wait here."

Moran fixed me in a dark stare. "See that you do."

He went direct over the gunnel and onto the bank, followed by Dobbs. Each of them consumed, one before the next, by some dark, hungry presence.

I didn't like Moran's parting remark, no doubt meant to remind me of *Eleanor*'s reputation among marines for leaving her own marines stranded onshore. It happened once, but once only, and on that same mission I was left behind, as well. On Minorca. Left behind by William Pogue, *Eleanor*'s midshipman in charge of the cutter sent to raid a farm. Not one year later Pogue stood before a firing squad, to be executed for his actions on that night. Heart shot out by marines chosen by Fleet Admiral Sley. The same marines Pogue had abandoned when he fled in the cutter. I vowed to die before I left Moran and his men behind.

The bowman was first to see it as we sat in the cutter, waiting anxious for the marines to return. A faint light, coming not from the fire set back from the river, but from somewhere above it. I thumbed my pistol to half-cock, watching some glow rising in the pitch black. A lantern? Not likely. So I listened for any sound, for a warning of what it might be. Listening for the Sukiyama, as well, for now the thing grew larger, an unknown threat heading for us direct. A most large object, spread wide as any topsail. I'd not ever seen such a thing, a glowing shape, adrift and floating as some low cloud. Of a sudden the drum stopped and the singing died away. I heard a voice, whispering low. Coming not from the Sukiyama, but from the strange radiance now hovering not twenty feet above us. A prodigious globe of some sort, entrapped in a great fishnet, with a wicker basket slung from a teeming array of cordage. A basket large enough to carry a small fire on board, its flames licking at the air, sending white smoke rising around the globe. A basket large enough to carry a man, though a man as yet unrevealed, but who now called down to us.

"You are from that ship in the bay. Yes?"

The oarsmen sat petrified, gripping their oars tight, stunned first by the apparition floating above us, and now by some unknown voice. The bowman called out sharp.

"Should I cast off?"

"No. Not without Moran and his men."

Another oarsman cried out. "Shoot it!"

"As you were," I hissed, even while drawing my hammer full back.

I called into the darkness. "Stand fast and say who you are."

A hurried response. "Nothing to fear. I am unarmed. A *tête-à-tête*, perhaps?"

French. A feather's touch ran cold along my spine and my missing finger throbbed, for now the voice rang familiar.

"Say your name."

No reply.

"Show yourself or I'll shoot you."

"I shall. But first you must wait. I am unfamiliar with this god machine."

Some dry rattle came from inside the wicker, and just as I made ready to fire, his voice called out merry.

"Ah! Yes, here we go then."

A rope ladder dropped from the basket, and a narrow man inched down. He wore no shoes. Left foot painted blue. Right foot painted red. Naked, but for a breech clout and a thin coat of whitewash. Red hair, long, and snarled as if some nest of snakes.

An oarsman whispered, "Ghost."

Another moaned, "Oh Mum. Oh Mum."

"Shut your mouths," I ordered. "He's no ghost. He wears a costume meant to terrify any fool witless enough to be taken in."

"Who is he?"

"Théophile Oignon. The Onion. The man who shot away my finger."

"Harriet? *Est-ce vous?* But yes, now I recall. It was your little finger, as I recall. Left hand. Still missing, is it?"

The Onion laughed maniacal, then stepped on the next rung, but caught his blue foot. The ladder swayed out and tilted the basket, if only slight, but enough for the small fire to light on the wicker. The cordage caught next, with flames creeping onto the netting. The globe caught fire instanter, and the ladder caught next. The Onion's hair burst into flames. Except it was only a wig, which he flung away just as the rope burned through, and he pitched headlong into the river.

No one cared overmuch if the Onion went in, for we watched aghast as the ladder burned away complete and the globe soared glorious into the night. Not for long. The fire leapt hungry, reaching for the lower skirt of the globe and consuming the whole thing at once, lighting the darkness in a wondrous display of crackling embers floating on the updrafts and drifting over the jungle.

The Onion coughed and sputtered as he struggled in the river, trying to reach us before becoming drowned, or taken under by some unseen creature. No one threw a line or offered to help. Instead, we only watched, all leery of his approach. Finally, he hooked an arm over the transom and stared up at me. Defenseless, yet with defiance glinting in his eyes. The man who'd run amok in the Indochine, who creased my left eye with a pistol shot fired at

Artesian Gate. Who killed Captain Cedric, my uncle, whose Prélat I now held. How fitting ... to dispatch this demon with my uncle's weapon. I brought the piece level, taking careful aim at the space between his eyes. Hammer still at full cock, my finger stroking the trigger and eager to test its pull. And yet . . .

I'll not ever know if I might have sent the hammer down, for just then Sergeant Moran hailed us from shore. I lit a glim. He stood not ten feet away, bearing the severed head of Corporal Dobbs.

18. The more things change

I sent every man ashore to help search for the rest of Dobbs. Moran secured the Onion to a cleat and I remained in the cutter, keeping guard over him. I lit a taper and brought the light close to his face. In the Mekong, he'd claimed never to change his name, only his look. Now his disguise had been washed away in the river to reveal him plain. This was the first I'd ever seen his true face. Difficult to read yet, at the same time, without airs. Coal black hair, cut short. High forehead with thin brows and staring eyes, dark, and set narrow. A nose pinched thin. Broken once, I think. High cheekbones. Colourless lips, and a tapering chin. He stared at me unblinking, then announced in his mocking tone.

"*Plus ça change, plus c'est la même chose.*"

"Speak English."

"The more things change, the more they stay the same."

"Now shut your mouth."

But I knew he would not. On the Mekong he'd talked near constant, and in this place he'd do much the same.

"I wonder, Harriet, how it is that you have come to this godforsaken river. But, even more, I wonder this ... did you hear it? On the river, just below the bend. Did you here it? You told me once you always heard it when there was a threat nearby."

The Sukiyma. I'd not told him of it, not ever. How could he know?

When I said nothing, he shifted awkward on the thwarts, examining his wrists. "I am unhappy. I did not expect this. To be trussed as a prisoner. Tied perhaps, but not bound so tightly. There is much discomfort."

To be sure there was discomfort, for Moran had bound his wrists with a slip knot. A thin cord, but strong, and cinched over tight. The Onion waited expectant for me to loosen his bonds. When I failed to oblige he only shrugged, and went on.

"You may not recall. We were on the Mekong." He looked around. "In such a stretch as this. The silent monk had given you medicine to relieve the pain of your missing finger. Too much medicine. You lapsed into a coma."

In the trees nearby some monkey screeched, and a flock of doves took flight across the river.

"It was then that you spoke it. The Sukiyama."

"I said shut your mouth or I'll shoot you."

"No. There is something you want to ask me. But if you kill me then you will never know."

Some animal stirred in the bush. A nightjar called. In the distance I heard Moran's voice. When Moran circled back, I told him to gag the Onion. I would still see his face but at least now he could no longer taunt. The search for Dobbs continued, but with no luck. I vowed to press on, at least until dawn.

Not long before first light we saw two white rockets rising simultaneous. Low in the west, just above the tree line, and likely coming from offshore. Moran came to ask what it was. I gave him the taper while I paged through my code book.

"Here it is. All white flares originate from *Black Joke*. Two white flares sent up together means they've lost contact with the ship they were pursuing. Not meant for us. Ignore it."

Moran pointed over my shoulder. "Look."

I turned to see one blue rocket climbing the night sky. Much closer, but still half a mile distant. I looked once more in the book.

"Blue rockets originate from *Eleanor*. Sending up just one means to carry on."

"Meant for us?"

"I don't think so. But we'll do as it says anyway. Carry on."

Moran led the men for another hour before returning to the cutter. Still nothing. He waited for me to speak, for me to be the one who called off the search. But I did not.

"We'll search for half an hour more. I don't want to leave Dobbs behind, but I have orders to return at first light. We'll be late, even as it is."

He nodded, looking grim, then led the search party back into the jungle. They returned without Dobbs. Moran stood silent, knee deep in the river, observing the tunic he'd spread across the head of his marine. I gave the order. We cast off, bound for *Eleanor*.

As eight bells of the morning watch rang out we finally hooked on at *Eleanor*'s entry port. I brought the Onion direct to the midshipmen's mess to cover his shame with borrowed slops. Now the Onion stood in the light pouring through *Eleanor*'s stern windows. I stood nearby; pistol still primed should he try to set upon the captain. I studied the deck where my uncle had bled out, shot and killed by the Onion four years previous. My uncle's blood still stained the deck, no matter how often Gleason holystoned the spot. The Onion strode across it, affording it not one look, but only clearing his throat before addressing Praether.

"Some would find it ironic, captain, for you and me to stand here in this cabin."

"You refer to our encounters in the Levant and then the Indochine. And that now, due to the treaty between our two nations we must try not to destroy one another. Tell me, how do you regard this meeting? Mere happenstance?"

"Nothing is by chance. I consider this audience as ... timely." He shrugged, if but slight. "Fated, perhaps." He frowned thoughtful. "Well, perhaps not fate, after all, but only the result of my sergeant's excellent night vision. He was the first to spot a cutter on the river heading for Gbowees."

"And you knew the cutter was from *Eleanor*?"

"Not at all. Only that it was sent from a frigate that, for some reason unknown to me, was trying to masquerade as a slave ship." The Onion frowned. "Why is that, captain?"

"I am not at liberty to discuss it, only that I operate under a Letter of Marque. Tell me why you were on the river."

"Of course. Since the cutter was headed for Gbowees I thought it was a chance for me to make contact."

"For what purpose?"

The Onion scoffed. "Do you think The One Body is the only crusade intent upon returning free slaves to Africa?"

"You are no more than an interloper, and to suggest that you have lately become an abolitionist is an insult."

"I have always been a champion of liberty."

"Nonsense. You are a mercenary, here for your own aggrandizement."

"And you, captain? Does not your Letter of Marque provide for your own enhancement?"

Praether coloured pink, a sure sign of his pique. "No. You are a paid assassin who in the past has committed unspeakable crimes. Now you proclaim to be one of us."

"But they were crimes committed in the defense of liberty, equality and . . ."

"Rubbish. I refuse to believe that it is your regard for equality that brings you to Cape Mesurado."

"I am not concerned with what you believe. But the fact remains, I have known of Cape Mesurado for ten years, ever since Louverture rose in rebellion on Saint-Domingue. I knew him at Gonaïves and we discussed Cape Mesurado as an option, should his uprising fail. He rejected the notion, but I did not, and came here when I heard news of Amiens. I remind you. I am no longer Napoleon's corsair, nor do I hold a commission in the *Marine Nationale*. I am free to operate as a free agent."

Praether's face soured. "I suspect you are involved with the Aro."

"I am. But just to rout them."

"What do you mean?"

"Just this. Five years ago, I deployed from Saint-Nazaire in command of a frigate ..."

"*Marat.*"

"Yes. *Marat.* A fine warship. Fast." He looked around. "Somewhat faster than *Eleanor,* and I would have overtaken her if not for the exceptional performance of your long guns. Some day you must tell me how you achieved such range and accuracy."

"Never. Get on with it."

"As you wish. While at Saint-Nazaire I also recruited one hundred nonpartisans. *Mon corps expéditionnaire.* Prussian and Swiss, mostly, but English, as well. I admit, a force of one hundred men has its limitations. But I had convinced the Emperor that one hundred well trained, well equipped, and highly motivated men fit my needs quite well. Easily transported and, once landed, they move quickly, and undetected. Inexpensive, as well. I equipped and trained them out of my own purse."

Praether discounted the concept. "A privateer in command of his own small army."

"An army eager to deploy. First Minorca. Then the Levant. And on to the Indochine. Regrettably, the mission took its toll. Typhus on Minorca. The loss of *Marat* at Amunia. Jungle fever on the Mekong. But for my sergeant, the rest of my expedition went missing at Song Mao. I had no choice but to withdraw from the Indochine."

"Your withdrawal was my intention."

"Yes." The Onion arched a narrow brow. "But what was it your Shakespeare said? A hit. A palpable hit. Yet not quite fatal." The Onion paused in thought, with a sulking expression at work on his face. "In this life is one not permitted to be of two minds? Or perhaps even more than of two minds?"

Praether began to pace, his boots ringing on the deck. The only sound in the great cabin, until he came to a stop square in front of the Onion. "Who beheaded Corporal Dobbs?"

"The Aro. They roam at will, and kill as they please."

"And you are complicit."

"I played no part in it. England and France are no longer at war."

"So now intend to wage war on the Aro?"

"Of course. But I can't risk engaging them on my own. Even though their weapons are primitive they have an unknown reserve of warriors. If any free slaves are to be landed at Cape Mesurado then the Aro must first be eliminated."

Praether turned to me. "He was in the hot air balloon that went up in flames?"

"I don't know what it was, sir, but the Onion was in it, and certain it went up in flames."

I wished the Onion had caught fire, as well, but knew better than to say it.

"Ah yes ... *la Globe Aérostatique*. A silk design of the Montgolfier brothers. Did you know that I brought the silk with me from the

Indochine and built it here, on my own?" The Onion sighed. "A pity to see such a beautiful creation consumed in fire."

On deck, the topsails luffed overloud. Praether paid heed, then resumed the discussion. "Why did you approach us in this way?"

The Onion shrugged. "At first the Aro thought I was only a trader. Only here to buy their goods. But so far we have not conducted business and now they begin to suspect my intentions. They watch me, and for me to approach you directly would raise an alarm. However, they are very superstitious. They ran like roaches when I rose in *la Globe* deep into the night. Quite amusing."

Hewitt knocked on the cabin door and stepped through. "Lieutenant Japhet sends his compliments, sir, and asks permission to go on the starboard tack."

Praether concurred, then once more addressed the Onion. "So now you mean to ask for our assistance."

"Such is my desire."

"I mistrust your desires. They come from a depraved mind. But, even though it galls, I find myself in agreement with you. The Aro must be reduced."

"If you doubt my desires then I invite you to at least confirm my intentions. Ask the Portuguese exile. He will verify that I have assumed the role of a trader."

"Very well. Mr. Harriet, fetch Silva."

I pressed the Prélat into his hand. "Take it, sir. I think you shouldn't be unarmed with this man in your quarters It belongs to you, anyway."

"I will." He took his Prélat. "Send in the sentry, as well. He will stand his post in here until you return."

I found Silva on the gun deck, along with Goodhoney, and led them both to Praether.

"Now then, Silva, there is another man in my quarters. Théophile Oignon. Mr. Harriet knows him as the Onion. Do you know him?"

Silva turned up his palms. "How do I know a person I can't see? But a voice ... by that I might place him."

The Onion spoke in English. "Of course. I am sure you recognize it. We have talked more than once."

Silva frowned. "My English is not good. But this voice, I know. It belongs to the new agent for the Aro ... since the last one has gone missing."

Praether aimed his pistol at the Onion. "If you are saying this man is in collusion with the Aro then I will shoot him here and now."

Yes. Do it. Shoot him here and now ... not three paces from where he shot my uncle.

The Onion only laughed, seeming indifferent to becoming killed. "My sergeant recently dispatched the former agent. He is very eager with his knife, my sergeant. Too eager, I fear. For now he's gone missing, as well. No matter, he's done this before, and has always returned to me. But, if you care to look for the agent, his body may still be floating in the bay. How opportune, don't you think ... for me to have replaced the man? Expedient, as you would say."

Praether scoffed. "Why would the Aro accept you?"

"Acceptance is not necessary, only greed."

I could no longer hold my tongue. "The Aro think he's a fire breathing demon, sir. Same as the Moi."

Once more the Onion laughed. "Ah ... the Moi. Slightly more savage than the Aro, though not as corruptible."

From the quarterdeck Japhet called to come about, and the watch stood ready to sheet their lines. Soon *Eleanor* heeled on her new tack, just as a hail came from the crosstree.

"Deck there! *Black Joke* hull down on the horizon. She's made a long hoist. Still too far for me to call it out."

Praether sent for Hewitt, and Hewitt arrived, looking pale. But the captain took no notice.

"Mr. Hewitt, go aloft with your code book and decipher *Black Joke*'s hoist. No lingering at the maintop."

Hewitt swallowed hard. "Beg pardon, sir, but, but . . ."

"Say it out, man."

Hewitt said nothing, but only ran for an open window and threw up.

Praether called out. "Good Christ. The man is sea sick."

I stepped forward. "Beg pardon, sir, but I don't think so. Going onto the shrouds makes him bilious. Certain he'll go, except he might throw up in his book. Shall I go in his place?"

"Yes, go you now."

I climbed on to the shrouds, nodding to the mast captain as he stood at the maintop. He reminded me never to look up, only down. I agreed, then climbed for the crosstree. *Eleanor*'s main mast swept the sky. The rigging stretched taut, the block and tackle straining. I looked down, hanging direct above the sea, near two hundred feet below. A gull hovered nearby, shrieking. I shrieked back, telling the thing never to look up, only down, then wrapped one leg around the royal mast and hooked an elbow through its deadeyes. *Black Joke* was no longer hull down. The wind blew a fresh breeze across her quarter, and her flag hoist stood out distinct. I took great care in writing it all down, then returned to the spar deck. Praether had come from the great cabin and stood waiting.

"They've taken the chase, sir. It's *Cycloop*. A gaff-rigged brig. Dutch slaver out of Rotterdam. No human cargo. She's been holed below the waterline. Hoyer asks for the carpenter."

The captain grinned. "Outstanding. Tell Hoyer to send me *Cycloop*'s captain." When the Onion joined us Praether narrowed his eyes. "Are you aware that Admiralty House has placed a bounty on your head."

The Onion feigned a laugh. "I am honoured. Tell me, what am I worth? Did you know the Consulate has set a price on your head, as well? Ten thousand francs. Perhaps I'm worth more. I must go below now and conjure a plan."

"Stay where you are." Praether paced on the companionway, then came to stop before the Onion. "Semyon. What happened to him?"

"Ah, that would be the private agent of King George."

"Harriet says he last saw Semyon with you. You were torturing the man."

"To save him."

"Do not mistake me for a fool. You were trying to extract information."

"I confess. I may have questioned him."

"He was privy to military intelligence. What did he tell you?"

The Onion shrugged. "Nothing. Not even at the end."

Praether raised a brow.

"Oh, I forgot. Semyon is dead. I buried him at Pleiku." A dark look. "I wonder. Did he have a wife? Some paramour? Perhaps a *mére*, longing to know what became of her son? She was with him at the end, you know ... at least in his thoughts. May I give you his last words?" He didn't wait for an answer. "'Please forgive me, mother.' Touching. I can only wish to have a similar experience when they pass judgement on my own misdeeds." He held a hand over his heart. "I have squandered my life, *mon gentil mére*. But I could not help it."

He sighed deep, looking regretful. Another mock, and Praether knew it. He rolled his eyes disdainful, even as the Onion spewed forth.

"I placed a marker on Semyon's grave. A small crucifix. But the jungle is ravenous. It consumes all. I will provide the location if you wish."

"I do not care where you buried the man. I want to know what you asked him."

The Onion raised a brow. "I never asked Semyon what he knew of fleet strength or deployment, if that's what you mean. Only about King George. His madness."

Praether shifted uneasy. "His Majesty is not mad."

"Of course not. At least not always. But Semyon knew him personally, and I pressed him for details."

"First you shot him."

"I didn't mean it. My aim is unpredictable. Forgive me."

"Then you tortured him."

"The ball shattered his ankle. *La gangrène* had set in. He was in agony. When I dressed his wound, it caused unbearable pain. I suppose that's when I would ask how well he knew King George."

"What, exactly, did you ask him?"

"Only if the rumor was true. And if it was true, then how often did the king lapse into madness. How long the spells would last, and if they could be foretold."

"Information to use against the Second Coalition."

"Of course. Except now there is no Coalition ... now that the

Treaty is in effect. No matter. Semyon was incoherent. He gave me nothing. Do you hold me accountable for his ruination?"

Praether tugged at his waistcoat. "I have recently reviewed the provisions set forth at Amiens. It appears that despite the bounty on your head, the terms prohibit me from holding you as a prisoner of war. But know you this. His Majesty, who you have just accused of being mad, considers this peace no more than an experiment."

The Onion nodded. "A doomed experiment, I fear."

"We shall see. But for now there exists an agreement between England and France, so it is our duty to uphold it. I do not know if Cape Mesurado is the best location to establish a free state. However, the two hundred souls on board *Black Joke* have waited too long. I have treated them like children. But they are not, and this is where they come ashore."

"Then you can expect the Aro to resist."

Instead of responding, Praether gestured for me to walk with him. We stepped downwind so the Onion couldn't hear. "He is not to be trusted. Take him below and confine him to the purser's quarters. Post a guard at the door."

Certain I would do it, though I wanted nothing more to do with him. I despised the man for his deliberate cruelty, and now felt my hatred boiling over. But then another feeling rose, from yet a deeper place. Shame. And dishonour. Mum said it was a sin to hate anyone. And now, to hate the Onion ... it would dishonour her life. And to shame Mum, that was an act I despised more than my contempt for the Onion. Of a sudden I recalled the incident at Dog Island.

No longer was I on board *Eleanor,* but standing once again in a dark stairwell looking down on a landing lit by the dim glow of a streetlamp pouring through a small window. I'd stood there once before, in some sort of lucid dream, but then, and of a sudden, shifting to a sunlit room with an open window and a pleasant breeze bearing the scent of lilac. Once more, the young man sitting at a desk. The last time he'd been writing. This time he only sat there looking my way. Except he didn't see, but was seeing straight through me. He stood and walked past me. I followed him into the adjoining room, a small and narrow space, with a couch covered in red baize. Two pillows. One shaped firm. The other split open and misshapen. The young man took the ruined pillow in both hands and slammed it on the wall. Again. And again. Until a woman came to stand at the door.

"Théo, my troubled son, what causes so much rage in you? Come to dinner now. I've made a nice *quenelle*."

Théophile set the pillow down, placing it just so. He walked to the door and joined his Mum but, before he passed, he turned to me. This time he saw me, and grinned demonic.

A most puzzling event, to be sure, and I'd recorded the matter in my ledger the next morning, at Mrs. Dolan's, hoping the incident might become clear, if I but wrote it down. No chance of that. And only now did it strike me ... that same ledger was now stowed in the purser's cabin. Well-hidden but, just the same, I must find another place to conceal it. The Onion, by his own admission, was unpredictable. And Captain Praether had his measure ... the man was not to be trusted. If anyone might find that ledger then surely it was the Onion. I should have killed him on the river. Or shot him grievous, just as he shot Semyon, and left him for the centipedes. Just then Praether tapped on my shoulder to disrupt my rumination.

"Mr. Harriet, pull yourself together."

I thought to give my standard response. Never to apologize, only strive to do better. Except it wasn't true. I could never strive to improve upon a thing that lay so far beyond my understanding. I might try to explain, but knew Praether would have none of it, so I let it pass and came to attention.

"Now then, repeat the orders I just gave you. I must know you understand what I want you to do."

I said them back.

"Very well. Check to make sure Oignon is locked in the purser's quarters."

I made direct for it, hoping to remove my ledger before the Onion might find it. I wanted to bring it to Elo for safe keeping. But the purser's door was locked, and I heard the Onion within. The man was reciting some French idyll. I dared not look for my ledger, not with him watching over me. I must wait to retrieve it, but I'd seek out Elo, just the same. Not for a potion, or for a cure, but for his steadfast presence, and to help me dispell this mare's nest.

Cycloop's captain was Ludo van Beek. A squat fellow, near fifty, grey hair, and a high forehead with a thick cowlick above his left ear. White brows arched high over watery blue eyes. He wore a stained brown frock, threadbare and of poor quality. His cracked wooden sabots knocked on the deck as he stood shifting his weight in *Eleanor*'s great cabin. Van Beek spoke English. And he spoke it slow enough for me record his remarks in The One Body's ledger. The questioning began with Praether's first concern.

"How is it you speak English?"

"Must. Only Dutch speak Dutch. Also, many years I serve on John Company vessel."

"Do you own *Cycloop*?"

"*Nee.*"

"Who owns it?"

"Cloth Guild. Amsterdam."

"Does this guild invest in the triangular trade?"

"Ja."

"Cotton?"

"Ja."

"From where?"

"Sea islands."

"Are you also invested?"

"Nee."

"But as its captain you have brought this ship here to barter for slaves and transport them on to Dakar."

"Ja."

"What is in your hold?"

Van Beek shifted once more. "Dutch trade muskets from Antwerp. Powder and shot from Naaldwijk Munitie, in Rotterdam."

"An unholy cargo. Also, illicit."

"I do not wish to be in the slave business, sir, but since the peace your navy has placed many of its officers on half-pay. Now John

Company has a long list to choose from."

"So they chose to pay you off."

"Last September. Now wife and son very sick." Van Beek bowed his head. "I have no wish to be a slaver, but I am destitute. I have no choice."

"Nonsense. One always has a choice."

"Ja. Two choices. The Guild owns the house we live in. If I choose not to sail, they put us out. If I choose to sail, they let us stay, and provide the stipend for my wife when I am at sea." Van Beek gestured with open hands. "Sea is what I know, so I take command of *Cycloop*."

"And now I will set it on fire and watch the thing blow up."

"Please ... take my men off."

"Of course. How many?"

"Twelve."

"I will press the lot."

"No. If I ask them to go with you, then they will go willingly."

Praether ordered van Beek led away, then turned to me.

"Make fair copy of his statement. Do it now. I wish to review it while the impressions are still fresh."

I enjoyed making fair copy, but this time I laboured with the task. I felt ill, or at least still benumbed by the Onion's reemergence. But I would not allow my disquiet to once more be the source of Praether's annoyance. To calm myself, I would concentrate. The steady scratch of the quill tracing methodic across the ledger helped put my mind at ease. And even more so when I came to record the number of men on board *Cycloop*. Twelve ... a number expressed by the numerals one and two. I could not but recall my family of numerals and knew they would relieve my anxious state. I saw them as a troop, once more coming to play Newbury Fair, and rehearsing their curious skit on the greensward. Here comes One, the smallest of them all ... no more than an infant. Two walks at his side. A kind number, always taking extra care of One. But now comes Three.

Willful, and disparate. Yet an angel of mercy ... when compared to the Onion. Enough! I could not shed the man's specter, and jerked in some sort of spasm, tipping my pot of ink. By chance the spill ran away from the ledger, and not toward it. Good fortune, as well, for I'd managed to soak the ink in my kerchief before it spilled to the deck. Even though Praether failed to notice my gaffe, this would never do. I made the last entry, blotted the page and returned the quill to its cabinet. Then sat with a purpose, waiting for Praether to dismiss me so that I might visit Elo. Except he didn't, at least not without additional orders.

"Lieutenant Strayhorne will take the barge and remove *Cycloop*'s crew. Lieutenant Fagen will follow in the longboat and prepare the slaver for demolition. He is ready to embark, and I want you to assist him. Go you now."

19. Rumor

I stood with Lieutenant Fagen on *Cycloop*'s quarterdeck observing the dinghy making direct for us, sent from *Black Joke*.

Fagen trained his glass. "Ajax at the tiller. Hoyer sends him. Claims the man is experienced with explosives."

I'd not thought much about Ajax since he'd gone with *Black Joke*, and now a question arose. Did he know the Onion was at Cape Mesurado, and now on board *Eleanor*? Likely he did. Shipmates are bound to spread any news, and this news would never go well with Ajax.

"Permission to meet Ajax at the entry port, sir."

"No." He snapped shut his scope. "Below a midshipmen's station to receive a rating at the entry port."

"I don't mean to speak out of turn, sir, but if Ajax doesn't know about the Onion then I think it would be best if I'm the one who tells him."

"Why?"

"Ajax was Captain Cedric's steward, sir, when the Onion killed him."

"Make your point. I have orders to blow up this ship and Praether wants it done smartly."

"It's just that Ajax and me ... we were the ones nearby, sir, when my uncle was killed. It was most awful. Ajax took it bad as me."

"As he should. A steward's first duty is to protect the captain."

I heard Ajax call out to ship oars. The bowman cast his line, and drew the boat in.

"Except now he might want to kill the Onion, to make amends."

Fagen scoffed. "I say let him. Ajax is the biggest seaman I've ever seen. He could break the Onion's back over his knee. And why not? No one trusts the Frog."

"No, sir. But I think Captain Praether wants to keep the Onion alive."

"No doubt to use against the Aro."

"And there was a price on his head, once. Maybe Captain Praether thinks there will be again."

"Bounty's the same. Dead or alive."

"But it's better luck to question someone when they're still alive, sir."

"Mind your tongue, Harriet. You speak out of turn."

"Aye, sir. I could also remind him that you're on board and in command of the operation, sir."

He began pacing on the companionway, trying, I think, to imitate Praether's manner. "Very well, meet him at the entry port."

A signal gun barked. We turned to watch a hoist from *Eleanor*.

Fagen groused. "Oh bloody hell. Praether wants to know what's keeping me. So be quick about it. I want you and Ajax on the orlop in five minutes. Reel off forty feet of slow match, and fifty of the quick. Run the cord through the orlop, straight to the powder. Go."

I met Ajax as he came on board. He appraised me with his grey, wide-set eyes. If he was pleased to see me, it didn't show. Not overmuch, at least. But at least he asked why I stood there doing nothing ... a familiar sign that he was only a bit displeased to see me. I thought better of telling him about Fagen being on board and in command. He'd know soon enough, so went to my own purpose for meeting him at the entry port.

"I've come to tell you a thing."

"The Onion."

"Then you know."

"Aye."

"What will you do?"

"I ask you the same."

I hardly knew, yet once more failed to mind my tongue, and the words spilled out. "I've become a fair decent shot with my uncle's Prélat."

"You are the worst shot in this navy. And we both know you wouldn't do it."

"Then I ask you not to bother with him. It would do neither of us any good."

Fagen called from aft. "Mr. Harriet! You and Ajax go below."

✦

Ajax stood in the orlop with his head bowed to prevent knocking on the beams, waiting while I made a count.

"Twenty trade muskets. Dutch made. Three canvas sacks marked as lead shot. Six kegs marked as black powder."

Ajax sniffed the close air, frowning. "That much powder should make my nose itch. Check the date."

Every keg was marked with the same milling date:

lotnummer: 51D-16

Naaldwijk Munitie, Rotterdam,

'01 juli

A date recent enough for the powder to still be fresh.

"It seems in order, Ajax. We best get on with it. Fagen won't like it if things aren't in place."

He raised a brow, just as Fagen came below.

"You take too long."

The deck creaked as Ajax shifted his prodigious weight. "Sir, I think we should open these kegs to see what's in 'em. They're of a proper weight, but . . ."

"Too risky. I won't open a keg until the fuse is ready to be inserted."

Gleason joined us. "Beg pardon, sir. Lieutenant Strayhorne's about to remove *Cycloop*'s crew and he needs your signature on the manifest."

When Fagen went on deck I asked Ajax what was the matter.

"Nothing."

"But if you think something's the matter, well, I don't wish to become blown up."

Ajax smiled, if but slight. "No one will be blown up. At least not by this lot. But we'll do as Fagen ordered, just the same. Reel out the slow match and string it on the companionway. I'll splice on the quick fuse and lead it to the kegs."

Fagen returned just as we finished. "We're the last on board. Get in the cutter and wait with Gleason. I'll make a final inspection, then touch it off." He studied the sky through the grating. "Harriet, give me your magnifying glass."

I gave Fagen my lens, then Ajax and I made smart for the entry port. Ajax secured the end of the fuse to a cleat and we went down into the cutter, looking up just as Fagen came to the rail.

"Harriet, mark the time."

"Fourteen minutes after one, sir."

Fagen focused the magnifying glass on the fuse. It caught instanter. He watched to make sure, then scrambled down, nodding to Gleason.

Gleason wasted no time. "Bowman, gaff us off. All oars in. Now heave, me lovelies. Handsomely!"

We made handsome indeed, and for all of a thousand feet, until we shipped oars and waited in *Eleanor*'s lee, still sitting in the cutter to witness *Cycloop*'s great explosion. Above us, the Eleanors lined the port rail, or climbed on to the shrouds, all of them keen for the great event, and all hard pressed to wager on just when *Cycloop* would erupt.

"Two sips says she goes off at one and thirty-nine."

"I'll take that, and say one and forty-four."

"I say we're too close. One sip if her dead fall hits us."

More wagers on how far any piece might fly.

"Five hundred feet. No more."

"No. She'll blow straight up and down. Seen it before."

"Where?"

"Jamaica Station. Took a Frog corvette and blew out her bottom with her own gun powder."

"How long now?"

I called out. "Ten more minutes."

Wat came on deck, fid still in hand. "Keep a steady watch. Fuses burn none alike."

I called out again. "Five more minutes."

At one minute to go all banter stopped, with each man shifting nervous, working his quid and waiting expectant for ... expectant for . . .

Fagen cleared his throat. "Mark the time, Mr. Harriet."

"Thirty-nine minutes past one, sir."

He turned to Ajax. "A twenty-minute burn, did you say?"

"Aye, sir. About that."

"Delayed fuse, then. Should be soon."

But it wasn't soon. Or at all.

Another ten minutes passed. Hewitt finally came to the rail, calling down to the cutter. "Lieutenant Fagen, the captain wants to see you in his cabin, instanter. You too, Harriet."

As I passed by, Hewitt forewarned me. "Tread light. He's in a fine pique."

⚡

Fagen and I approached Praether's quarters most expeditious, barely giving the sentry time to come to attention and pass us through. The captain stood gazing out the stern windows. No wringing of hands. No pacing about. He only stood there, no doubt venting his spleen. We came to attention, and Fagen spoke.

"Reporting as ordered, sir."

Praether turned to us, glaring first at Fagen, then me. No outward sign of what he might be thinking, but likely unsettled by how this misstep would be perceived by Whitehall. They would blame Admiralty House for the failure. Then Admiralty House would disavow any knowledge of our mission, since HMS *Eleanor* operated under a Letter of Marque. Next, Captain Praether would be held accountable. Except the captain had not been present on board *Cycloop*. Lieutenant Fagen had been in charge of the operation. But Fagen would pass the blame down to me. Some might then expect me to assign blame to Ajax. He was, at least in the order of things, under my observation, if not my command.

I'd not pass it down, though. Nor would I take responsibility for the inglorious muddle we now found ourselves in. And also wondering, though I dared not speak of it, if that fuse might still lay

223

there smoldering on *Cycloop*'s deck and might detonate before much longer. No. I'd stand for Ajax. For it was Ajax who first cast doubt upon what was really in the kegs marked as black powder. Such an investigation was sure to take place. Not anytime soon, though, since we were far removed from London. As for now, Praether wasted no time, and went straight to the nub.

"Lieutenant Fagen, I ordered you to blow up *Cycloop*. Why have you not done it?"

"That was my intention, sir, but I think the fuse might not have been spliced properly, and it burned out before reaching the powder."

"Who spliced the fuse?"

"Ajax, sir. Though I didn't observe him. I had other duties."

Praether turned to me. "Did you observe Ajax splicing the fuse, Mr. Harriet?"

"No, sir. I was running the slow match up the companionway. Ajax stayed below and spliced together the two lengths of fuse, the slow to the quick, and then he brought it to the powder." I paused, for now came the matter that would give rise to second thoughts. I took a deep breath and went on. "Except Ajax ... he wasn't sure it was black powder in those kegs, sir."

Praether scowled. "Why would he think that?"

"Because of his nose, sir. He said black powder made it itch. But it didn't itch."

"I see. So what did he think was in those kegs?"

"No one asked him, sir. And he knows better than to speak out of turn., sir."

Praether raised a brow. "Very well. Fetch *Cycloop*'s captain. Maybe he will know."

Van Beek stepped in, his face purple as some eggplant, and creased deep as a prune.

Praether addressed him. "Captain van Beek ... the kegs in your hold, the ones marked as black powder, did you ever inspect them?"

Van Beek shut his eyes, replying mournful. "*Toegeven*."

"What?"

"I say to admit of it."

"Admit what?"

"Not gunpowder."

"Then what is it?"

"Charcoal. No sulphur. No saltpeter. Only charcoal."

Praether began his pace, holding his hands behind his back and wringing them fretful. Three times past the stern window before stopping to address the Dutch man.

"It was marked as black powder. Was it to be traded as such?"

"Ja. Charcoal not cheap, but costs less than gunpowder. Look the same."

"Therefore, more profit for the Cloth Guild."

"Ja."

"I could arrest you for unfair trade, van Beek. But, since there is nothing fair about slavery, I will leave this be, and may even commend you for your unknowing support of abolition." He called for the sentry. "Escort this man to the officers' mess."

Van Beek was led away, and the door stood ajar. We heard a great uproar coming from just beyond. The door flew wide, with Ajax frogmarching the Onion into the cabin and slamming him hard to the deck. The Onion jumped up with a clasp knife ready at hand. He took Ajax's measure, then moved in. The giant stood ready, his massive fists flexing. The sentry charged in to stand between, his musket at half cock, and the tip of his bayonet pressing on the Onion's heart. A standoff, until Praether broke it.

"Drop the knife or I order him to shoot."

The Onion hesitated, if but for a heartbeat, yet long enough for the marine to draw back full. The hard snick convinced the Onion, and he flung his knife on the deck. Praether kicked it away, then faced Ajax.

"Explain yourself."

"The man's a spy, sir. He found that hidden bulkhead in the purser's quarters and was going through it. The guard caught him with a ledger and reported it."

I shifted uneasy, for there was no other ledger but mine stowed behind that bulkhead. The man had just seen the record of my private thoughts, and certain he now fed upon my private observations.

The Onion moaned some false lament. "I don't like being confined, you see, and was trying to find a way out. But instead I found a ledger, with a string of curious entries. Shall I recite them, captain?" The Onion cared little if Praether might reply and continued. "The first page had just one entry. Only one line, but rather captivating."

I shuddered, knowing by heart what I'd written on the fist page, and that now the Onion knew, as well. He cleared his throat, then spoke the line.

"There are some who covet what you have and would destroy you for it."

He looked straight at me, his eyes expressing some sort of shared awareness. I thought he might dwell on that first line, but he went on.

"The next few pages are some sort of strange litany. If I have it right, they're no more than a childish fancy involving numbers. Tell me, Harriet, what number do you think I impersonate?"

I remained silent.

"You fail to reply, so I will tell you. At some point in my life I have played every number in your little drama." He turned to Praether. "Relating this fantasy of your midshipman tires me. May I sit down?"

Praether would have none of it. "Remain on your feet."

"How inhospitable. Very well, where was I? Oh yes, the ledger. It also contains an absorbing account of ... of a night visitor. Me, I do believe." He paused, as if in some street play. "But you must ask Harriet about this." He laughed then ... a most owlish screech.

Praether slammed his fist on the desk. "Shut your mouth or I'll have you gagged." Then he turned to me, raising a brow. "Is this your ledger, Mr. Harriet?"

"Aye, sir. It was given to me by a gentleman crossing the channel to Calais. I've since used it as a journal."

"Nothing classified?"

"No, sir. Just my observations."

The Onion affirmed. "Not at all classified. But still of great interest, at least to the midshipman. To me as well. I wonder, has Harriet ever spoken of his ... hmm, how shall I name it? Of his intuitions?"

Praether stepped forward. "Enough. You abuse the freedom I have granted you. From here on you will be confined to the chain locker."

"That is repugnant. I promise to commit suicide."

"A pity. But I doubt you would do it. The marine could have killed you, but you chose to stand down."

"A different moment." He arched a brow. "You should know a thing before I take my life. The black powder in *Cycloop*'s hold. It's only charcoal. Her crew said as much. They speak Dutch, of course, and I understand some of what they say. '*Alleen houtskool.*' That's what they say. Only charcoal."

"You play the smug informant, but your information comes too late. I know it is only charcoal."

"But do you know how to make use of the knowledge? How you might turn this *alleen houtskool* to your advantage?"

Praether said nothing.

"I thought not. You are no less than ordinary, Praether, yet no more. Forgive me, but you are uncreative."

⚡

If van Beek was telling the truth then his ship contained no black powder, only charcoal. Even so, some officer would still be required to volunteer for the unlucky task of reboarding *Cycloop* and determining just why there had been no detonation. But, to be safe, Praether chose to wait a bit longer before sending anyone. A few hours of good light still remained, and a few hours was deemed enough. During the wait, he convened a council of war. Captain Praether, Lieutenants Fagen and Hoyer, the Onion, and myself. No midshipman would likely be included in a war council, but I was included only to record the proceedings. Praether began with a warning to the Onion.

"I will permit you to explain what you have in mind. But, if what you say is no more than an attempt to avoid the chain locker, I will know it soon enough. Begin."

The Onion bowed. "Begin, indeed. Begin to stride across the stage of all West Africa in the shared command of a new coalition."

"Rubbish. I remind you that you are for hire and serve at my pleasure. Get on with it."

"Then I will start with the Aro's headman. N'tonga."

"What did you just say?"

"Ah! You notice my clicking skills. Very difficult to produce. It's the Khoi-San dialect, from the Niger-Congo."

He repeated the name, N'tonga, while somehow making the sound of a sharp click coming from his mouth.

"N'Tonga. I'm rather fond of the sound. Perhaps I should do what Semyon did and change my name for each mission. Reinvent my name to produce some such a clicking. *Théo à la Clique!* What do you think, captain?"

"Get on with it."

"Yes. I stray off course. Two days ago, then ... that was when N'tonga came out of the jungle and asked me to arrange for an exchange. He knew a ship would be calling soon at Cape Mesurado, and he has twelve fresh captures."

"He holds them at the rapids?"

"No longer. He moved them after you sent a reconnaissance. When the time comes, he will bring them to the bay. But he will rise to the bait only if he sees crossed muskets on the landing, along with powder and shot. Twelve slaves for the entire shipment."

Praether smiled. "And if the powder is nothing but charcoal, then the Aro will present less of a threat."

"Yes, but N'tonga himself is the main threat, and the promise of modern weaponry is the bait to tempt him from the jungle." The Onion raised a brow, arched high and thin. "I will rendezvous with him again to make final preparations."

"When?"

"Tomorrow, at first light. On the river below the rapids." The Onion sighed. "A stinking bilge of a river. I still smell it on my skin.

Tell me, why would your cartographers name it after a saint? I would have disliked Saint Paul. I think we are too much the same. Yet I would never name a sewer after him. The Stinking River would be more fitting. Or perhaps . . ."

Praether pounded on his desk. "You waste time."

"Forgive me. So then, at this appointment I will confirm that a slave ship has been sighted and will soon call. Oh!" The Onion knocked on his forehead. "A brilliant thought! Perhaps you can make use of *Cycloop* for this operation, since you've failed in your efforts to destroy it. *Le voilà!* See how I've just turned your ineptitude into your good fortune."

Praether tugged at his waistcoat. "Your goad falls short. But in spite of it, I may very well use *Cycloop*."

"Excellent! When should I have N'tonga deliver his goods?"

Praether started to pace again. "Tell him to bring his prisoners to the landing tomorrow, at noon."

"Very well. Have you any feathers?"

Praether stopped in mid stride. "Enough of your idiocy. Take this fool and place him in the chain locker."

"No, no. Please hear me out. For this sortie I must create a diversion. I shall play the First American!"

"What?"

"Oh, I forgot to tell you. I once played the Indian. At Fort Liberty. A splendid performance. I wore a set of sumptuous feathers. Very convincing."

"A disguise?"

"You insult me, captain. It is no disguise, but the grand masquerade. You may regard it as *la garantie*."

"What do you mean?"

"N'tonga will expect the Onion to join him at the landing. He doesn't love the Onion, though, and if given the chance he would detach my head as a trophy and feed the rest of me to his men."

"I question why he has not done so already."

"One reason alone. Ever since I eliminated his last agent, N'tonga needs me to conduct his business. I always stay one step ahead, of course. My balloon rising in the night served a dual purpose. I wished to make contact with an unusual ship arriving off Cape Mesurado, which has turned out to be you. But even more, my balloon struck fear in N'tonga's men. Him as well, I think. And now, for the Indian to make an appearance, and wearing a war bonnet? This will make N'tonga take pause, and then he walks blindly into our ambuscade."

"You mean to kill them?"

"Only N'tonga. He's the only one who matters. His men are nothing without him. They will quickly dissolve into the jungle. After that, the next move is yours."

Praether turned to gaze out the gallery windows, thinking overlong before giving reply, and with his back still turned to the Onion. "You say the next move is mine, as if this were some game. But it is not. And I remind you that we are no coalition. I will not reveal my plan. At least not to you." Praether called for the sentry. "Take this man forward and secure him to the foremast."

"I am discouraged."

"Should I send you to the chain locker, instead?"

"Not necessary. I will try to console myself. And my feathers?"

Praether turned to me. "Mr. Harriet, do we have any fowl on board?"

"Several ducks, sir, for the midshipmen's mess."

The Onion sighed. "I love *le petit canard*, but he is too humble."

"What else, Harriet?"

"Gleason has laying hens, sir."

The Onion wagged his head. "*Sans distinction.*"

"Is that it, then?"

"Oh. And the peacock that fell in love with Lorca at Yawri Bay. He bought the thing."

"Ah! *Le peon!*" The Onion near swooned. "My new war bonnet! Made from the plumes of a peacock. Ravishing!"

Praether cut him short. "Shut your mouth, Oignon. Harriet, what did Lorca pay for that bird?"

"One bob, sir."

The Onion crowed. "I will pay more! Forty *centimes.*"

"Do you have it? You came on board wearing no clothes, as I recall."

"But my knowledge is invaluable. Permit me to use it as collateral."

"The true worth of your knowledge has yet to be determined. However, and against my better judgement, I will send you Lorca's peacock." Praether called for the sentry. "I am quit of this man. Take him away and shackle him to the foremast."

Praether waited for the door to close before going on. "Now then, Lieutenant Fagen, I think you know how I shall rate your performance in this operation. At least so far. However, there is still time to improve upon yourself."

"I am eager for it, sir."

"Then you volunteer to return to *Cycloop*?"

"With a will, sir."

"I thought as much. So here is the situation. It is vital to our mission that the Aro are not allowed to be in possession of black powder. It may very well be that the powder kegs in *Cycloop*'s hold contain nothing but charcoal. But we do not know it for sure. Therefore, before we proceed it is incumbent upon us to discover the truth of the matter.

"Incumbent upon me, sir."

"Indeed. So you will return to *Cycloop* and examine each keg, as well as every inch of unspent fuse. Take van Beek. Watch closely for his reaction when you tell him he must come with you. If he is indifferent, then likely he has told the truth. Now repeat what I just told you."

Fagen said it back.

"Very well. Once all is in order on *Cycloop*, fire one white flare and I will send van Beek's crew. Van Beek will sail the ship under your command, and you will bring it to anchor in the bay."

"And if van Beek refuses to go with me, sir?"

"If he balks, he may very well be lying to us. Then, as Lady Praether was inclined to say, we shall cross that bridge after we burn it. Go now. I want you on board *Cycloop* before twilight."

The captain turned next to Hoyer. "How many from *Black Joke* are here on *Eleanor*?"

"Only two, sir. Kofi and the girl."

"Collect them and return to *Black Joke* immediately. Make preparations to land your passengers. When they come ashore, I dare say their lives will once more be worth living. Questions?"

"No, sir."

"Then go you now."

Finally, to me. "No need to make fair copy of this meeting. You are dismissed."

♭

I made direct for the purser's quarters to retrieve my journal. It lay on the desk, opened to the first page.

There are some who covet what you have and would destroy you for it.

Words spoken by Mr. Lau, that I later entered in my ledger. And now most likely read by the Onion. Not a good thing. I thought it best to find a new hidey-hole. But the storage bin under my berth would never serve. Nothing remained hidden for long in the midshipmen's mess. Any mate would see me stow the thing. Someone was sure to read it, and then laugh at my odd notions. Once more, I thought of Elo. Some small space tucked away in his surgery. For the last two days I'd meant to visit him, and now I went to his surgery, with my journal in hand.

He sat at his bench, stirring some odious remedy in his crucible. He didn't look up but, just the same, he knew it was me.

"Expect you before now."

"I've been kept busy. What are you making?"

"Infusion of birch bark."

"For courage?"

"No. For Wat. Arthritic."

"He'd never ask for medicine."

"No. But I see him work. Watch his face. See much pain. Make this for him without him asking."

"I don't think he trusts your concoctions."

"You give to him. You his mate." He glanced at my journal. "What?"

"My journal. I kept it in the purser's quarters but the Onion found it when he was locked in. Will you keep it for me?"

"Ja."

"Except you mustn't read it."

"Ja. I read."

"Oh. Well, I suppose. I've told you much of what's in it already so I guess it won't matter. And ... there's something more."

Elo snuffed his burner and set the crucible aside. "Ja, something more. Caligula."

"What?"

"Rome tyrant, long time back. Mad. I think Onion is like that one."

"What do you mean?"

"Same malady. Caligula and Onion. Have same thing. *Dementia Precox.*"

"Finnish?"

"Latin."

"What is it?"

"When two people live inside one head. First one is tyrant. Like Caligula. Second one maybe a papist saint. Like Joan of Arc. Always war. No peace."

"None for for me, either."

"Something is inside your head? The Sukiyama?"

"Some times, but not always. But the Onion, it seems he's always there. Can't you see, Elo? First Minorca. Then Amunia. And the Mekong. He was even at Dog Island."

"Onion at London?"

"Only a specter in some sort of strange dream, with him pounding on a wall and his Mum unable to soothe him. Now he's here at Mesurado."

"Following you?"

"I can't think how he'd know I'm here."

"People know this place."

"Maybe. He told once about being on Saint-Domingue when the slaves rose up. Except the Onion's no abolitionist."

"Are you?"

"I never thought about it. About slavery, I mean. Not until I smelled a slaver. But I doubt the Onion cares about fighting the slave trade."

"Depend on who talking inside head." Elo leaned in and spoke low. "And Caligula ... that one talk loud."

He gave his medicine one last stir, then brought a small clay pot from under his bench and set it next to his crucible. "Maybe Onion looking for Sukiyama. Wants Sukiyama inside his head to chase Caligula away. Chase other voices, too. Stop war if only one voice speak." He poured his potion, careful slow. "You tell Onion about Sukiyama?"

"Never. But after I became shot on Minorca I woke up in a hut. An old woman gave me something to drink. I slept heavy and must have called out. Onion made his camp there, in the hills above Mahon. The old woman and Yadra ... they cooked for his camp. I think the Onion came there often. He might have heard me calling out."

"Who this ... Yadra?"

"A girl. She saved me. She held me when I was afraid. When I shivered at night. I loved her. But the Onion ... he shot away her little finger."

"Same way he shoot you?"

"Yes. But then he hanged her."

"Ja. That Caligula." Elo corked his clay pot. "Now you find Wat. Give him this. Drink when pain hurt too much."

"I'll do it. Will you find a safe place for my journal?"

"Ja."

♭

Wat never stood a watch. But a sailmaker works near continuous, for even a fresh suit of sails is in constant need of repair, and *Eleanor*'s working canvas had long since begun to weather. On my way to find him I recalled what Wat once told me about sail making, that a sail must be cut and stitched with great skill and with an experienced hand, so the wind can shape it into a certain form. He called it a foil and claimed that any proper made foil is a pretty thing to see.

On the companionway I looked once more into *Eleanor*'s rigging to study the shape of each sail, with every sail cut perfect true to send her chasing on the swell. All told, *Eleanor* carried twenty-nine sail ... from her thunderous main course down to the least of her studding sails. That's a great spread of canvas, and with each sail filling handsome whenever laid on. And as soon as Wat repaired one sail he'd go straight to the next, so he might be working at any place where there was enough space. I found him on the gun deck, with the fore royal draped across the forward battery.

"Wat, I've brought you something."

He took the pot and sniffed at it. "Medicine. Loblolly make it?"

"He did."

He gave it back. "Don't want none."

"But he say's it's for your arthritic."

"No thank 'ee." He set down his awl and wrung his hands. Gnarled and painful to look at.

"Do they hurt?"

He only sat there cracking his knuckles and working his quid.

"Why won't you take it?"

Wat spat his plug overboard, then muttered but a word. "Gnome."

"What?"

"Earth dweller. That one might be a earth dweller."

"Why do you say that?"

"Seen one before. At Ormalu. Long white hair. Blue eyes. Same as Inari."

"To be sure the loblolly's of a different sort. I can't guess he means you any harm, though. But if you don't want it then I'll take it back."

When I stood to go he tugged at my sleeve.

"Wait, Mr. Harriet. I've a thing to say."

"What?"

"There's a rumor."

"What rumor?"

"Sailmaker on that Dutch ship ... he speak some English. He say the treaty fail."

"Treaty of Amiens?"

Wat only nodded.

"What makes him think that?"

"Last month, when *Cycloop* weathered the Hook at Rotterdam, he seen the Royal Navy boarding all Dutch and French ships anchored in the Meuse. That what he say."

"Do you believe him?"

"Not for me to believe, or not."

"Either way, you need to tell someone."

Wat gave a snort. "I tell you." He picked up his awl. "Captain of the foremast ... he want this sail ready to furl on by next watch. So you go along. Take the pot with you."

20. The rest is history

Black Joke's cutter rode high in the water, secured at *Eleanor*'s entry port, with her crew waiting for Hoyer. *Eleanor*'s barge stood alongside taking on the Dutch crew, all of them watching hopeful for *Cycloop* to send up a white rocket. I joined Hoyer as he waited for Nary to bring Kofi and Binta to the waist. Soon the lad came from below decks with Kofi in tow, but not Binta.

"I looked everywhere, sir, even behind Lorca's stove, but I can't find the girl."

Hoyer turned to me. "Any idea where she might be?"

"Did you see the orange cat, Nary?"

"Aye, Mr. Harriet. It's under the long boat. I'll go fetch it!"

I disguised my grin with a slight frown, amused by Nary's misplaced zeal. "That won't be necessary. The girl and that cat have become best mates so where you find one you may find the other. Try looking all the way under the long boat."

Nary went off, just as *Cycloop* sent up its rocket. The Dutch crew gave a thin cheer, and the barge cast off, leaving *Black Joke*'s cutter in its wake.

If I dared speak to anyone about what Wat just told me, then Lieutenant Hoyer was the one, and now was the time. But for a midshipman to advance any rumor coming from a tar might risk the displeasure of an officer. Even so, to overlook Wat's story and then have it turn out to be true, that would not bode well, either. Besides, I could speak simple plain with Hoyer, so I took my chance.

"A word with you, sir?"

"What is it?"

"Wat just told me a rumor he heard from *Cycloop*'s sailmaker, sir, and I think it may be worth reporting."

"Tell me."

Hoyer listened without interruption before making reply. "Well you can be sure that by the time we hear it, the men have gone on to their next diversion. There's no doubt the peace is fragile, but I wonder if we can believe it's already failed." He squinted thoughtful. "Still, it would do no harm to take it as a cautionary tale."

Just then Nary returned, with Binta in hand. Hoyer sent her into the cutter to wait with Kofi, then turned to me.

"A conscientious lad. He'd be at wit's end if he hadn't found the girl this time."

"Aye, sir."

"I suspect you're at wit's end, too, for reporting Wat's story. But I think you've done the right thing. If I was remaining on board I'd pass this along to Captain Praether. Now you must tell him yourself, and I suggest you do it soon. Tell him you spoke to me first."

Gleason came to report. "Beg pardon, sir, but the last of the ration's about to be swayed into the cutter. Should take ten minutes."

Hoyer only nodded, studying *Black Joke*, now making full and by, and not a half-mile astern. *Eleanor* took a rogue wave on her beam, and we shifted on the deck to avoid the cargo net.

"A fair ration of manioc in that net, sir."

"Should be enough to last them a month once they go ashore. If they're careful."

"I wonder what will become of them, sir. I mean, after we leave."

Hoyer frowned, as if reluctant to reply. "Mr. Harriet, this is for your ears only. I do not mean to presume, but it seems our captain has taken on the role of father protector of these souls."

"He treats them like children, sir."

"He does. However, I've made an effort never to condescend, but to try for an even exchange whenever possible. Measure for measure, and of equal value."

"Does an Englishman measure value different than an African, sir?"

"It can't be denied. But the real difference is that when all's said and done, they're landsmen, and we're sailors. What a landsman knows holds little value to a sailor. And vice versa."

Gleason gave the call, and we stepped back from the rail to watch the cargo net laden with a dozen sacks of manioc rising off the deck.

"But I suspect that what an Englishman knows, sailor or not, provides little worth to a West African. Even so, I've observed them for the last month now. I've see how they are willing to exchange their sweat for their sustenance. With a bit of good fortune, they might find their way. If they don't destroy themselves first."

"Sir?"

"There are warring factions among these people, Harriet. And in this they are very much like the English and French."

Gleason gained the tumblehome nimble quick, and shot through the entry port.

"Cargo's secured, sir, but you need to sign for it."

Hoyer signed the manifest, returned our salutes, and departed in the cutter. And I went in search of Praether. But he hailed me first.

"Harriet. Walk with me."

Together we made down the companionway and onto the gundeck. We threaded our way through the men, all mustering for first watch. But, now that their captain walked among them, their horseplay ceased immediate. Praether acknowledged them as we passed by, then addressed me.

"Be so kind as to state our current position."

"At today's noon sighting, thirty of July, 1803, I recorded six degrees north by ten degrees west, sir."

"Much the same as for the last month. It seems your duties as a master's mate are not quite demanding for the moment." He pulled a small ledger from his coat. "Take this, if you will."

I took it.

"I know you maintain a personal log, along with your ship's log. Now you will maintain a third. An unofficial record to be kept for The One Body. Open it. You will see that I have already made several entries, but my left hand has become somewhat numb, and my cursive worsens. But yours is clear and consistent. So now you will pick up where I left off. But first answer me this, if you will."

"Aye, sir."

"Since *Eleanor* was first put into service, we have come upon Théophile Oignon no less than three times. The first, at Minorca, it seemed by chance. The second was perhaps by coincidence, yet even then I began to speculate. Maybe the man had some interest in *Eleanor*. She is a fine war ship. No doubt the French would love to capture or sink her." Praether drummed his fingers on the rail. "But now I think different. I do not think Oignon has an interest in this ship. I believe he has an interest in you."

The wind shifted a point, and he peered into the rigging to study her top hamper. Once satisfied, he turned to me once more.

"So I must ask you. What is this interest? And how would he know to find you here?"

Praether was my captain and commander. Certain he had the right to know anything I could tell him. Certain I would try. But, just as any captain will, Praether expected facts, not speculation. Not some strange notion discussed by Elo and me.

"I'm trying to find out, sir. It's all most confusing and unclear. But I think you're right. Or at least close to the truth of it. The Onion wants something of me."

"And do you have it?"

"I think so. Except it's not mine to have. It's ... something beyond any sextant or compass."

Praether narrowed his eyes. "By that do you mean it is beyond reason?"

"Aye, sir."

"Very well. I suppose that must do, at least for the moment. Come. Your first entry begins now. I must catechize Oignon."

♭

The Onion leaned against the foremast; his right leg shackled to an eyebolt. An oakum basket lay at his feet. He cradled Lorca's peacock in his left arm, stroking its long neck, with its tiny head tucked under a wing.

When the Onion saw us, he pressed a finger to his lips. "*Mesmérisme.*"

Praether would have none of it. "Gibberish. What are you doing?"

The Onion knelt on the deck and set his bird in the oakum ... cooing for the thing and stroking its neck one last time.

"I have placed *le peon* in a trance and return him now to the roost I've just built for him. I am a saint. Yes?"

Not by half. But then I recalled what Elo said, and spoke before thinking.

"Joan of Arc. Maybe the Onion believes he's like Joan of Arc, sir."

"Absurd. And if I want your opinion, Harriet, be sure that I will ask for it. Now then, Oignon, account for yourself."

The Onion beamed over bright. "Not absurd. Perhaps I was Joan of Arc." Then he scowled. "As for now ... *le peon* lies content in his nest."

"A bird in a nest. This preposterous costume is your plan?"

"Once more I remind you, captain. It is no costume. It is the grand masquerade. When the time comes, I will once again put *le peon* in his trance, secure him in this nest, and then wear them as my war bonnet."

"To what end?"

"For when we conduct our business with N'tonga. I'm quite certain he'll be distracted when *le peon* displays his train. Have you seen *le peon*'s display? It's rather fine, but for one feather that seems to have gone missing."

"I will not have it. You are deranged even to suggest this mad scheme."

"I think not. N'tonga will be nonplussed by such a spectacle and he will drop his guard. Yes, I know. I have not become the first American, as I first intended. A setback, but I must go on. If I do not redirect N'tonga's attention, then I feel strongly that he will attack us at the first opportunity. Something is required to divert him."

"We shall see. But first you need to meet him at the rapids. How well do you know this language he speaks? What did you call it?"

"Khoi-San. I communicate not very well. N'tonga is amused with my clicking." The Onion shrugged. "No matter. Slaves for weapons is rudimentary."

One bell sounded, eight-thirty in the evening, and the first watch began. Praether tugged at his waistcoat. "Enough. Be ready at first light." He turned to go. I followed on, but at the midshipmen's

241

mess, he hauled short. "Record this last conversation with Oignon. Now. Do it now while it is still fresh. That will be all."

Except it wasn't all. Hoyer expected me to tell the captain just what I'd told him, and to tell him soon. I cleared my throat and spoke out.

"Sir?"

"What."

"I've something to report."

"Say it."

"I spoke to Lieutenant Hoyer just before he left, and he said to tell you."

"Go on."

Praether listened intent, his hands held behind his back, pacing forthright on the mess deck.

"Who knows of this?"

"Lieutenant Hoyer thinks everyone below decks knows it by now, sir."

⚡

Six bells rang in the last dog watch. Seven of the evening. I stood before Lieutenant Fagen as he addressed me sharp.

"As *Eleanor*'s First Officer I'm required at this council. Lieutenants Japhet and Thousand will be here shortly, but a midshipman has no business in a captain's quarters." His face darkened with mistrust. "So why are you here?"

"My duties include serving as Captain Praether's recording secretary, sir."

"An enviable post." Fagen grew tense. "Praether has become your patron?"

"I don't think so, sir." Then, before I could hold my tongue. "Ask him yourself."

A remark verging on disrespect, and no doubt Fagen meant to set upon my impudence, but just then came a knock, and then another. The door swung wide. Japhet and Thousand stepped through, and for the next few minutes they took turns discounting the rumor of a failed peace, with none of them considering the consequences if such a thing was true. As expected, I was ignored, so went about setting a taper on Praether's writing stand and dressing my quill.

Being ignored by his superiors is not uncommon for a midshipman. Not a bad thing, though, for it gave me pause to reflect on what Mr. Lau might say about this turn of events, be it rumor, or perhaps involving some grain of truth. He might have reminded that all officers in the Royal Navy must take any portion of the truth and turn it to the Crown's advantage. A good starting point, but where would it lead? To be sure no one would ask me. Also, a good thing, for certain I had no answer.

Fagen fumed away, and soon harped on a new subject ... the low standing of an African slave. "I believe in the Great Chain of Being, gentlemen. And in that chain the African is hardly above an animal. Far below an Englishman. Do you not agree?"

Thousand, a quiet and solitary officer, said nothing. But Japhet responded with a question of his own.

"If you don't mind me asking, Fagen, but if you feel that way then why do you serve on this ship? Surely you knew what we were about before you signed on."

"I did not. I remind you that Praether read out his Letter of Marque only after we weathered Ushant. Far too late to do anything about it. Besides, in the last year this damnable Treaty has reduced many of us to half-pay. My father would go hungry if I'd not been offered a commission on *Eleanor*. Even so, I doubt very much if I would have signed on if I knew we were to sail under The One Body's banner." Fagen curled his upper lip in a sneer. "Even if we've done little to advance its cause."

I looked at Lady Praether's portrait, still hanging from the bulkhead. The first time I'd seen her likeness, I thought she was a beautiful woman. But when she came on board at the Solent and I saw her in true light, I thought her homespun, if not unbeautiful. But now, since her untimely death, her portrait once more held an allure.

She'd not have liked Fagen's latest remarks, spoken in the same quarters she once shared with her husband. And she would likely never have allowed her husband to sign Fagen if she'd known the man's rancour. Yet Fagen was right about us not doing over much. We'd relieved *Elizabeth Carton*'s abandoned slaves at Cape Verde, but only to send them on to Saint-Domingue with Dame-Marie, instead of returning them to Africa. Then we'd captured *Black Joke*, and now meant to land her human cargo, here at Cape Mesurado. A questionable undertaking, and with any measure of success coming only with the Onion's cooperation. A dubious alliance, and I thought it an ignoble one.

The wind shifted a point, increasing to a moderate breeze. The sails luffed continuous. On the quarterdeck Strayhorne called to sheet the lines and the starboard watch beat feet to man their stations. A most thunderous din. After all were in place I was once more left to my musings.

Was I the only one to see this collaboration with the Onion as dishonourable? To join forces with a recent enemy? One who Elo compared to some mad Roman emperor, or a papist saint burned at the stake? Once again, I puzzled why the Onion was at Cape Mesurado at all. Surely not only to disrupt the slave trade. More likely he was here to hunt me down. Or, more likely yet, to follow the Sukiyama ... to possess it for what it might afford him. To relieve him of his madness. Of a sudden, a name occurred.

Semyon. The Onion's prisoner on the Mekong, and wounded grave. In his delirium Semyon might have let slip some shard of information. The Onion knew he was a prized agent of His Majesty and had access to the Privy Chamber. Perhaps Semyon suspected that King George was possessed by the horrors of the slave trade. He said near as much while on board *Eleanor*, hinting that, at some point during his madness, His Majesty would speak of deploying ships, each provided with a Letter of Marque and sent to eliminate the slave trade in West Africa. Possible. But then the king would soon forget and would say no more of it until his next spell.

Beyond that, Semyon knew Praether was a well-connected abolitionist who would be keen to volunteer *Eleanor* for any such duty. And that I would likely join him, since it's not uncommon for a master's mate to stay with his ship. If Semyon had let such information slip, then the Onion might well have made note of it. Even so, the Onion's appearance at Cape Mesurado remained cloaked in mystery, one to be revealed only by the Onion himself, though I guessed he never would.

Just then my ramblings were cut short by Strayhorne's bark. "Haul away!"

In the great cabin we all leaned to port, waiting for *Eleanor* to respond. Japhet called Fagen out. "And now, Fagen? What say you now?"

"I say that, even as I doubt it, I now wish this rumor to be true, and that Amiens has failed."

"So we can return to the business of war?"

"No. To the glory of it."

The sentry slammed the butt of his musket on the deck and we all turned to see Captain Praether enter, with Nino Silva and Daniel Goodhoney close behind. We came to attention.

"As you were, gentlemen." He turned to me. "This briefing is now under way. Harriet, take this down."

I set my ink pot on the writing stand and dipped my quill.

Praether cleared his throat. "First I will remind you that we are supposed to be a slave ship. Continue to wear common slops and try not to conduct yourself with an obvious military bearing. Understood?"

Understood.

"Now then, this operation will consist of several stages. The first stage is under way. Oignon has departed for his meeting with N'tonga. He will stay with the headman tonight and bring him to the meeting tomorrow."

Praether began to pace. "For the second stage I have made an adjustment. Our meeting with N'tonga will no longer take place at the landing." He looked to me. "Bring the Cape Mesurado chart."

Praether spread the thing on his table, and we all watched as he traced his finger along the Saint Paul River, coming to a stop at its mouth.

"There is a sandbar, just here. It does not appear on any map. Three hundred feet long and roughly seventy feet wide, running parallel to the shore, and with an elevation of no more than three feet at high tide. The bar lies about fifty feet offshore and is completely devoid of vegetation. More than enough sand to land

Eleanor's barge. This is where we shall conduct our business with N'tonga."

Praether stood back. "Step forward, all of you. Make yourselves familiar with this place. It has no name. It did not exist when this chart was drawn, and no doubt it will be gone before the next chart is made. But, for the duration of this operation, I have given it a name. Ararat. Befitting, I think. No doubt you will recall that Ararat is where Noah came ashore."

After we studied the map, Praether continued.

"Oignon claims that N'tonga is leery of the water, and there is a strong current running between Ararat and the mainland. Strong enough to make N'tonga even more cautious, and he will likely become distracted. That is why I have chosen this location, instead of the landing. I am quite certain N'tonga is eager to acquire his weaponry, but if he wants his goods then he has no choice but to arrive by boat. Same as Sergeant Moran and his marines. They will accompany you in the barge and await orders to overrun the sand bar. But the timing is critical, and they must remain unseen until given the order. So I have told Gleason to rig a tarpaulin for the barge, and for the marines to remain under cover until given the signal to attack."

The tiller groaned, and I caught my ink pot just before *Eleanor* heeled to port. Praether folded his chart before going on.

"As for Oignon, be sure to watch what he does. When he deems the time is right, he will give a signal. He claims to have trained his peacock to display its feathers on command. That will be the signal for Moran and his marines to charge on to the sandbar and take control. Questions?"

Japhet cleared his throat. "I don't think a peacock can be expected to display its feathers on command, sir."

Praether nodded. "That is what I told Oignon. But he says it will, and argues that such a colourful display will be sure to divert N'tonga's attention. And this will be the signal for Moran to attack. But you are certainly right, Japhet, therefore I have provided an additional signal, in case Oignon's peacock is useless." Praether turned to Fagen. "Now hear this, lieutenant, in addition to the peacock, Oignon has agreed to tap his foot on the sand three times. That will be the sign for you to send in Moran. More questions?"

Silence ... until the faint report of a cannon found its way down through the grating. We all cocked an ear, waiting for another report. None came. Likely it was a signal gun coming from *Black Joke*, or *Cycloop*, calling attention to some flag hoist ready to be sent up. Praether was about to go on, until Hewitt stepped in.

"Lieutenant Strayhorne's compliments, sir, and he wishes to report a hoist from *Black Joke*. It appears they've sighted a ship on the horizon, bearing on Cape Mesurado."

Praether turned to me. "Go on deck. Find out what you can."

I found Strayhorne clinging halfway up the gaff vang, better to glass the approaching ship. She'd just made a final tack that would stand her into the bay. Strayhorne studied it for a moment longer, then snapped his scope shut and scurried to the deck.

"Harriet, has the captain been informed?"

"Aye, sir. He sent me to take your report."

"Very well. You may tell Praether it's a Dutch snow, and she's towing a yellow boat with a high bow ... maybe a carronade mounted on it. Looks to be some sort of galley. Or a xebec. I've counted six gun ports on the snow, and I don't like her aggressive maneuvering. I've ordered the men to stand by. Go handsomely now, and inform the captain."

No need, for Praether joined us on the quarterdeck. He wasted no time. "I do not know what that Dutch captain intends to do, but if he plans to intercede then Hoyer has little time. Send a hoist to *Black Joke*. Tell Hoyer he must enter the bay immediately."

Fagen came on deck.

"Fagen, return to *Cycloop* and make ready to accept N'tonga's prisoners. Be sure to stay well clear of that Dutch vessel. If it becomes necessary, then break off and run for Freeport. We will rendezvous there in one week."

"Beg pardon, sir, but even if we're stripped down to look like a slaver, we still carry more cannon than a snow, I suggest we make a fight of it. Sail between *Black Joke* and the Dutch."

Praether studied the Dutch ship, with her transom now in full view and revealing her name. *Hector.*

"I commend you for your fighting spirit, Fagen, and will mention it in my log. But as you can see, *Hector* has just gained the weather gauge. So we must now rely on Hoyer to devise his own plan. Go."

When Fagen departed, Praether called for Japhet. "I intend to negotiate with *Hector*'s captain. But if civil discourse fails then we must defend our interests. Beat to quarters."

Midshipman Hewitt turned the ten-minute glass and the sand started to run. Praether watched the decks clearing for action with a sharp eye, even as he called for me.

"Mr. Harriet, state the full time and date, if you will."

"Four minutes of two, sir, in the afternoon watch of seventeen July, eighteen and three."

"Make a note of it. Now take down my next statement, to be entered into my log."

"Yes, sir."

Praether came to attention. "Sixteen months ago this ship engaged in a battle that no longer needed to be fought. As a result of that action several men died, and many were wounded. All from a lack of communication. Unfortunately, this lack of communication still exists."

Lieutenant Japhet came to report. "Sir, all bulkheads removed and secured."

Praether went on. "Therefore, I have no choice but to act in accordance with my faith, for I have cause to believe that the Treaty of Amiens has failed."

Once more Japhet came to report. "Water butts topped off. Gun deck sanded. All guns primed and ready to run out."

Praether glanced at the sand still remaining in the glass. "You are very slow."

Japhet made double quick for the helm. Praether continued with his statement.

"Even though there has been no official word that England is once again at war with the French Republic, I feel duty bound to bring my guns to bear on any and all enemies of the Crown. Be they known, or greatly suspected."

Japhet approached once more, this time looking pleased. "All sections reporting, sir."

"Very well. Stand to."

I coughed polite. "Do you wish to say more, sir, for the log?"

"One last thing. I have previously done no more than restrict the movements of the French agent, Théophile Oignon. But immediately after he has served his purpose on the sandbar, I will place him in irons and hold him as a prisoner of war."

And for the murder of Semyon, as well, I thought, but knew better than to say it.

"Will that be all then, sir?"

"That will be all. Carry on."

We stood at the starboard rail, watching *Hector* close on *Black Joke*. To be sure, the snow was small, and lightly armed, but she still outgunned *Black Joke*. Instead of bringing the fight, or trying to run, Hoyer hauled his wind.

Strayhorne spoke out. "A mistake."

Praether rapped his knuckles on the rail. "No. It is a ploy. *Hector's* captain has no idea of how many are on board *Black Joke*. No doubt Hoyer intends to keep them well hidden so as to lure the Dutch into boarding. When they grapple on he will overwhelm their boarding party and before they can disengage, he will amass on *Hector* and take her for a prize."

It may have worked, but for *Hector's* captain, who was a cautious man and ordered his boarding nets raised, then turned out a squad of marines to repel boarders. A cautious man, but also aggressive, for just then a gout of yellow-grey smoke disgorged from *Hector's* chaser. The round sent up a waterspout not twenty yards off *Black Joke's* bow. Hoyer went on the leeward tack, then ordered the topgallants set, in an attempt to outrun *Hector*. But, even as *Black Joke* heeled on the next swell, the Dutch ship fired once more. The round threw high, smashing on *Black Joke's* main topmast. A lucky shot. But unlucky for *Black Joke*, for the mast toppled and hung in the rigging. *Black Joke* fell off the wind, and before she could fill, *Hector* began to close.

The Dutch ship managed to fire but one more round, though, for of a sudden the wind failed, leaving *Black Joke*, *Hector*, and *Eleanor* as well, becalmed and wallowing in the troughs. Hoyer wasted no time, and sent his men aloft. They formed a bucket brigade and began dousing the sails with sea water, better to catch any wind that might still linger. *Hector* did the same but, in spite of her efforts, the Dutch fell behind. Hoyer saw his chance to increase his lead by setting out his boats and towing *Black Joke*. Praether saw what Hoyer was doing and set out our own boats to narrow the gap between *Black Joke* and *Eleanor*.

The Dutch fell even further behind, until they finally recalled their boats. Hoyer had managed to avoid capture, and at the same time bring *Black Joke* into the bay. A fine showing, and the Eleanors gave a cheer, followed instanter by a groan, for just then the yellow xebec towed by *Hector* cast off its line, making direct for *Black Joke*, oaring methodic, and at considerable speed. The xebec required no wind, and slipped into *Black Joke*'s wake most deliberate, its one carronade aimed at her transom and its crew prepared to send a twenty-four-pound shot ripping through the entire length of *Black Joke*. A deadly attack, and Hoyer had no way to fend it off. He knew what was coming. To prevent a needless slaughter he chose to strike, and to become a prisoner of war.

Soon night fell on Cape Mesurado, and we lost sight of both ships.

♭

Even with the loss of *Black Joke*, the slave exchange on the sand bar was to take place the next day, at noon. But Praether had other plans.

"Keep N'tonga waiting. Wait until evening."

And so, the next evening, an hour before nautical twilight, I stood on Ararat with Lieutenant Fagen. Wat had come along, taking the final stitches for the tarp, even as Sergeant Moran and nine of his marines remained under cover. As soon as the barge ran aground, the crew began crossing muskets on the sandbar, then stacking powder and shot. Once in place, the Onion, now wearing his headdress, and N'tonga, bearing a ceremonial spear and a gunny sack, stepped from the tree line and climbed into a small dugout. N'tonga's warriors followed in a larger dugout, transporting a dozen slaves. Once all was in place on the sandbar, the Onion convinced his peacock to display his train. At first it seemed to waver, but then gave a crow, more the sound made by some crying baby, followed by a glorious display. All stood transfixed by the sight. Fagen, as well. And the moment came and went for Moran to attack. Only when the Onion tapped his foot on the sand did Fagen remember to give the command. But even before Moran and his squad could charge onto the sand bar, N'tonga opened his gunny sack and withdrew a severed head dripping with blood. No doubt a sign for his warriors to make some move of their own, and they came howling straight at us, freezing my blood in shock. But they rushed by me, and instead went charging at Fagen. The prisoners all cowered and moaned in terror, and the Onion stood among them, shrieking for all to hear.

"Mon sergent! Vous avez tué mon sergent!"

He drew his pistol and fired at N'tonga. An errant shot, and he drew his second pistol, just as N'tonga hurled his spear. Not at the Onion, but at Wat! I pushed him aside as the spear hissed by. The Onion's second shot hit full on N'tonga's forehead, thudding with a most awful sound, and blasting his brains out the back of his head. When N'tonga fell, his men put down their machetes instanter and lay in the sand awaiting their death. Except for one warrior who stood defiant. Sergeant Moran ran for him and knocked him to the ground. When he tried to get up, Moran drove his bayonet clear through his throat to impale him on the sand. Moran wasted no time, but only left his musket stuck in place, drew a pistol and led his squad farther on to the sand. Another gun went off. Not a Brown Bess, though, and not nearby. Something bigger, and fired from a distance. I turned to see a boat rowing for us. It came from out of the low sun and, as I squinted, a gout of smoke spewed from its bow gun, soon followed by another report and the buzz of grape shot filling the air. The round came from a swivel gun mounted high on the bow of an oared boat. The yellow xebec that had forced *Black Joke*'s surrender!

Moran formed his marines to counter the attack. Another gout of smoke, and once more the air whined as a swarm of wasps when the grape shot screamed past. This time a marine fell. But a mate helped him to stand, and he returned to the line. Moran walked up the line and then down, making light of the xebec's efforts.

"They shoot no better than blind pigs, lads." He was about to bark out more orders but noticed Fagen and me standing near the crossed muskets. He trotted over. "Beg pardon, gentlemen, but since there's no available cover on this place I think it would behoove you both to make yourselves smaller targets by assuming a position very flat upon the sand."

A good thought, and we complied. Moran hurried back to his men.

"All right, me lovelies. Three more strokes of their oars 'til they're in range."

I raised my head to count the strokes, waiting for Moran to give the order.

"Ready! Fire!"

The first rank fired a tight volley, followed close on by the second rank, and then the third. I can't guess that any of their rounds could have thrown high. Some went wide, though, only to splash harmless in the bay. The rest fell short, and not one man in the xebec folded, prompting Moran's disgust.

"A sorry display, lads. But at least you backed them off. Stand down and save your powder and shot."

I went to see about Wat. Still the heart of oak, though he did let me help him stand. If only some.

The sun dipped on the horizon. The Onion knelt in the sand, cradling his sergeant's severed head and peering into the bay. "We cannot get off this bar and the Dutch dare not approach. An impasse."

Fagen called out. "Not for long. *Eleanor*'s standing in. *Hector*, too."

Moran called out as well. "Well damn my eyes ... and both flying a white flag."

⚡

Eleanor's longboat indeed flew a white flag, and Captain Praether stood in its stern, taking his seat just as the oarsmen shipped oars. Praether came ashore, tugged at his waistcoat, then turned to observe a boat coming from *Hector*. Soon it beached on the sandbar and a tall figure, wearing the epaulet of a Dutch captain, waded ashore. He brought a lieutenant, a midshipman and a ship's boy with him, along with a lantern, a small table and two wicker chairs. They wasted no time in arranging the furniture on the high ground. When all was in place, the lieutenant put a match to the glim, for by now the sun had gone well down. A good thing the land breeze stirred, for the sand fleas had found us.

The Dutch captain surveyed the sandbar before coming to sit in one of the chairs. Then, in the dim light cast by the lantern, he waved for Praether to join him. After exchanging a few words, Praether called for Fagen to approach. Me, as well.

"You are in command of *Hector*?"

"Yes. I am Dayan. And you?"

"I am Praether. In command of *Eleanor* and *Cycloop*. Permit me to introduce my First Officer, Lieutenant Fagen."

"And this is de Groot, my lieutenant. Before we begin our negotiations, I must first say . . ."

Praether raised a hand. "No. First I must ask if the English and the Dutch are now at war."

"The situation is tenuous, but when I left Antwerp two months ago our countries were still in observance of the Treaty."

"Then why did you attack a ship flying an English flag? A ship under my command?"

Dayan stiffened. "I attacked because it was my duty. *Black Joke* is a large slave ship, and to come across a slaver of that size at these coordinates is an invitation for me to investigate, regardless of nationality. I remind you that I fired a warning shot. But Hoyer paid no heed, and instead took flight. He left me with no choice but to engage. As for *Black Joke* being under your command, that is irrelevant, even though I was not aware of it until she struck. Under the circumstances I'm sure you would have done the same."

"I will not divulge what I would have done. Nevertheless, please continue."

Dayan took several long breaths before he spoke. "I was about to say, captain, that it was wise for you to call for negotiations before this went any further."

"I wished to prevent an international incident. I seems we both suspect that the Treaty of Amiens has likely failed, but neither you nor I know it as a fact. Better to proceed as if it is still in effect."

"Agreed."

"Tell me something. Van Beek speaks English well enough. But after hearing just a few words from you, I know your English is native. Would you care to explain why that is?"

"I was born in your English colonies. New Amsterdam. But make no mistake. I'm Dutch. The Royal Netherlands Navy has sent me to safeguard Dutch interests along this coast. There's been talk of an English privateer operating in these waters, so I came here to investigate."

"I see." Praether retrieved a scrap of foolscap from his coat and placed it on the table. "My terms. May I put them forth?"

"Proceed."

Praether sat back in his chair. "First. The forces you and I command are of approximately equal strength. Do you concur?"

"I do. And to continue these hostilities would risk mutual destruction."

"And to no end. It is only a sandbar."

"Then why have you claimed it?"

"I do not claim it. I only wish to make use of it ... for the return of African slaves to their native soil."

Dayan examined his nails. "Go on."

Praether shot his cuffs. "Second. If you agree to not interfere with me landing *Black Joke*'s human cargo on this sandbar, along with their supplies, then I will release *Cycloop* to you. Will you consent to that?"

"No. If I agree not to interfere then you will not only release *Cycloop* to me, but also disavow any claim on *Black Joke*."

"Impossible. If I do not retake command of *Black Joke* it will likely reenter the slave trade."

Dayan peered into the bay. "It's very dark. I can't quite see *Black Joke*, though I smell it even from here. It's an old vessel. Crossed the Atlantic many times. I think it's lost its value, both to you and to me. Yet neither of us is willing to give it up."

"Then together let us burn it to the waterline."

"A good compromise. However, I insist that you depart these waters within twenty-four hours. And know this. If I should learn that the Treaty has been revoked I will make every effort to engage you if our paths cross again."

"Understood. I will make preparations to get underway. In the morning we will land our passengers and then we will burn *Black Joke*. Is that amenable?"

"Yes."

Praether nodded to Moran, and the sergeant slipped into the dark. Praether brought his face to the lantern light. "My last point. An exchange of prisoners."

Dayan waved a hand. "Captain Praether, I hold Lieutenant Hoyer and six of your men. You hold no officer of mine, or any of my men. So who is there for you to exchange?"

Praether raised a brow. "Someone of great value. If not to the Dutch, then surely to the French."

Praether made a sign, and Moran brought Théophile Oignon in from the dark, hands tied at his back.

$$\maltese$$

It took all the next day to land *Black Joke*'s passengers, and to offload their provisions. Great joy and celebration. Chaos, as well. Silva arrived on the sandbank to help matters along. He tried to instill a sense of order. But even with Goodhoney's help, it was still a most tumultuous undertaking.

That evening the prisoner exchange got under way. *Hector*'s boat arrived. Hoyer and six Eleanors waded ashore. I stood with the Onion, his hands no longer bound.

I spoke without looking at him. "Why did you come to Cape Mesurado?"

He said nothing, but instead withdrew a small wooden ball from his coat. The size of an orange, shaped from pieces of rosewood and black walnut, each piece carved fine, and locked tight into place.

"Perhaps I came here to give you this."

He offered it to me, but I stepped back.

"I'll take nothing from you."

He turned it in his hand to reveal a carved inscription. Sukiyama. My breath caught. "What is this?"

"*La solution.*"

"I don't wish to know it. Not if it comes from you."

"It won't come from me. Only from you."

He held it to my ear and shook it gentle. "Something's inside."

"What?"

"I don't know. Perhaps someday you will discover the way to unlock it. Then you will know. Take it."

But I did not.

He said no more, only placed it on the sand at my feet, and left with the Dutch.

Epilogue

The Treaty of Amiens was doomed before the ink even dried on the page. Napoleon had never really considered an amicable resolution to his war with the Second Coalition. And, for its part, Great Britain felt threatened by its loss of control on the continent, as well as the sudden loss of revenue. The Treaty's death knell sounded on May 18th 1803, just one month before HMS *Eleanor* encountered the Dutch snow, *Hector*, at Cape Mesurado.

In February of 1803, Jean Dame-Marie and nineteen survivors from the slave ship, *Elizabeth Carton*, made landfall on the north coast of Saint-Domingue. Dame-Marie never went ashore, choosing instead to live on board *Villa Real*. But he used the sovereigns provided by Captain Praether to buy eighty hectares of land, then gave it to the people he had delivered to the new world. They started a farm there, deep in the hill country, and in his honour they named it Dame-Marie.

The two hundred slaves on board *Black Joke* were successfully landed on the sandbar ... the one Captain Praether had named Ararat. However, their fate, as well as that of the sandbar, remains unknown ... lost in the flow of time, and of the river.

Landing *Black Joke*'s human cargo was *Eleanor*'s last operation along the coast of West Africa. She departed Cape Mesurado on July 19th, 1803, returning to her home port of Portsmouth to undergo a refit, and then resume her role as a Lively Class frigate in His Majesty's Royal Navy.

Once Captain Praether returned to Portsmouth, he posted the letter he'd written to the Right Honorable Charles Fenton Mercer. But, due to the renewed hostilities, now referred to as the Napoleonic Wars, his letter did not arrive in Fredericksburg until the spring of 1805. Mercer took the proposition under advisement but did not act upon it until much later. And only then with the assistance of Daniel Goodhoney and Nino Silva, who had set down roots along the Saint Paul River. Their combined efforts did, in fact, return a limited number of free slaves to Africa. But, from the very start, the experiment struggled with a high mortality rate, along with fierce internecine rivalries. Even so, Cape Mesurado has since evolved into the modern-day capitol of Liberia, Monrovia ... named after the American President, James Monroe.

As with many operatives, there is no official record of Théophile Oignon. He did go with the Dutch, in the prisoner exchange conducted on the sandbar. However, it seems the Onion never reappeared in France. He remains a mystery. Much like the Sukiyama.

Concerning the Onion's parting gift to Owen. At first, Owen Harriet left the small wooden ball on the sandbar, repulsed by the notion of accepting anything whatsoever from the Onion. But Owen's good mate, Elo Inari, convinced him to take it, if for no other reason than that it was extremely well crafted, and felt well balanced in one's hand. Also, the Onion was correct, for that wooden ball concealed an arcane secret.

As did the artifact that Mr. Lau helped translate for the Society of Antiquaries of London. As it turns out, Mr. Lau's rubbings from the fragment of a certain stele, subsequently lost in the desert at Amunia, played an integral role in deciphering the Rosetta Stone. But the glyphs on that fragment also predicted an event quite disturbing and blasphemous. An event so inimical to our concept of world order that Mr. Lau chose to speak of it but one time, and then only to Owen, whom he knew well, and trusted with instinctual certainty. Mr. Lau claimed to be a natural philosopher, a humble man born of the Enlightenment, and inspired by the truth writ large. Yet he feared the truth etched into that lost fragment. And when asked where he stored the rubbings, Mr. Lau would only say that he had destroyed them. But he did not. Instead, he tucked them away in the garret of Mrs. Dolan's Room & Board, still waiting to be discovered. As with the Age of Enlightenment, Mr. Lau's own light had also begun to fade with the coming of the new century. But he did make one final voyage, to visit the grave of the man he most admired. Benjamin Franklin, buried at Christ Church Burial Ground, in Philadelphia.

After killing Owen's brother, Dunstan Steep ran to his father's holdings near Salisbury. Constable Erth sent word to the sheriff there, and Dunny was arrested, charged with murder and transported to Derby for arraignment. At the assize he pleaded not guilty, with his London barrister claiming that his client was the victim of untimely circumstance. The prosecution then failed to produce any factual evidence, and Steep was acquitted. Soon after the trial, though, his father, Squire Steep, disavowed Dunny. Not for being a steady drain on his purse, but for being the laughingstock of all Newbury, a bastard child whose red hair and fair skin marked him as the progeny of some other man.

After Cape Mesurado, Owen Harriet returned to Newbury for extended leave. While there, he and Rebecca Stanhope were married. One might say their marriage had become ... expected.

Soon thereafter, Owen went on to take the exam for Master's Mate. On his first attempt, he failed miserably. Something to do with voicing his opinion when not asked to do so. But on his second try he managed to hold his tongue. He passed with highest marks, received his Certificate, and was offered a berth on one of several frigates, *Eleanor* among them. The rest is history.

Glossary of Nautical Terms

ballistics - the science of projectiles and firearms

banded jacky - a style of plug tobacco popular in 1798

beam end - a ship listing more than 45 degrees

beam reach - to sail at a right angle to the wind

beat to quarters - to clear for action

belay - to stop

belaying pin - a short wooden stick stowed in the pin rail and used to secure a rope

bicorne - a two-cornered hat worn by naval officers

binnacle - the stand on which the ship's compass is mounted

blue jackets - the term for sailors trained to fight at close quarters

bosun - slang for boatswain, a sailor in charge of deck operations

brig - a square-rigged, two-masted sailing ship, a ship's gaol

brigantine - a ship smaller than a brig

broad reach - to sail with the wind coming from behind but at an angle

Brown Bess - the standard musket for British armed services during the Napoleonic era

bulkhead - an upright wall within the hull of a ship

bunt line - a type of knot

canister - lead balls packed in a can and fired from an artillery piece at short range

capstan - a winch used to raise the anchor

carronade - an artillery piece intended to be fired at a short range

cathead - a beam extending from the port and starboard bow used to secure the anchor

cabin boy - usually about twelve years old, duties include serving the captain of the ship

carlin - a wooden spacer secured between the beams of a ship

chains - a series of deadeyes used to secure shrouds at the mast tops

chandler - a merchant selling maritime supplies

chip log - a piece of wood used to determine a ship's speed

cleat - a stationary metal or wooden device used to tie down a rope

close-hauled - to sail close to the wind, sailing with as little angle as possible

come about - to change course

companionway - the stairs or steps in a ship

corsair - a privateer

coxsun or coxswain - a steersman man serving as boat handler, a captain's steward

crosstrees - a wooden support used to secure the shrouds at the top gallant mastheads

crossjack - the square yard used to spread the foot of a topsail where no course sail is set

davits - a crane used to bring objects on board (usually used in tandem to handle boats)

deadeye - a wooden block with holes

Dispatches, London Gazette - periodicals used to report on military engagements

dogger - a commercial fishing vessel

downhaul - the running rigging used to lower a yard

dragon - a firearm, usually a sawed-off blunderbuss fired as a pistol

fathom - a measure of six feet

fid - a sailmaker's tool used to stretch grommets before inserting reinforcement

fife, fife rail - a small flute usually played at the rail around the mainmast (fife rail)

fifth rate - a frigate armed with 24 to 40 or 50 guns

fighting top - the platform resting on the top of any section of a mast (topmast, mast top)

first rate - a ship armed with 98 guns or more

flog - to whip, usually with a cat-o-nine tails

full and by - to be close hauled with sails filling

futtock shrouds - the shrouds gathered below the mast tops and crosstrees

gallery - a small walkway aft of the great cabin

galley - a ship's kitchen

glim - slang for a lantern

grape shot - ammunition similar to canister shot, used for anti-personnel

great cabin - the captain's quarters located aft on the gun deck

grog - a drink, usually about one-part rum to four parts water served twice daily

gudgeon - the female part of a fitting used as a hinge (see pintle)

gunnel (gunwale) - the upper edge of the side of a ship

hand - to furl a sail (hand and reeve)

halyard - a rope used to raise a sail, see running rigging

hawser - a large rope used for mooring or towing a vessel

holystone - a block of sandstone used to scour the deck

HMS - His (Her) Majesty's Ship

hornpipe - a lively dance

hull down - a ship seen with the hull still below the curvature of the earth

Indiaman - a merchant ship serving in the East India Company (see John Company)

in irons - when a ship's bow is headed directly into the wind

in ordinary - a naval vessel out of service for repair or maintenance

jeer - a block and tackle used to handle sails

John Company - East India Company

jury-rig - a temporary repair

king post - the spoke on the wheel indicating when the rudder is steering straight ahead

lambda - a ship's longitudinal position

langrage - the debris fired from an artillery piece to cut through rigging

leadsman - a man assigned to measure water depth with a long rope weighted with lead

lighter - a small harbor vessel

loblolly - a surgeon's assistant, apothecary

long gun - a long range artillery piece

lubber - a landsman, the lowest rating on a ship, a land lover, a green crew member

lubber's hole - the opening used by a lubber to gain access to a mast top

mast top - the platform resting on the top of any section of a mast

marlin spike - a hand tool used to reeve or unknot a rope (see spike)

midshipman - the lowest rank for an officer in the Royal Navy (ensign)

monkey rail - a light railing surrounding a mast

neap tide - a minimal tide occurring just after the first or third phase of the moon

Nore - the mutiny occurring in the Thames Estuary in 1797

oakum - old rope fibers used for caulk

orlop - the deck covering the hold of a ship

outlier - a ship detached from the fleet serving as a lookout

pintle - the male part of fitting used as a hinge (see gudgeon)

pitchpole - to sink a boat bow first

point of sail - the relationship between direction of wind and direction of ship

quarterdeck - the last quarter of a ship's top deck, now called the bridge

queue - a braid of hair popular among sailors

ratlines - the horizontal ropes tied between shrouds used as the rungs of a ladder

reeve - to prepare or mend a rope (hand and reeve)

roads - (inner roads, outer roads) the open expanses in a harbour where ships anchor

rope walk - a long shed in a chandler's shop used to store and measure out rope

running rigging - the ropes employed to raise and lower yards

running - to sail with, or nearly with the wind

sailing master - the chief navigational officer, also responsible for the best use of sails

salt - an experienced sailor

sea - a sea refers to heavy weather, the sea refers to a body of water

scupper - a hole in the ship's side to ship water overboard from the deck

sheave - a hole or a space for a rope to run through

sheet bend - a type of knot

sheer hulk - the hull of a decommissioned ship used to transfer heavy loads to another ship

ship's bells - the bell rung every half hour to measure the time elapsed in each watch

shroud - the standing rigging employed to keep masts standing upright, port and starboard

sheet - a rope used to trim a sail

skeg - the trailing edge of the keel where the rudder attaches

slops - the clothes worn on a daily basis while at sea

slow match - a slow burning fuse

smack - a small fishing boat used off the coast of Britain

smasher - slang for a carronade

snow - a square rigged vessel with two masts

spanker - a boom sail rigged fore and aft at the lower mizzenmast

Spithead - the mutiny occurring at Portsmouth in 1797

spike - see marlin spike, or to ruin an artillery piece by ramming a spike in its touch hole

standing rigging - the shrouds and stays that stand in place to support the masts

stay - the standing rigging secured to keep masts standing upright, fore and aft

stepping the mast - to erect and secure the mast to its vertical position

strake - the overlapping boards making the hull of a boat

studding sails - the additional sails extended beyond the yard ends

tack - the course of a ship

tacking - the zig-zag pattern of sailing into the wind

taffrail - the railing on transom

tar - a sailor

topmast - the platform resting on the top of any section of a mast (fighting top, mast top)

transom - the aft wall of the stern

tumblehome - the curvature of a ship's hull from waterline to gunnel

waist - of a ship, midway between the bow and the stern

watch - the blocks of time served on duty (first watch, morning watch, etc.)

wear ship - to tack away from the wind

windlass - see capstan

xebec - a small sailing ship common in the Mediterranean

About the Author

L ee Henschel Jr. was born in Minneapolis, Minnesota, and began his writing life when he was twelve. He is the author of two previous volumes of *The Sailing Master* saga: *Book One, Coming of Age*, and *Book Two, The Long Passage*. Lee's poems and short stories have been published in numerous literary journals and anthologies, including *Lost Lake Folk Opera*. His collection, *Short Stories of Vietnam*, was published in 1982.

"Each day I give thanks for any writing talent I've been given, and I vow to honor the gift, to nurture it, and to share it."

—Lee Henschel Jr.

Made in the USA
Columbia, SC
02 September 2019